STUMBLING
ON THE SAND

Jenna Rae

Bella
BOOKS

2015

Bella Books, Inc.
P.O. Box 10543
Tallahassee, FL 32302

First Bella Books Edition 2015

Editor: Katherine V. Forrest
Cover Designer: Judith Fellows

ISBN: 978-1-59493-461-2

Other Bella Books by Jenna Rae

Turning on the Tide
The Writing on the Wall

Acknowledgments

I am very grateful for the patience of my darling Lee and of my sweet, beautiful giants Josh and Ben. Thank you for occasionally reaching into the abyss to pluck me out and offer me love and finger foods. Maritza, Becca, Morgan, Mary, Brigid, and April—thank you for being your kind, loving, accomplished selves and for putting up with my neglect and distraction. Medora MacDougall, thank you for being insightful and supportive.

I won't tell you Katherine V. Forrest is brilliant, because you already know that. What I will tell you is that she had the patience to read my ugly, lumpen draft and see something worth salvaging from that mess. Her insight and clarity were instrumental in making this a much better book and me a much better writer. Katherine, thank you. I will try not to be such a gushing, awkward fan girl when I am fortunate enough to see you next.

Thank you to the smart, dedicated, talented team at Bella Books and to our peerless leader Linda Hill. Karin Kallmaker, thank you for your patience and energy, your talent and humor. Thank you, members and leaders of Golden Crown Literary Society, for creating a cohesive community where once there were scattered readers, writers, editors and publishers. Frankly, I'm still a bit scattered, but there isn't much you can do about that.

I want to thank the reader. Your time is valuable and your choices many. Thank you for investing irretrievable minutes and hours to this story. I hope this book and others make your lonely, perilous journey feel less lonely and perilous. I wish you every joy.

About the Author

Jenna Rae also wrote *Writing on the Wall* and *Turning on the Tide*. She is immersed in her current reading, writing and learning projects and is grateful as always when her loved ones tap her on the shoulder and usher her briefly into the real world for meals and work and coffee.

CHAPTER ONE

San Francisco Police Department Inspector Del Mason stood next to her partner, Tom Phan, and looked down at the body at their feet. The sun's first clear rays had burned through the morning's mist and framed the crumpled figure in golden light, but there was no way to imagine the bruised, bloody boy was a drowsing angel come drifting down to terra firma.

Del spoke first. "What a shitty way to die."

"Not exactly a great place either." Phan gestured at the nondescript industrial buildings and parking lot that framed the crime scene on aptly named Shotwell Street. "Gang, you think?"

Both eyed the nearest building, leased to a limousine company. It displayed no identifying graffiti for the Mission District gang currently laying claim to the street that housed their newest case.

"No tagging." Del examined the kid's skinny arms and neck. "And no ink. Hair's wrong too."

"We'll check anyway."

"Of course. I'd say he was dumped." Del spoke as she tapped notes into her phone. "Male, juvenile. Five-seven, a hundred pounds or so. Fifteen or sixteen. Hispanic, maybe?" Del examined the mashed remains of the boy's features and shook her head. "Cheap T and jeans, dirty. Hair's several days greasy. Outgrown too. Homeless, I'd guess. A pro?"

"Eh." Phan typed into his own smartphone. "Fully dressed. Not much blood on the clothes. Almost none on the sidewalk. I agree, he was killed somewhere else and dumped here. He could have been re-dressed after. Time of death will be important. Could be a working boy, like you say. The john got out of hand? Or the pimp. We'll see if there was sexual assault. Was he a junkie?"

"I don't think so." Del pointed at the body with her phone. "Skinny, but I'm not seeing tracks or meth mouth."

"Okay. Anything else? Right. Let's divvy this up. I'll canvas the street kids if you'll take the shelters. You check the missing kid files, I'll do the trafficking database. Deal?"

Del nodded, crouching to take a closer look at the victim while Phan continued. "Tuesday's usually not too busy, morgue-wise, so if we have a name—"

"Yeah. Hold on." Del noticed a small scar on the boy's earlobe. She sprang up and stepped back from the body. She shook off Phan's hand when he touched her arm. November's early morning chill suddenly hit Del.

"What's up?"

"I recognize him," Del said. "Mikey, Mikey Ocampo. Rendered unto the tender mercies of the juvenile justice system five or six years ago."

He looked at her in concern. "Why do you remember him? He was that bad?"

"No." Del rubbed her face. "He was that railroaded."

"Yeah?"

"Not exactly the highlight of my career."

"Are you okay?" Phan again reached out a hand and again Del shrugged it off.

"No. He was a nice kid, he got fucked over." She eyed the bruised boy at their feet and shook her head. "I can't believe he's dead."

"Wanna tell me about it?"

"No." Del scrubbed at her newly shorn scalp, feeling the tight blond curls resist her fingers. "Shit. Yeah."

* * *

"Why do I get all the kids?"

No one in the homicide division responded to newly transferred Del Mason, not even to rib her for whining. She grabbed a couple of items from what had just become her desk before heading to the nearest interview room. Seated at the only table was the social worker, a prototypically bleary-eyed civil servant. Her graying roots, dark-ringed eyes and sallow complexion proclaimed the weight of her workload, while her dirt-grimed, white, Disney-themed Dooney and Burke satchel bespoke a happier, more hopeful past. The two women exchanged nods, not bothering to introduce themselves, and Del considered how to proceed. After too many years in sex crimes, Del had hoped not to spend any more time interviewing traumatized kids. Wasn't that what her transfer to the homicide division had been about?

Curled up in a ball in the corner was a kid who let his eyes flick in her direction for only a second. Looking much younger than the eleven years claimed on the patrol officer's paperwork, Mikey Ocampo was maybe the size of a normal eight-year-old, underweight not in the way of a rapidly growing child but of a chronically underfed one. His eyes were black holes burned into sallow skin. His nose had been broken at some point and not fixed. He would have breathing problems his whole life, however long that was. His toes pressed against the thin, straining fabric of his too-small, cheap canvas shoes and looked close to poking through. His faded blue sweatpants were too short by a few inches, and bunched around his narrow waist. His T-shirt was so worn it was almost transparent. He'd chewed his fingernails to the quick. Mom wasn't just poor, then. She was neglectful, maybe abusive. Was she an addict, an alcoholic?

Del forced her muscles to relax. The kid's antennae were out, though his eyes stayed focused on the floor in front of his bunched legs. He was trying to decide how dangerous she was. Not whether or not she was dangerous, how much so. She couldn't show any of what he expected to see, tension or contempt or disgust. She had to stay as neutral and blank as possible without seeming indifferent. Del sat on the floor a few feet away from the boy, careful not to look at him or move too quickly. She pulled out her phone and checked her messages, pushed her hair back off her forehead, turned off the ringer, put her phone away. The boy watched her out of the corner of his eye.

She pulled out a toy car and set it on the floor. Mikey was too old for toys, or thought he was. But Del would bet he hadn't had a lot of age-appropriate playthings when he was little.

"My friend gave me this." Del spoke as though to the opposite wall. "We're not friends anymore but I still kept it."

The boy eyed the die-cast plaything.

"She gave it to me when I crashed my real Mustang. It was red like this. God, it was beautiful. It took me three years to get it running, only drove it for six months." Del smiled wryly, still not looking at Mikey. "I guess I thought I was a NASCAR driver. Went too fast around a curve and totaled it. Walked away without a scratch, but I destroyed the most beautiful car I've ever owned."

The boy shifted an ankle and spoke in a barely audible voice. "I got in a crash once, it was me and my mom. We didn't get hurt too bad. Just like here." He pushed back his hair and showed her a jagged scar that ran up his ear and disappeared into his hairline. "My mom thought she was a NASCAR driver too."

"Funny, how we see ourselves isn't always the way we really are."

Mikey shrugged.

"It's a good memory, the day she gave it to me." Del pushed the toy with her fingertips. "Means a lot, when somebody does something nice for me. It's always kind of a surprise."

Del pulled out a couple of candy bars and put them both on the floor. "You pick."

Mikey waited nearly a minute before choosing the milk chocolate bar. He slid it closer but left it on the floor next to his hip.

Del took the remaining candy and pointedly ignored the boy while nibbling a corner. Eying her, Mikey picked up his and peeled off the outer wrapper without tearing it. He smoothed the paper, folded it, put it in his sweatpants pocket.

Del was yanked back to fourth grade, when she got a perfect report card and the teacher gave her a candy bar. She opened it like this kid, trying not to tear it. She remembered how strange it felt, eating a candy bar like a regular kid.

It was like the toy car. Elise did nice stuff for Del all the time when they were together. She used to buy Del all kinds of gifts, just cards and treats, little things like the toy car. Del wondered if Elise knew how much she appreciated those affectionate gestures. Other girlfriends had been like that too, always buying some little present for her, showing up with surprises and treats. Thoughtful gestures Del had never acknowledged beyond cursory thanks—how had she gone from a grateful kid to a selfish adult? Del shook off the strangeness left behind by her recent breakup. It had been slow and protracted and nearly silent, like most of her breakups. And there had, she realized with a pang, been far too many of those.

"Maybe if I was nicer, I don't know." She cut off her thoughts with her words and her words with a snapping chomp of chocolate.

"You blew it." The boy's voice was muffled by a chunk of candy.

"I really did."

"You could say you're sorry." This was a gift, and Del nodded in thanks and agreement. The boy let his legs uncurl and stretch out in front of him.

"I probably should."

"But you're not going to." The boy's sidelong glance was knowing.

"No." Del gave a rueful laugh, and the kid smirked in response. They watched each other's faces fall.

"Sometimes sorry isn't enough." Mikey let his candy hand drop. He looked for all the world like a lost toddler, and Del swallowed hard.

"Accidents happen, mistakes too," she offered.

"He's dead, isn't he, Mr. White?"

Del waited until Mikey turned to look her full in the face.

"Still alive, last I heard."

"I kilt him." He let go a great hiccup and started crying.

Del turned away from the kid, knowing his tears humiliated him and that he didn't want her to see them. "He's still in surgery."

"No." He wiped his nose with his arm. "I'm a killer."

"Are you?" Del tilted her head. "Did you want to kill him?"

The boy shook his head and tears scattered.

"Did he hurt you?"

A shrug, then a denial.

"Did he hurt your mom?"

Mikey curled his arms around his head, one hand aloft to keep the candy safe, and his snuffling turned to choked sobs. Del waited him out.

After a few minutes, the boy settled down and tried to regain his stony expression. It just made him look unbearably vulnerable.

"Tell me."

He turned to face Del, curling his legs to the side. She turned and mirrored his posture, only vaguely aware that she did so.

"Mr. White's a total prick."

When the boy checked for a response to the word, Del just nodded.

"He's always doing weird stuff. He made my mom—she's had a real hard life. Had me when she was only fifteen. Nobody ever helped her, not even her parents, they just threw her out. They don't care about her. Or me."

Del nodded again, her face open and neutral.

"She works real hard. She's the assistant manager at Chicken Shack, plus she works at the carwash sometimes." He wiped his nose again. "But they don't pay that good. So we're broke all the time." Mikey's eyes searched Del's. "We moved here so my mom could be a manager. She's a real good worker, they said so."

"Must be, to get a promotion to assistant manager."

"But the rent here costs too much." He lapsed into silence, staring at the candy bar in his hand like he wasn't sure how it got there.

"It's too much for most everybody, Mikey. It's crazy. Puts people in a real bad spot. Any other problems besides money?"

"Problems?" Mikey reddened. "Mr. White started hanging around, talking to my mom and stuff. She didn't like it, but he let her pay the rent late sometimes. It took most our money to move, plus she had to pay bail for Brian."

"Her boyfriend?"

"Yup, but he went to jail anyway. So then she didn't have no money from him, plus he wasn't there to keep Mr. White away. He showed up this morning, bugging my mom."

"What happened?"

"They started fighting. Mr. White was bugging her for money. He was weird. He asked if I was mixed. He asked if she only likes white guys, you know, 'cause Brian is white. She told him to leave me alone, and Mr. White got real mad. He called her a whore. Mom slapped him and he punched her, real hard. Then he, like, grabbed her and took her to her room and locked the door." The boy's gaze drifted away. "She was crying, I tried to help her. Tried to open the door but it was locked."

Del nodded.

"She told me, get to school, leave me alone." The boy shook his head. "But she's the one that wanted me to stay home to keep him away. I think so. Maybe he came by before when I was at school, I don't know."

Del let him ponder that for a moment, knowing he would return to the story.

"Then Mr. White comes out. He goes in the kitchen, eating my mom's food. You know? Like it's his food. There's not enough already, now he's gonna eat our food? He figured he could just do whatever he wanted."

"He had no right to be there."

"He had no right." Mikey nodded, making sudden tears fly. "He doesn't own us."

Del swallowed painfully.

"Brian left his gun when he went to jail. He kept it on the fridge, it was still there. Mom knew she could trust me not to touch it."

There was a shred of pride in this, in being the one man his mother could count on. Del nodded, squeezing her mouth tight.

"But I—"

"Go on, Mikey."

"Mr. White told me to go to my room. Like he's my dad or something. I asked, real polite, can I please get my school supplies off the fridge—Brian put the gun in a cardboard box. Is he gonna get in trouble? He's not supposed to have guns 'cause he had trouble before in Visalia."

Del shook her head.

"Mr. White said I could get my homework stuff. 'Cause I knew how to act. He said most Filipinos are too uppity." The boy reddened. "I said he was right, I called him sir." His eyes pleaded for her understanding.

"You had to go along with him, just for a minute."

"I had to. I think I had to. Anyways, I took the box to my room. I took out the gun. It was real heavy, I didn't know it would be so heavy. I thought maybe if I waited a while, he would leave and I wouldn't have to." The boy looked at the flickering fluorescent light in the ceiling, and Del held her breath. Now he would lie or tell the truth. He was deciding, and she didn't want to interrupt. After nearly a minute, the kid shifted his feet and shook his head.

"But he wouldn't leave. I couldn't let him hurt my mom again."

"I get that."

And she did. The kid was just old enough to feel like he had to protect his momma. And the other side of it was there, too, in Mikey's clouded eyes. A mean man hurt the one person he loved, and he wanted that mean man to pay. That wasn't hard to understand either. The question was, how much of the shooting would legally qualify as self-defense, and how much would be considered revenge?

"He told me to come in the kitchen, but I didn't want to." Mikey held out his hands. "I had the gun, and I didn't want to, but I could hear my mom crying and I didn't want him to get mad and hurt her again. I didn't want to."

"You felt like you didn't have a choice."

"I shot him," Mikey announced. "It was heavy. I couldn't make it work at first." He reddened. "Mr. White was laughing at me. I was crying, and he said I was an uppity little bitch and then I figured it out, I slid the thing, and then I shot him and he was surprised, and he got up and he slapped me and I shot him again. Then he fell down and there was a lot, a lot of blood. A lot, all over."

"You were scared he would hurt your mom again."

The boy nodded.

"Were you scared he would hit you again?"

Mikey nodded again.

"After he fell down, did you call for help?"

"They told us at school, call nine-one-one. I didn't want to kill nobody, I just didn't want him to hurt me and my mom."

"Okay. Did your mom come out to the kitchen after you shot Mr. White?"

"Yeah. She started screaming. She ran over and fell, 'cause the floor was all wet. She fell down all in his blood, and I was on the phone with the nine-one-one, the lady couldn't hear me and I dropped the phone. My mom was freaking out and she just sat there screaming so loud and crying and she wouldn't look at me, there was blood on her."

"Where is she now?"

"I don't know. She left. She don't have a car and they put me in the police car by myself."

"Okay, Mikey. Thanks for telling me."

"What's gonna happen to me?"

"I'm not sure exactly. You'll probably have to answer the same questions I just asked you a bunch of times. Other than that I'm not sure."

She looked at the social worker, who continued to stare at the wall and ignore them. The woman looked ten paces past tired, had probably been up for a couple of days. Was she high? Del examined the social worker's eyes, skin, posture. Not high, maybe. Just checked out. It happened a lot with cops, social workers, teachers. The very people kids in crisis needed the most. But that was the problem, wasn't it? Too many fucked-up families, too many kids in one emergency after another and too few resources to help them with. It was a soul eater, trying to empty the ocean with a slotted spoon.

"Where's my mom? Can I see my mom?"

"Yeah." Del shook her head. "I don't know. I'll see if she's here, okay?"

"She hates me now, I know it."

There was a scrabbling sort of knock, and a tiny, baby-faced woman pushed in. Both eyes were blackened, her mouth torn up. Her tropical-print sundress was darkened with smears of dried blood.

"Mommy!" Mikey rushed into his mother's arms, nearly knocking her over.

"Baby, my baby, oh God, my baby!"

Del eased out of the room and exchanged grimaces with seasoned Homicide Detective Inspector Dave Leister. It was he who'd approached her, asked her to talk to the kid.

"Good job softening up the kid for me, sweetheart."

Del nodded her thanks. Leister was a member of an older generation that still seemed to see women as secretaries, assistants, babysitters, nurses—helpers, not equals. He wasn't trying to be condescending, she reminded herself. He was in his sixties and ready to retire and doing his best to adapt to a new detective who was not only a woman but also taller than he, younger and fitter than he, and not only college educated but also clearly a dyke. It was a lot to take in for a member of the old guard who remembered the good old days of white male cops standing on their own private side of the thin blue line.

"Why's this in Homicide, if the vic isn't dead yet?"

"Doc doesn't think White'll survive surgery, brass says it's more cost-effective to just give it to us."

"Well, that's just dandy."

"Kid's not a killer," Leister commented. "Thanks for opening him up, but I kinda wish you hadn't."

"I feel you. Get the mom in for a rape kit, take as many pics of her injuries as you can. See if you can get an interview with the ex, Brian. Climb up the ass of the landlord. If he really did go after the mom, he may have priors. Get Mom's statement now—it'll make things better for the kid if we can say they didn't have time to confer."

"Any other advice, oh brilliant one? Thank Christ you're here to tell me what to do. This bein' my first rodeo and all."

Del colored. As the newest and most junior member of the team, she shouldn't be telling anybody what to do, and she knew it. Hadn't she just been trying to see things from Leister's point of view? She felt like an ass.

"Sorry," she offered as Leister turned away.

Retreating to the ladies' room, Del washed her face and hands with cool water. Kids were the worst. Whether they were the victims, suspects or witnesses, they always got to her. Like they got to everybody probably. Del had considered, more than once, using her response to kids as a kind of litmus test. Once they didn't get to her anymore, it would be time to get out. She'd been on the force for fifteen years and knew she'd grown harder because of the job. But the kid got to her, so she figured she was still good.

Examining her reflection in the mirror above the sink, Del thought she'd better get a haircut before her wild blond curls completely obscured her blue eyes. She noted that every one of her forty years was etched into the fine lines that highlighted her clearly defined features. She noticed her only blue pullover was starting to fray along the shoulder seam. She stuck her tongue out at herself. She'd been out of uniform for over a decade but still didn't have enough clothes or enough time and patience to go shopping for more.

Back in the hall, Leister waved Del toward the interview room, filling her in on the update: the landlord had survived the surgery, but barely. Nonetheless, Homicide was still working the case, and the captain had assigned the two of them, as expected.

"I should have seen this coming." Mikey's mom wailed into the bunch of tissues she clutched. Mikey was crushed to her, nearly strangled by her short arm. "I never shoulda moved here!"

Leister eyed Del with alarm. She gave him a nod and watched him rock back on his heels in relief. Mariposa Ocampo was Del's to deal with now.

"Ms. Ocampo? Mariposa, right?" Del offered her a cup of water. "My name's Del, and I've been getting to know Mikey. Can you and I talk? Please?"

"What's gonna happen to my baby?"

"Depends. I want things to go as well for Mikey as possible. I need your help to do that."

"Oh, no, I know how this works!" The woman pointed up at Del. "You cops wanna lock up my boy and throw away the key! You're not going to pin this on my Mikey, no way!"

"It's hard to trust us, I get that. But I promise you, I want to help Mikey, not hurt him. He's a nice kid, we don't want to see him—"

"You stay away from my boy and stay away from me, I want a lawyer!"

"Okay, whatever you say, but we can help Mikey more if you just talk to us, I promise."

"I look stupid to you? Huh? I wanna lawyer for my Mikey!"

"Okay, Ms. Ocampo. Here's my card. When you and the lawyer are ready to talk to us, you can call anyone in the department, but I hope you'll call me. Mikey seems like a really decent kid, and I'd like the chance to help him and you."

Del forced herself to walk away. There wasn't much she could do now. She sat at her new desk and eyed the senior detective who'd dragged her into his mess. The kid would go to some juvenile detention center, CYA camp, some version of kid jail. Then what? Either he went to prison because his sentence was longer than seven years, or he was released at some point and sent out into the world as a product of the juvenile justice system. Or he got in one too many fights defending himself from the bigger kids and got a longer sentence. Or he got tried as an adult, and he turned hard and angry, picked up a whole new set of skills helpful only in prison and criminal circles. The kid was screwed.

Del grabbed a blank report and started filling it out, trying to decide how she could have handled things better. The captain's administrator, the only other female employee on the premises that day, sashayed up to Del's desk with a pained look on her face.

"You okay, honey?"

Del nodded and kept writing. She got the distinct impression Patty was a relentless gossip and troublemaker, and Del wanted no part of her or her games.

"Kid's cute, isn't he?"

"Yup."

"What do you think of the mom? You think she's cute?"

"I didn't notice." Del had been working in the Mission station all of five minutes before Patty had started trying to draw her out about her sexuality. It was getting tiring after only a half day, but Del had to give the woman her due—she was persistent. Maybe, Del thought with a smirk, Patty should have been a detective.

"Landlord gonna make it? What's his name? White? Ernie White? His mom owns the properties and he just drives around in his black Lexus—did you see that thing? The techs were going on about it—and collects the rent. Sounds like he collects more than checks, huh?"

"You sure seem to know a lot about this case, Patty." Del stopped and fixed a stare at the admin's wide blue eyes.

"Oh," Patty purred with a little wiggle, "I know everything that goes on around here."

"I'll keep that in mind."

"You, you're a closed book. Maybe you and I should go for a little welcome-to-the-station drink, huh? It can make a big difference around here, having a friend."

"What do you mean?"

"Oh, nothing, really. Just remember, honey, I have the ear of the most important men in this city."

"I've heard you have a lot more than their ears, Patty," put in Leister.

"You don't need to run interference, Inspector Leister." Patty was pouting now. "I bet Mason here knows just how to handle the ladies." She flounced away in a huff, soaking up the chuckles that sounded from around the squad room.

Del kept her head down and continued writing her report. She'd been fielding unwanted flirtation, jealousy and resentment from her first day at the academy and still had to remind herself to rise above it all. She knew she needed to grow a thicker skin so she wouldn't feel betrayed when the only other woman around tried to throw her under the bus at every turn.

"Thanks for your help," Leister offered. "I couldn't get the kid to talk to me. Needed a woman's touch."

"Sometimes they're scared of men." Del rubbed her forehead, pushing away annoyance over her colleagues consistently dismissing her skillset as a product of her gender. "Not your fault."

"Well, maybe we can work this one together."

"Yeah, okay." Del was wary. After several failed partnerships, she knew better than to take any olive branches without checking for signs of poison sumac.

"Landlord's rich and kid's poor, Mason. I assume you know how this thing ends."

"Does it have to? Justice isn't exactly blind to the color green, I know, but Mikey's no murderer."

"Agreed. But face it. Kid's screwed. Especially if White dies."

"Cheery." Del put down her pen and looked at her would-be partner. "The thing is, it never shoulda happened. The boyfriend's gun should have been confiscated when he was popped. The mom should have been safe, the kid should have been safe. The landlord should have been locked up before the kid ever met him. I bet Mariposa Ocampo wasn't his first victim."

"If the kid's telling the truth. She did look pretty banged up, but that coulda been a new boyfriend. You know how these women are, they can't go five minutes without a man."

Del ignored this and watched Leister to see if he would follow up.

"Maybe we could find other victims," Leister mused, jotting down a neat to-do list in a small notebook. "Since White—actually, it's his mom. Mrs. White owns a dozen properties in low-rent neighborhoods. Her son doesn't have a real job. He supposedly manages the properties, and she has a lot of tenants. We should run those tenants down."

"If we establish the landlord as a repeat offender, we might be able to help the kid."

"Put the victim on trial." Leister nodded. "You learned that in sex crimes I guess."

"Pervs and their lawyers do it to rape victims all the time." Del stared at him, fighting her rising hopefulness.

"We'll see." Leister raised an eyebrow. "Listen, young lady. We'll try, that's all we can do. It's easy to get all worked up, especially for a woman and especially when it comes to a cute little kid."

"I'll try not to lactate all over the station."

Leister's wry smile was an almost-apology. "This is gonna get ugly," he warned.

"Yeah," Del responded. "Don't they all?"

She and Leister ran down every tenant in every property White's family had ever owned. They high-fived when they got word that Ernie White had opened his eyes and was out of his coma. Del questioned the smug little twerp every time the doctor and his sharp-featured mom reluctantly let her in the room. After every interview Del felt like she should take a ten-hour shower.

"Mariposa says I forced myself on her?" White raised his light eyebrows over his eerily light blue eyes and shuddered as if with distaste. "That girl ain't pretty enough to flirt with, much less sleep with."

Del had to swallow her anger. White was exactly like many other sexual predators she'd interviewed, and she'd questioned hundreds of them. He was glib, arrogant and careful to protect the only person who mattered to him—himself. She sat back, ignoring the way the visitor's chair dug into her shoulders. White was blond, with lax muscles, weak features and a suspiciously orange tan.

"Oh, come on," Del teased, smirking, "I know you're a spoiled rich guy, but pussy's pussy, isn't it?"

"Vulgarity?" White smiled, relaxed and easy in his smug self-assurance. "Amateurish. I'd hoped for something a little more interesting."

"What do you find interesting, Mr. White?"

"The same things most evolved people do," White drawled, smiling easily. "Beauty, intelligence, humor, spontaneity. A challenge."

"Ms. Ocampo was a challenge?"

White rang for the nurse.

"If you really enjoy a challenge, why do you only rape women who don't have the option of going to the police for help?"

"I'm losing my patience, lady cop. Mason, was it? I'm starting to not like you."

"Because I'm not some scared little pauper who shakes in her boots when you look at her?" Del smiled, despite knowing her needling was irritating the subject instead of getting him closer to opening up. She switched tactics. "Come on, Mr. White, what if you just said the shooting was an accident? You don't have to admit any wrongdoing at all. You don't get anything out of the kid's life getting ruined. Please? He's just a little boy. A nice little boy."

"And then what? You spend the rest of your pathetic career trying to bust me for a crime I didn't commit?"

Del's hesitation made White laugh. He waved her away as a nurse came bustling in.

"You think I'm an idiot, don't you? Lady, you're nuts. Now get out of my room unless you're planning to make yourself useful and blow me."

Del tried to rein in her disgust, as much with herself as with the so-called victim. White was exactly the sort of asshole she couldn't stand, and her years working sex crimes had done little to help her gain the equanimity needed to work a guy like him. If anything, investigating sex crimes had convinced her that the world was filled with people like Ernie White, who got away with their crimes, usually against women and children, far more often than most folks realized.

"You should have talked to White," she told Leister when reviewing the failed interview with him. "I let him see what I think of him. Not to mention, he has no respect for a lowly woman."

Leister, seated and looking up at Del, smiled.

"You don't look that lowly to me."

Del took the olive branch with good grace, offering to buy him an end-of-the-workday beer and drawing him out in the nearest shithole cop bar. Once he'd decided Del was okay, Leister let down his guard and only occasionally acted like she was his secretary. She figured that was about as good an outcome as she could hope for.

As the case progressed, Del tried to build rapport with the shooting victim. When this didn't work, she poked at Ernie White as often and for as long as she dared, and she never got more than a smirk or a smile or a veiled innuendo to confirm what she knew was true, that Ernie White was a dangerous rapist and that Mikey Ocampo shouldn't be convicted of attempted murder for shooting him.

At some point, White's mother hired an attorney who got Del and Leister barred from talking to him without his lawyer present. Whenever they tried to talk to him, they were accused of badgering an innocent victim. When they tried to talk to Mikey, they were refused access to him. Mariposa Ocampo wouldn't talk to them. They slammed themselves into one brick wall after another to no avail for the next several weeks and only occasionally swapped complaints and self-pitying rants over beer or burgers.

Del tried not to resent it when Leister backed off as he got closer to claiming his well-earned gold watch.

"It's a rigged game," he told Del one evening as they sat at their respective desks, hers piled with computer, phone, a half-eaten sandwich, reports and office supplies, and his bare of everything but a computer and a phone.

"I know." Del rubbed her forehead. "But it doesn't make this right."

"No," Leister agreed. "It doesn't. But the reality is what it is. The sooner you learn that, the longer and happier you'll live. I'll bet you five bucks the mom ends up helping the prosecution more than the defense."

Del knew better than to take that bet. Mariposa had refused the medical exam, wouldn't speak with Del or Leister, wouldn't let them have access to Mikey and of course couldn't afford a private defense attorney. White's lawyer, an overpriced blowhard with no conscience, tricked Mariposa into saying the kid had been playing with the gun and had accidentally shot the landlord when he came by to fix the dripping faucet in the kitchen.

"Why would she do that?"

Leister shrugged. "The guy's a trickster, you know how they are. Got her all mixed up, that's what they do. It's all over now."

Del wasn't clear why Mariposa thought this lie would help her son. Some cynical part of her wondered if there'd been some secret exchange of money, but a cursory examination of Mariposa's finances showed no proof of this. The lie paved the road to Mikey's conviction. Once the mother had said White was just a conscientious property manager and that her son had shot him, it was easy enough for the prosecutor to get the kid to admit he'd shot White on purpose. Del didn't comment when Leister crowed his bitter, cynical I-told-you-so. She just nodded.

There wasn't even a trial. Del was on her own by then because Leister was off enjoying his well-earned retirement, fishing in the Bahamas and golfing in Arizona. She tried to help Mikey's public defender, but he just flipped through the file for all of thirty seconds before consulting for a few minutes with Mikey's guardian ad litem and agreeing to the DA's deal: five years in juvenile detention.

Once the deal had been struck, Del was out of it. There was nothing more she could do for the kid. By then Mikey Ocampo was just one more person she felt she'd let down. Del had kept track of Ernie White for three or four years, but then he moved to another city and became just one of several predators she'd vowed to keep an eye on. She had a vague desire to keep tabs on Mikey but had no wish to watch him grow scarred and hard. Not seeing him let her think maybe he could beat the odds. She knew there had to be kids who came out of juvenile justice systems and went on to be productive citizens. She preferred to leave alive her hope that he would be one of them.

Now, five years after he got sent up for shooting his mom's rapist, Mikey Ocampo was dead at her feet.

CHAPTER TWO

"How was your day?"

"Frustrating, mostly." Del shook her head to forestall Lola's questions. "Yours?"

"I finally finished the stupid second book and sent it in."

Del smiled. "Stupid?"

Lola rolled her eyes. "Hopefully I'll feel better about it after the editor hacks it up. I don't like anything about it right now."

"Did you feel that way about the first one?" Del watched her maybe-girlfriend, maybe-ex-girlfriend weigh the question. Even frowning, Lola looked closer to twenty than almost forty. She had the fine-boned features of a doll and huge hazel eyes that seemed to glow in the light of early evening. Lola looked troubled, as she so often did lately. She had been agonizing over her sophomore novel for the entire year and a half Del had known her. She wished the book was the only thing troubling Lola, but she knew better. Most of the tension in Lola's small frame came from their relationship.

Lola looked at the ceiling as if searching for an answer. "I guess not. Maybe it's just that I didn't actually imagine anyone reading it. It was mostly therapeutic. Now I feel like I have some responsibility. Expectations. People hoping I'll do better than I'm really capable of and some people hoping I'll fail. Either way, it feels like a lot of weight. Not that my writing is the center of the universe. I just don't want to miss something important because I don't really know what I'm doing. What if I make a mistake and let down the story?"

"Maybe you should have a little faith in yourself."

Lola offered a wry smile. "That's not as easy as you make it sound. But you're right. I'm just a little self-conscious. As you know."

"But you use the pen name. Nobody, including the lunatics, knows Lisa Miller is you. Doesn't that help?" She watched Lola process this and smiled when Lola pursed her lips and shook her head.

"Not really."

"Could I read it?"

"Oh." Lola made a face. "Maybe after it's had some work done. It's still pretty rough."

Del tried to keep her tone casual. "Well, if and when you're ready to share it with me, I'd like to read it."

Lola made a noncommittal sound and looked at her like maybe she'd rather be burned alive than hand over her manuscript. Del pondered the implications of this apparent reluctance. Was Lola really so self-conscious, or was it about their relationship?

Just the week before, their friend and neighbor Marco had asked Del how things stood between her and Lola, and she'd been unable to answer.

"Are you together or not?" Marco had stared at Del as she shrugged, his wide brown eyes studying her with a gravity that chilled her.

"I don't know. I hope so." She still wasn't sure. Lola had every reason to tell her to go to hell, but she didn't. They'd been in a strange sort of relationship limbo for weeks, and it was wearing on both of them.

She should ask Lola now, while they were talking about it, but she hesitated. What if Lola offered her mild, gentle regrets and said they were just friends? Del rubbed her forehead. It was silly. She should be able to ask a simple question and get a clear answer. But what would she say if Lola asked her the same question? Things between them had been confusing from the beginning. They'd lived together for a few months, but mostly because Lola had been afraid to stay in her own house alone after being attacked in it.

Del had thought things between them were mostly fine, but one day Lola had suddenly moved back in across the street to her own home. Del wondered if she would spend the next ten years watching Lola from across the street and wondering how to close the distance between them. Would they ever really connect again? Had they ever really connected in the first place? There were times she wondered if everything between them had been one-sided, and Lola had just been playing along out of politeness or fear. And it wasn't only Lola's feelings she questioned. Sometimes she wondered if part of what appealed to her about Lola was how different she was from Janet. There were moments she considered the possibility that she and Lola were doomed as a couple simply because Lola was not Janet.

"You're not scared to be here alone anymore." Del smiled an apology for the non sequitur. It had been several months since Lola had been back in her own house, but they had never had an open conversation about that fact.

"What?" Lola scrunched her delicate features. "No. I mean, I haven't forgotten what happened. I have nightmares. But I'm dealing with it. I should have been strong enough to deal with it back then. Maybe things would have started differently between us if I had. Now I'm trying to leave the past in the past."

It seemed Lola was better at putting it all aside—the trauma of being stalked, of finding her mutilated pets, of being terrorized by a madman—than Del was. She looked at the kitchen and saw traces of violence on every gleaming surface. She could almost smell the blood and the fear. She'd always wondered how victims who'd been attacked in their homes went back to living their daily lives. But here Lola was, cooking dinner and writing her books and making coffee and all of the normal things. It was like nothing ever happened. Maybe that was good. Maybe that was healthy.

Lola gestured across the table at Del's plate. "How's the chicken? I'd never cooked it in the roaster before. Do you like it this way?"

"It's good. Juicy."

"Listen, can we talk about it?"

Del wished she'd turned down the last-minute invitation to dinner. "Talk about what?"

"Really?" Lola made a face.

Del shrugged an apology. Of course she knew what Lola was talking about. "Janet."

"Yes. Janet." Lola sat back. She ran her fingers through her short, dark hair. "Don't you think we should?"

Del nodded again. She'd been surprised when Lola suddenly cut off her hair, going from nice, silky lengths to the sporty little pixie. It was pretty. It suited Lola's delicate features and small build. But there was something about the haircut that made her seem different. Del wasn't sure she wanted to examine what that was. She realized with a start that it wasn't just Lola's hair that was different. The shy little mouse was increasingly willing to give voice to her opinions. That was, she reminded herself, a good thing. She wanted a partner and not a shadow. Part of her attraction to Janet had always been Janet's iron will. Why was it so much less comfortable for her to deal with Lola's blossoming autonomy?

"I need to know where we stand," Lola said. "Whether we're together or not. Whether you still love Janet or not. Whether you still love me or not. You know we need to talk about it, and you've been putting me off for weeks. I need to know where we stand."

"Right." Del chewed her lower lip. Lola's questions were perfectly reasonable, and she knew it. They were the same questions she wondered about herself. But she felt her obstinate streak pushing against her better judgment. "I told you, I don't love Janet. Not anymore. I do love you. Isn't that enough?"

Lola crossed her arms. "You're saying what you think I want to hear. You're not even thinking about it. I need you to really look at this and tell me the truth. No sugarcoating, no placating, no patronizing."

"I'm not—"

Lola cut off her denial with a snort. "Your ex-girlfriend landed on our—excuse me, on your—doorstep out of the blue. She told us she was in mortal danger, and from the minute Janet showed up you started pulling away from me. You were clearly still in love with her. It looks like you've been in love with her this whole time."

"You're acting like this is my fault," Del protested. "I didn't invite her in, you did."

Lola chopped the words with her hand. "Stop. Janet brings a serial killer to us, and we both nearly get killed, and you're acting like none of it happened! Between Janet and Sterling, there was enough craziness—you were kidnapped, Del. I was kidnapped. Janet was like a little puppetmaster. She played with us like we were toys. You do acknowledge that, right?"

Del nodded, transfixed by Lola's red face and darkened eyes and loud voice.

"I thought it would be good for you to see Janet in prison. I thought it would make things real for you. But I have no idea what it did to you. You won't say a single word to me about it. How am I supposed to feel about that? How would you feel in my shoes? What am I supposed to think?"

Del chewed her lower lip. "You're right. I know you are."

"So talk to me."

Del took a deep breath but couldn't put how she felt into words. She shrugged helplessly.

"What happened when you went to see her? How do you feel about her?"

Del hugged herself. "I went to Chowchilla but she wouldn't see me. I talked to one of the corrections officers, Nan. She met me in the parking lot after her shift. She's a friend of a friend. Janet's not exactly thrilled to be incarcerated. Of course. But Nan said she's adapting."

"You're worried about her," Lola asserted. "That's understandable, no matter what happened. You care about her. I just—"

Del gave a wry grin. "You know what's funny? I'm not actually that worried about Janet. I was at first, but according to Nan she's fine. She's smart and manipulative and savvy. Plus she has money. It doesn't save her from the basics but I'm guessing it does insulate her from the worst of it. Janet is nobody's fool. She's probably running her own personal crime ring out of her cell by now. She's eligible for parole in just a few years, and with a good lawyer she'll get it. She has more than enough money to pay for a good lawyer."

Del watched Lola decide to sidestep the bigger issues and focus on a minor detail. "How can money help her in prison?"

"A lot of female prisoners have kids and moms depending on them. They need cash and Janet can help with that. Prisoners want snacks and smokes, drugs, alcohol. It's all available if you have money. Nan said she has weekly visitors, and they probably work for her. Maybe a financial advisor and a lawyer. Trust me, Janet's a survivor. She knows how to work a system, and prison's just another system."

Lola stared at Del, her brown eyes tinged with green and a little bit of gold. Her mouth was drawn in tight, and Del really wished she knew what Lola was thinking. But Lola merely nodded at her to continue.

"I took your advice and went back home to Fresno. The trailer park we lived in is gone. My folks are gone, I don't know where. I haven't seen them since I was a teenager. I don't even know if they're alive or dead. Maybe they went back to Texas. Who knows?"

"You're a cop. Couldn't you find them if you wanted to?"

Del pushed her hand across her body as if to deflect the question. "I guess I'm still trying to decide if I want to. Things were a little rocky between us. I'm not sure I want the drama they would probably bring, especially after everything that's happened. Does that make sense?"

Lola nodded slowly.

"How about you?"

Lola gave her a questioning look.

"Well, aren't you curious about your birth parents? I thought it was interesting that you wanted me to look into reconnecting with my parents, but you've never really talked about finding yours."

"Oh!" Lola sat back. "I have to think about it."

"Okay." Del sat back too. "Fair enough."

"Nice job turning the tables," Lola said, crossing her eyes and sticking out her tongue.

Del laughed and shook her head. "Listen, you're right. I owe you a real conversation about all this. But it really has been a shitty day. I don't wanna get into anything heavy right now."

"You never do." Lola rubbed her eyes. "Are you ever going to talk to me? Or are you just going to keep freezing me out until I give up?"

Del blinked and snapped her mouth shut. "You're ambushing me," she said. "Is it really so unreasonable to say, now isn't a good time for a serious talk? Can't we plan a different time to have the rest of this conversation? So I have a minute to breathe?"

"Okay. Fine." Lola leaned forward and tried to hold Del's gaze but Del looked away. "Maybe you could tell me why today was so frustrating."

Del shook her head. "I'd prefer not to."

"Well, all right then, Bartleby." Lola sat back, dropping her napkin and pushing her plate away with an ugly scrape.

"Don't get wound up," Del said. "I'm just in a lousy mood. People do that sometimes. Everyone can't live in Happyland all the time."

"I'm not asking you to live in Happyland. I'm asking you to talk to me. A lot has happened. That whole nightmare, that happened to both of us. To us together. Can't we just talk about it? Please? It doesn't have to be today, but—"

"Good."

"What happened, Del?"

"Nothing." Del stood and cleared her place, avoiding Lola's gaze.

"You think I'm mad at you about Janet. You're closing off from me because you don't want to have to hear me complain about it, but I won't. I don't blame you. I just want to—"

"I love you, you know that, right?"

Lola seemed to sense that she was being shut down. She pressed her lips into a thin line before sighing heavily in what looked like resignation. "I love you too."

They exchanged a perfunctory kiss and hug.

Del was shocked by the relief that washed over her as she loped across the street to her own home. Two minutes later, she picked up the phone.

"Hi, Del, what's up?"

"I just wanted to say I'm sorry. You were nice enough to have me over and I was a jerk. I didn't even thank you for dinner. Forgive me?"

"Always," Lola murmured. "I'm not trying to push. I just want to connect with you again, you know?"

"I know you're right. We should talk. I'm just not ready. Can you wait a little longer?"

"I guess. I just—we can't keep putting things off like this."

"Yeah." There was a long pause.

"You don't want to talk about it."

"Sorry." There was another long pause. "I'm a bit ragged right now."

"Why? What happened?"

"A kid was murdered. I can't see any way I'll find his killer. They beat him to death, just smashed his whole face, and dumped him in an alley. He was half starved, living on the streets, I think. He deserved better. He was a nice kid, you know? And I already—he just deserved better."

"You care about people, Del." Lola's voice was soft. "That's what makes you good at your job, isn't it? But the way you talk about him, he was special. Why?"

Del laughed brokenly. "You always ask the question I don't want to think about."

* * *

"'Mission Women Terrified, Police Stymied' is what they're saying."

Standing as if in an early morning prayer circle, the officers listened to their boss rant. Del resisted the urge to glance at her partner, whose comically attentive look was a good distraction from this stupid meeting about a peeper. What she wanted was to hear about Mikey Ocampo's autopsy. A quick peek at the clock behind Captain Bradley told her it had only been a little more than twenty-four hours since she and Phan had been called to Shotwell Street, but she had a feeling Mikey's case was, despite their efforts, already cold. And now this.

After again reading the headline aloud, Captain Bradley glared at the cobbled together special investigative unit for a long minute. He had arranged extra patrols and a series of programs on self-defense. He'd set up a hotline, had warning flyers posted around the area, and saturated the social media sites. He was hosting weekly community forum meetings and making sure they were covered by the media. He'd put a series of female officers in front of television cameras to plead for help with the investigation. Bradley had requested updates on the local sex offenders. He'd pulled every available investigator from every nonessential task.

Finally the captain waved them off as if in disgust. As the officers wandered back to their desks, Del exchanged glances with Phan. Within seconds, Mission Station was again filled with the usual babble of voices and ringing phones and fingers pounding on keyboards. Though she couldn't see it from her seat on the second floor of the station, Del knew that, only feet away, Valencia Street bubbled with a more melodious mix of sound and movement.

"Bradley's doing everything possible," Phan said. He shook back his long hair, and Del suppressed a smile. Phan wore perfectly ironed oxfords with perfectly ironed trousers and gleaming loafers. He was clean-shaven. His desk was perfectly organized. He was controlled, disciplined and appropriate. His one indulgence was his hair. Long, slightly wavy, and thick, his mane was always beautifully cut and his one source of vanity. When he was tense, Phan would touch his hair or shake it back or toss it like he was a restless pony.

"True. But everyone's still freaked."

"Well, you know how it is."

"Peepers aren't dangerous," Del started, meeting Phan's eyes. They finished the sentence together. "Until they're dangerous."

In the fifteen months that she and Phan had been partners, Del had come to appreciate the easy connection between them. She'd had a lot of partners over her twenty years in law enforcement. Some had been mentors, a few had been nightmares, but most had been men she'd had to work hard to build rapport with. Almost from the beginning, she and Tom Phan had been able to bypass the power struggles and misunderstandings that can get in the way of successful teamwork.

She wasn't sure what it was about Phan that made him so easy to deal with. He was a little senior to her in both age and experience, but he was a true partner. He was smart, so that helped. And he was confident enough not to need her to stroke his ego. He didn't seem to find her threatening or off-putting or inferior. She smiled at Phan and saw his easy grin spread across his wide face. Then he frowned over her shoulder, and Del turned to see why.

"Come on!" This came from Milner, an inspector recently passed over for promotion for the fourth time. "A couple of sluts got nervous, somebody took a peek at their tits? Big deal, close the fuckin' blinds, you don't wanna get looked at. No common goddamn sense!"

"Milner," Bradley barked from somewhere behind Del. "My office, pronto."

"Jesus jumped-up Christ. Here we go again. 'Make nice-nice with the bitches'—I've heard this speech a hundred fuckin' times."

No one responded.

"Milner's an ass," Phan put in quietly as the partners watched Milner strut across the station.

"Burnout."

"You don't think he was always a jerk?"

"Maybe." Del gave a wry smile. "I know peepers can escalate, I just think we may have bigger fish to fry. Like Mikey."

"I know." Phan pointed at his desk as if to remind Del of their sixteen hours of work the previous day and the dead ends they'd chased down in trying to solve Mikey Ocampo's brutal murder.

Del rubbed her thumb absently on the case file. "I owe him. I can't let him down again."

"I get that. When we get the autopsy report we'll focus on the kid, okay?" Phan tapped his desk as if to punctuate a change of subject. "Listen, how dangerous do you think our peeper could be? Does he have a record? Is he single, married? Can he hold down a job? Is he afraid of girls, too socially awkward to get a date? Or is it more complex?"

"Why're you asking me?"

"You worked sex crimes a lot longer than I did. Bradley said, back when he was matchmaking, you had some kinda amazing arrest and conviction record, sex crimes superstar."

Del shook her head. "Bullshit."

Phan nodded. "Mason, throw something out there. It's not like you to hold back."

"I don't know enough to say much." When Phan merely stared at her, Del shrugged in resignation. "You want my worthless, no-insight-included guess?"

"Disclaimer noted."

"The guy is single, a planner. Has a low-level job with limited face-to-face. Smart. Arrogant. Disdainful of women, threatened by women. Possibly religious, it reinforces his gender fuckery. Innocuous, polite, not overtly creepy."

"That's pretty detailed for an off-the-cuff guess."

"Probably bull. Broad strokes based on nothing."

"Right." Phan made a face. "If he's afraid of women, why not just look at porn?"

Del sat back in her worn desk chair. "Maybe he does, but porn isn't intrusive enough. Voyeurs are turned on by the fact that the victims can't consent to their watching. The invasion of privacy, the violation, is the important thing. Forbidden fruit, you know, stolen candy is sweeter. He's a naughty boy. The secrecy and violation are the turn-ons, maybe more than the actual women."

"I don't know about that," Phan countered. "Naked ladies are pretty enticing. And remember, we lowly men don't have your evolved sensibilities."

Del gave the obligatory snort and motioned at him to continue.

"Putting that aside," Phan grimaced, "so our guy decides to walk around, look in a window here and there, maybe getting shot or arrested, over staying home, looking at porn? Doesn't track."

"No, it doesn't." Del shrugged. "I can't explain it." She thought for a minute. "Hey, maybe there's porn tailored to peepers. You know, simulated peeping."

"Why not? There's every other kind."

They went to Anton Jones, a computer expert in the department. He interrupted their rundown of the case with a shake of his head. His wide eyes regarded them with wry good humor.

"Right," he said. "You know I actually work here, right? I've been collating data on this for days. The pattern isn't distinctive enough to offer much in terms of narrowing the pool of suspects. But you already know that. So what's your angle? What do you want from me?"

Phan filled him in on their question, and Jones wrapped his thin arms around his long, narrow torso before answering. Del watched his face relax into a wide, amused smile.

"You want me to find out who's looking at peeper porn?" Jones shook his head, still smiling. "Do you have any idea how much porn there is? How much of each type? How many possible versions of peeper porn there must be? And I can't look at who's downloading anything without a warrant, you know that. Yeah, sorry, guys, no can do."

Del made a face. "What about identifying individuals who download excessive porn?"

Jones laughed so hard he reared back in his undersized chair and almost hit the back of his head on the colorful *Dr. Who* poster he'd recently hung in his tiny cubicle.

"Come on! What's an excessive amount of porn? Phan, you like to look at naked women, right? Shit, Mason, don't you? I sure as hell do. And it's legal. You want to know who's looking at what? You need something real. Give me a name, an address and a warrant, I can tell you every keystroke in the guy's history. But until then, there's no way."

Disappointed, the partners thanked Jones and left his little kingdom. As they walked away, Del heard Jones muttering something about "excessive porn" and chuckling. Back in the larger space they shared with the other Mission Station officers, Phan and Mason wrote a list of questions they needed to answer to identify the peeper.

"You feeling hamstrung?"

Del nodded. "He's invisible. In such a big city, a guy like this disappears."

There were over a hundred registered sex offenders in the Mission District—not, unfortunately, an unusual number for a neighborhood of that size and density. Del and Phan and several other investigative pairs combed through the records with both care and urgency.

"Hey," Del called out to her partner later that afternoon. "I say we send out an email asking all the detectives in the area for the names of sex crime suspects not arrested or convicted within the last year."

"You're shitting me!" Phan threw his hands in the air. "Do you have any idea how many pervs that is?"

"What else can we do?"

"Oh, I don't know, maybe we could just count the grains of sand on the beach."

"You know I'm right," Del said, arching an eyebrow.

"Doesn't mean I have to like it." Phan mirrored her expression, and Del smiled.

"What?" Phan frowned at her.

"What, what?"

"You're smiling at me. I don't like it."

Del rolled her eyes and ignored Phan to focus on sending out the request for updates.

The responses came pouring in within minutes, and she was struck by how many officers were immediately able to name multiple suspected rapists who'd never been booked, much less imprisoned. Del and Phan created a spreadsheet that detailed the specifics on each suspect and asked Captain Bradley for a couple of warm bodies to input the data. He agreed, and within an hour they were watching the spreadsheet grow to cosmic proportions. Setting aside the pedophiles, they were able to cut the number in half, but it was clear there were a lot of sex offenders roaming around. Their pool of suspects was a flood.

"Makes me sick," Phan snapped. "These assholes get away scot-free."

"You know how rare it is for a rapist to spend a single night in jail?"

"Too fucking rare."

"Got that right." Eyeing her partner's glower, Del decided not to follow up with the statistics. As the father of an adolescent daughter, Phan was increasingly wound up about crimes against women, and Del wasn't interested in distracting him further. Her mild-mannered partner could respond to most things coolly, but woe to the bad guy who laid a single hand on sweet young Kaylee Phan.

"I'd help you get rid of the body," Del said impulsively, mostly joking.

Phan's ghastly smile told her he'd followed her line of thinking, and she wished she'd kept her mouth shut.

Though they continued to look at hundreds of suspects, no one stood out. As dinnertime came and went, Del and Phan put aside their work on the peeper case and focused on Mikey Ocampo's murder. After reviewing their notes and the list of possible interview subjects, they went over what little they knew.

Phan flipped through the photos from the crime scene. "Okay, let's lay out a timeline from the time you met him to now."

"He got five years in juvenile detention in Stockton and was released after four. Mom died, breast cancer, while he was still locked up. A year ago Mikey got released to a group home."

"Did he even get to say goodbye to his mom?"

"I don't know." Del shook her head. "She didn't have health care with any of her jobs, and it looks like either the cancer got too far before it was diagnosed or she couldn't afford treatments or didn't know how to get help. I didn't hear about her death until later."

"Okay. So Mikey goes from juvie in Stockton into a group home here in the city," Phan prompted. "After a few months of getting along fine—he's going to school, passing his classes, no arrests, no fights, no disciplinary actions, no red flags—one day he just runs away. No dirty drug test? No pregnant girlfriend? No bullies in the group home? No pervy adults in his life?"

"Nothing. So far. He was in the wind for months before his body was found." Del exhaled loudly. "We have to reinterview everybody. The counselors, the social worker, the group home kids, teachers, students at the high school, neighbors. Somebody knows something."

"He's never been to any of the shelters?"

"Nope. Not the churches either. No hospital visits. No connections." Del ticked off the fruitless investigative inquiries. "No arrests since that one five years back. No known gang affiliations, in juvie or out of it. None of the street kids seem to know him, at least they won't admit to knowing him. I don't know if Mikey was gay or straight or bi or trans, religious, agnostic, a health nut, a musician, a nerd, anything. Now the forensic scraps."

"Scraps is right." Phan pursed his lips. "Okay, the postmortem didn't add much to the picture. No recent sexual assault or sexual activity. Scrambled face, you saw that. It looks like he was beaten with fists, kicked, and hit with what might have been a golf club. Evidence of earlier abuse, physical and sexual. Scarring, healed fractures, a couple of missing teeth. Positive for pot and ecstasy, but he wasn't a junkie. Dehydrated, empty stomach, both of which could mean he was held at some point or just that he was hungry and thirsty because he was homeless. HIV negative. No hep, no gonorrhea, no ongoing disease or infection. Wrists show some abrasions from restraints, looks like they used rope. And that's about it at this point. If we had anything—"

"Right." Del again looked over the photos of Mikey's body and of Shotwell Street. She saw nothing new. "Killed somewhere else, like we thought."

"Yeah. Dead for six hours when we saw him. Some transfer of clothing fibers, plus maybe carpet from a trunk. Like the rope and the golf club, nothing distinctive, no identification of either unless we have a comparison. Nothing useful in terms of the location of the actual assault or which vehicle was used to move him. We need a suspect before the forensics are useful."

"Nobody knows him, nobody remembers him, but somebody tied him up and then beat him to death around midnight Monday night." Del pushed back her hair. "Why?"

"And was the destruction of his face to slow identification, or was it a personal thing?"

Knowing Phan didn't expect an answer, Del stared at the most recent photo of Mikey they had been able to find. It had come from a kid in the group home. In the photo, taken nine days before his disappearance, Mikey and five other kids stood behind a wide, scarred oak table. Someone must have done something silly right before the photo was snapped, because all of the kids were laughing. Del stared at Mikey's open, gleeful expression, his short, neat haircut, his black T and long, ropy arms. He was at the back of the group and was mostly hidden by another kid, but he looked happy. He didn't look like a kid who was about to run away and disappear from view. He didn't look like a kid who was only months away from being murdered. He looked like a regular teenager.

Del searched the photo for clues—regarding his relationships with the other kids, his emotional state, his physical wellbeing, anything—but all she could glean was that he seemed in the picture to be happy and to be comfortable with the other kids. No one seemed to know anything meaningful about Mikey, and she was determined to figure out why. They spent a couple of hours going over what little they knew and dividing up the to-do list on Mikey's case.

"We'll go over it all again as soon as we have anything else, I promise."

"Okay," Del muttered, closing the file. "Back to the pervert."

"Oh goodie," Phan said under his breath. They repeated many of the same steps they had just gone through with Mikey's case: reading the files, taking notes, looking for patterns and differentiating features, and making to-do lists.

"Who is this peeper?" Phan asked.

"Apparently he's nobody." She pointed at the computer to indicate the burgeoning database of potential suspects. "He's everybody."

"Could be more than one guy," Phan offered.

"Yeah. Or it could be the same guy in disguise. We have too many pervs, too many different descriptions, too many of everything but solid leads."

"Too many hours adding up to nothing." Phan slapped a file down on the pile. "I'm taking Alana out tonight. Wanna join us?"

"Thanks, but I'm gonna go home. I've been promising to make Lola dinner for months, and I owe her for Janet and Sterling."

"None of that was your fault."

Del shrugged. "I dated a crazy woman. At least some of that is on me."

Phan laughed and shook his head. "Mason, if dating crazy women is a crime, then I'm due for a couple of life sentences."

Del rolled her eyes and grinned. "Okay, it's definitely time to get outta here. I'm actually starting to think your jokes are funny."

They'd almost made it out of the station when Bradley barked out their names.

"Got another one, and I want you two over there."

Del led the way to the parking lot.

"My turn to drive," she said, and Phan grunted in agreement.

On their way to interview the latest peeping victim, Phan called to cancel dinner with Alana, who was none too happy. Phan rubbed his eyes.

"I'm glad the victim called it in, but there's gotta be a way to balance this job and having a life."

"I wish someone would figure it out." Del eyed the fannypack-sporting tourists jaywalking in front of them. Based on the direction from which they ambled through traffic, she guessed they were on their way back from viewing the colorful Clarion Alley Mural Project, situated just across busy Valencia Street from the Mission Station.

Phan grunted. "I wish someone would figure out why so many of the victims didn't call us until Bradley started doing the media blitz asking women to come forward."

"Being a woman means constantly being judged. Harshly. You're never good enough. You're always in the wrong and it's other women as much as men." She huffed as she braked to avoid a cyclist who cut in front of her in the descending mist that characterized San Francisco's late-autumn evenings. "Shit. Imagine not knowing if the cop you talked to would be Milner. No wonder they underreport."

"If a woman came to me to report any crime, I'd treat her with respect. If a man came to me, same thing. Whoever." Phan's tone was mild, but she felt his tension. "Just 'cause I'm a guy, that doesn't mean I'm a pig."

"I know." Del smiled. "But you are a rare and wonderful creature, that most mysterious and mythical being, the truly evolved male."

Phan grunted and scratched his chin. "And they may figure, all he did was look."

"Yeah." Del eyed the night sky, wondering if the peeper was in one of the houses they were passing at that moment. "All he did was look. Not enough to bother with, according to Carter."

She and Phan had already met with sex-crimes specialist Angela Carter with a plan of going over the case files and building a profile. This had been days earlier, when they'd first been pulled into the widening investigation, and the cold shoulder they'd gotten still rankled.

"Listen," Carter had muttered, looking up from the files after a cursory glance. "Odds are this is as much as he does. I mean, he hasn't even spoken to one victim or gone inside. He's not exposing himself to them. Yeah, the guy's a creep and I hope you catch him, but even your victims didn't think it was enough of a problem to bother calling it in."

"You don't think he's escalating?"

"Well, he's getting physically closer to the domiciles. But is he still running away when they see him? Seems like it. He's not trying to get in, that's the main thing." Carter had stood and stretched. "I don't mean to sound callous, you guys, but I've got six rapes and four abuse cases on my desk and a partner out 'cause his wife had a kid. I hope your guy doesn't hurt anybody. I hope you catch him. Until or unless he escalates, I can't do more than that. Get a good sketch if you can, tell people to put in motion-sensor lights and close their drapes and hope for the best. Everybody on the damn planet has a cell phone with a camera, so why don't you have a photo? Maybe we have bigger fish to fry, right? Mason, you know what I'm saying, I've seen your arrest numbers. You wanna come back here, you're welcome, as far as I'm concerned. This loser? Get someone to take a picture of him. Call me when he yanks out his dick or refuses to leave or tries to get inside a victim's house. Until then, I have to go interview a foster kid who was rescued from a sex trafficker and has now sexually abused at least three other foster kids. So, you know, I'm kinda busy."

"Ridiculous," Phan muttered as they neared the latest crime scene, and Del knew he was still thinking of Carter too.

Del was thoughtful. "I don't think I could work that division again, could you? Fucks you up. You see a six-year-old raped by her dad, and you have to baby her in to get a med workup. Interview the whole family, look for other victims, talk to the so-called experts, write up a report. Then the kid recants, her mommy told her to. Mommy calls her a lying slut right there in front of you. That's just another day, there'll be another one tomorrow or sooner. Peeper seems like nothing."

"And—"

"And I get it. I'd rather work Mikey's murder than this."

"We both would. And I understand that he's especially important to you. I get why."

"Which I appreciate." Del made a face. "But we still have nothing."

The normally sunny Mission District was by this time blanketed in the heavy fog that arrived each November. Behind the damp shroud, Del knew, were the shops, restaurants and homes that served as the backdrop for a swirling mass of human dramas.

Housing one small human drama was a diminutive beige house on Guerrero Street. It was dwarfed on both sides by three-story stacks of flats. Linking the apartment buildings and their sandwiched neighbor was a matching set of black wrought-iron gates. Each sported a hefty keyed lock. Pausing before they ascended the half-dozen stairs that led to the front door, the partners eyed the home's points of entry.

"The front windows, maybe living room and kitchen," Phan noted.

Del murmured in assent before pointing at the narrow gaps between the small house and its neighboring apartment buildings. "So either the guy looked in one of those windows or he got past one of the gates."

A baby-faced patrol officer Del had never met let the pair in and offered a brief summary of what he'd learned before disappearing to the front of the house. The living room was tiny, with barely enough room for a small couch and chair. A budget television hung over the rounded fireplace. The home was tidy, with a notable absence of clutter. Del examined the pictures on a small shelf above the entry tiles: beaming mom and dad with young college graduate daughter, smiling women in fancy dresses, pretty little girl in Catholic school plaid.

The victim came out of the bathroom, red-eyed and pale. She was a pretty, thirtyish Hispanic woman sporting a chic, short hairstyle and a thick pink bathrobe and matching fuzzy slippers. She had a small bandage on one knee but wasn't limping.

"Hi, I'm Inspector Del Mason. This is my partner, Inspector Tom Phan."

"Hi. Sofia Gonzalez."

Del and Phan exchanged a glance, and he withdrew, mumbling some nonsense about a perimeter.

"Can I get you some coffee? Tea?" Sofia Gonzalez gestured at the couch.

"Actually, how about we sit in the kitchen? Is that okay?"

"Sure. It's bigger anyway. Tea all right?"

At Del's nod, Sofia Gonzalez led the way to a small white kitchen that was almost completely bare. It looked more like a display used to advertise cleaning products than a place where people might cook or eat.

"Ms. Gonzalez?"

"Sofia, please. Chamomile okay? I have to work in the morning, and it's late." The petite woman glanced at the wall clock as she put on a teakettle. She sat at the table and started fussing with her hair.

"Sofia, Inspector Phan and I are here to help you."

"Yes."

"I know you already talked to Officer Chang, but I need to ask you to do it again, and don't worry about telling me too much or taking too long or repeating yourself, all right?" She sat back, pulling out her notebook. The cellphone didn't work in interviews; witnesses and victims seemed to see note-taking on a phone as texting.

"Okay."

"You came home," Del prompted, and Sofia gave a nervous laugh.

"I came home from work." She stopped, shrugged. "It sounds—"

"Where do you work? What do you do?"

"RN. The burn unit at Mercy."

"Whew. Sounds like a tough job. Pretty hot in there, right?"

Sofia laughed. "It really is." She sobered. "But of course our patients don't usually have a lot of skin to keep them warm."

Del nodded.

"It was a rotten day, to tell you the truth."

"How come?"

"We lost a patient, a really amazing guy. We knew there was almost no chance he'd survive so it wasn't a shock, but still. He suffered so much for so long and then his heart finally gave out. My friend Luz, we work together, we both know better, of course. But he was special, we got attached to him. After all those weeks. All that suffering, all that time, and then he just died."

"I'm sorry."

She shrugged.

The two sat in silence that was broken by gurgling from the teakettle. Del watched as Sofia made their tea and brought the cups to the table.

"How do you get over something like that?"

"Ha." Sofia shook her head. "You figure it out, be sure and let me know."

"Yeah." Del nodded. "Right back at you."

Sofia took a sip from her steaming mug, sitting back with her legs crossed. Del mirrored her posture.

"There are so many people like us," Sofia offered.

Del gestured at her to continue.

"We do these jobs, wanting to help, wanting to make a difference. Then we get attached to people we don't even know personally. Then they die or do something stupid or whatever, and we're a mess. And we keep coming back for more."

"Masochists, obviously."

They shared a grim smile. Sofia Gonzalez was, from what Del could see, easy to like. She was empathetic, smart, appropriately responsive. She'd be a good witness, in the unlikely event of a court case. Phan showed up and hovered in the doorway to the kitchen, waiting for Del's casual nod. He came in and leaned against the kitchen counter.

Del nodded at Sofia. "So you came home feeling lousy. You came directly home?"

"Around four. It was really foggy, which did not improve my mood. Worked a double. I should've gone to bed early, but I wasn't that tired. Actually I was starving, wanted to eat something before my shower. I always take a shower when I get home." She laughed. "Sorry. Am I making sense? Now I'm tired."

"You're doing fine. What'd you eat?"

"Oh!" She laughed again. "Toaster waffle with peanut butter. You know, single-girl food. I ate it standing up. Pretty sad, right? My mom would be horrified. I went to my room, undressed. I only have the one bathroom, I put on my robe first, so I didn't have to take my clothes from the bathroom." She waved at a door off the hallway that divided the living room and bedroom on the left side of the house and the bathroom and kitchen on the other. "So I'm putting on my robe and I see a face at my window. I scream like some stupid teenager in a horror movie, and he's just standing there staring at me."

Del waited. Sofia pushed back her hair and shrugged.

"I started to run into the hallway, but I bumped into the bed. All the rooms here are what realtors like to call 'cozy.'" She took a deep breath. "He *laughed*. I fell down, and he was laughing and I got mad. I grabbed something, I think it was a shoe, and I threw it at the window. He just stood there laughing at me, and my robe was falling open, and I started crying."

Del nodded, not wanting to interrupt.

"Oh," Sofia groaned, covering her face. "I get up, and he's looking at me, like, why are you crying?" She shook her head. "And I'm scared again. He starts fussing with the window, like he's trying to open it, and I start screaming, and I run to the front door. I go to open it, and then I'm thinking, no, he's outside, and then I'll be outside too." She shrugged.

"It's natural," Del put in. "You don't want to be near the guy."

"Exactly." Sofia shrugged and took another sip of tea. "And the fog was so thick, I couldn't have seen a thing anyway. So I grab my cell and call nine-one-one. I stay in the kitchen, and by the time that first cop gets here—Officer Chang—the guy is gone." She crossed her arms. "This is so stupid. I watch the news, I have an alarm, I know there's a creep out there watching women, but I didn't think it would happen to me. I thought he did his thing at night, plus I guess I figured these guys like looking at young girls, you know?"

"What did he look like? Can you remember?"

"Oh," she closed her eyes. "Youngish. Baby face, big cheeks. Dark eyes, you know, sleepy eyes, bedroom eyes? Pointy nose, small chin. High forehead, light brown hair, thinning on the top. Widow's peak. Hardly any eyebrows." She shuddered and then took a sip of tea. "The thing is, he looked totally harmless. Really. I mean, if I saw him on the street or in a store or something, I wouldn't even notice him. He seemed totally innocuous. Well, except I thought maybe he was touching himself. Now that I think about it, I'm not sure he was. Maybe I just assumed he was."

Del looked down at her notes. "When he laughed, could you hear him?"

Sofia thought for a moment before she shook her head. "Actually, he covered his mouth with his hand, like a little girl. Oh, he had a ring on his hand!"

"Left or right?"

"Um, right. A plain gold band, like a wedding ring, but it was on the middle finger of his right hand."

"Big hand, small?"

"Um, smallish."

"White guy?"

"I don't know. Medium everything. Totally a blank canvas. Seriously, the more that I think about it, the guy looked like somebody who'd get beat up by a bully. I don't know why I was so scared." She was laughing nervously.

"Sofia, if I saw a face at my bedroom window, I'd be scared. I don't care how harmless the guy looks at Starbucks, at your bedroom window, any stranger is scary. Calling for help was absolutely the right thing to do. Is your bedroom at the back of the house?"

She nodded. "And my side gates were locked last night. I know because I have to check. The kids in the neighborhood know I work a lot, if I leave one open the yard turns into a Belushi movie."

"Is there a lock on your bedroom window?"

"Yes, and I put a stick in it."

"Good. Sofia, did the guy look at all familiar to you? A face you've seen before, maybe?"

She shook her head. "Honestly, he was pretty bland. Invisible, you know? I could have seen his face a dozen times somewhere else and never remembered it. Not ugly, not handsome, not anything." She rubbed her eyes. "I think he's been here before."

Del frowned. "Tell me about that."

Sofia glanced at Phan and looked down. Phan took the hint. He made some excuse to leave the room, and Del nodded at Sofia to continue.

"I should've—I don't know. I called the police station on Valencia, not nine-one-one. It didn't seem like an emergency. Anyway, I'm not sure it was the same man."

Del nodded slowly. "Maybe you could walk me through that, the whens and whats, okay?"

Ten minutes later Del was scribbling her cell phone number on a card—something she hadn't done but a handful of times before—and handing it to Sofia. "Anything else? Okay, thank you very much for talking to me. We rely on folks to tell us what's going on, and I'm sorry you didn't get a good response the first time. If anything hinky happens, will you please call nine-one-one and then me?"

"I will," Sofia promised, glancing at the clock. "Is it okay if I get dressed now?"

As they headed back to the station, Del rolled her head from one side to the other, cracking her neck.

Phan muttered, "Seeing the victim like that."

Del nodded. "Makes it feel more like a crime than a nuisance."

"She's a nice lady."

"I agree, and she shouldn't have to feel scared in her own home." She hesitated. "Listen, I think it's interesting that the guy's been there before, maybe. She saw movement in her backyard one night a few weeks ago, but it was really dark and she wasn't sure. She called the station and got someone—

I'm guessing Milner—who told her to buy curtains. She was embarrassed, almost didn't call us this time."

Phan was quiet for a moment. "You'll put this in the report?"

"Of course. Makes you wonder how many others there are who'll never call in. How many just move in with their boyfriend or move back home or buy a gun or just lose sleep or drink or whatever. Because they think they can't call us or we won't take them seriously."

A few minutes later Del and Phan watched Bradley process their verbal breakdown of the interview, including the fact that Sofia Gonzalez had been rebuffed weeks earlier when trying to report a peeper. After making notes to himself, Bradley visibly waved this aside and focused on the current issue.

"Is this another escalation in the peeper's behavior? The backyard, trying to open the window?" Bradley's gaze bounced from Del to Phan and back again. His eyes were red-rimmed, his tie askew. Like the detectives, he'd been at the station for over sixteen hours and was still not finished for the day.

Phan gestured at Del, who shrugged.

"Hard to tell. He might have had an impulse to help the vic. He laughed when she fell down but he might have been startled. People laugh when they're nervous. She started crying and he might have felt bad."

"Hm." Bradley tilted his head. "You make him sound pretty sympathetic."

"No, he's a creep, but he doesn't seem all that overtly dangerous at this point." Del shrugged. "It doesn't sound like he was trying to get in to harm her physically."

"Maybe he doesn't think of himself as a bad guy," Bradley put in.

"Well. Maybe not." Phan cleared his throat. "We think we need more specifics before we can really guess at his motives."

Making a face at his relentlessly ringing phone, Bradley rubbed his forehead, waving them off.

"I actually feel bad for the guy," Del said, gesturing at Bradley as they left his office.

"Oh, shit." Phan made as if to feel her forehead. "You feeling okay?"

"Bradley's doing a decent job, other than the results. Now he has to deal with a nonresponsive officer. If that goes public, the investigation goes to hell along with our reputation."

Phan grimaced. "How many other women called and got the same response, or didn't bother calling in because they figured they'd be flicked off? What if Kaylee was off at college and something happened and she didn't call because of that?"

Del wondered about Phan's tendency to frame every crime against a woman around how his daughter would feel if she were the victim. While it made him a more sympathetic listener and more responsive investigator, what was the personal cost to him? How did it shape his relationship with his daughter?

"I've been thinking." Del rubbed her forehead. "Men are taught from infancy that women exist for their stimulation. Their sexual satisfaction. Their ego gratification. How does a guy know when he's won? When he gets to sleep with whatever women he wants. Sex is just a way of keeping score. You win a war, you get the women as prizes. You claim the land by raping the women and making them have your kids. The more money you have, the easier it is to get a beautiful young wife. If you're an athlete, supermodels will sleep with you. Women are booty for the most successful pirates. Then we act surprised when men treat women like things instead of people." Del eyed her partner. "I always wonder what it is that makes a guy like you."

She watched Phan stifle a defensive impulse. "What do you mean?"

"Well," Del inclined her head. "You seem to think I'm a person. Your daughter's a person. Alana. Lola. You even think your ex-wife is a person. So tell me, how did you come out all right?"

"Seriously?" Phan stopped and eyed Del. "How come I'm a man but not a sociopath? Is it that hard to figure? Have you met so few guys that aren't assholes?"

"It's not that." Del hesitated. Clearly she'd put a foot wrong, but she wasn't sure how.

"I'm fucking with you." Phan grinned, tossing back his shaggy hair. "Most guys are assholes for a good three or four decades, maybe longer. That's why I'm teaching Kaylee how to shoot."

Del rolled her eyes. "She'd be better off learning how to fight hand-to-hand."

"Oh, she's learning that too." Phan's smile widened. "Trust me."

"I do." Del held Phan's gaze.

"You're a good partner," Phan said. "I don't think I've ever had a better one, and I've been at this even longer than you have."

Del grinned. "You are pretty old."

"Fifty." Phan took a deep breath and made a face. "God, I never imagined myself surviving this long. Of course, I never pictured myself as a cop when I was young. You?"

"Oh, I'll never make it to fifty." Del grinned at Phan's impatient huff. "Yeah. I think I wanted to be a cop from the time I was a teenager. I always wanted to be one of the good guys, you know? Help the little guy, stand on the side of the angels, all of it. I still feel that way."

"I bet you were a giant pain in the ass when you were a rookie."

Del laughed. "I'm still a pain in the ass."

Phan smiled and then sobered. "He is escalating."

"Yeah." She shook her head. "We've got six women, including Sofia, coming in tomorrow to work on a sketch. A lot more interviews with pervs. The media is even sorta helping us. There can't be a woman in the area who doesn't know to close her drapes, lock her doors, watch out for strangers. I don't know what else to do now."

"I do." Phan stood. "We go home."

"We didn't do shit tonight but take an interview and find out we dropped the ball."

"We're done. I'm sorry, but it's midnight and I'm done."

Del knew he was right. Still she stayed a while after Phan left, trying to think of another way to find something, anything, but they'd already covered the basics. Too tired to do more than go over the same old ground, she finally gave in and went home.

A couple of hours later, heading to her bedroom, Del thought about the latest victim, Sofia, coming home tired and frustrated, just like Del, and having to deal with the peeper. Del fantasized for a moment that the guy was in her yard, looking in her window. She would catch him and make sure he got locked up. Or was that arrogance? She hadn't been able to get away from one tiny ex-girlfriend, so how could she think she'd be able to get the peeper? Del had to remind herself that she'd apprehended plenty of bad guys and hadn't ever had a problem doing her job as well as any other cop. Janet had gotten the drop on her, and it could have happened to anyone, Del huffed to herself.

She saw a lump on the bed then and stiffened. How had she not sensed there was someone here? Her hand went to her weapon and her breathing went fast.

Then her hand dropped. The figure on the bed was Lola. What was she doing? They hadn't been lovers in months. Lola didn't even live in this house anymore. She'd left without notice and moved across the street to the house that had once scared her. She certainly hadn't spent the night in Del's bed since then. Del's stomach hurt. She'd been devastated by Lola's decampment and still didn't understand it. She blinked away sudden tears, wishing she knew how to connect with this beautiful woman she still loved.

Lola whimpered then, in the grip of yet another nightmare. Del eased onto the mattress and held her, calmed her for the duration of the dream. She hadn't held Lola like this since her haircut and rubbed her lips gently against the soft, short strands. It was like baby hair, and it smelled like Lola—lavender and vanilla and something else. For months Del had sat across the table or across the room from Lola and craved the scent and the feel of her. Their brief hugs and kisses had only made Del feel lonelier. She squeezed her eyes shut, not wanting the grief and frustration of the last months to spoil this little bit of intimacy.

It was absurd—could she really only feel close to Lola when she was asleep? She drew back and looked at Lola, who was finally relaxed. The moonlight painted her a silvery blue, and

Del was flooded with tenderness. She wished she could change things, make Lola's bad memories go away and make her own bad memories go away too. She wanted to wash them both clean and start all over again with no hurt, no guilt, no disappointment, no regrets, no scars. If she could, she would keep Janet from showing up to wreck everything, stop Sterling from killing all those women and trying to kill Lola. She would stop Sterling from shooting her and stop herself from taking it out on Lola. She would, as long as she was at it, keep Christopher James from terrorizing Lola. She would also keep Orrin Beckett from marrying teenage Lola and abusing her. She would make Lola's parents keep her and take care of her, and she would make her own parents keep themselves together enough to treat her right. In the magical world where she was all-powerful and had a time machine, Del would make everything perfect for both of them. If she could do that, would they be together now? Would she sleep next to Lola every night? Would she be able to give Lola what she needed if nothing else got in the way?

Del flexed her shoulders, feeling the pull that she knew came from not doing the physical therapy exercises for nearly a week. Scars don't go away, she told herself. Damage doesn't get undone. Lola had once said something about that, hadn't she? Del wished she'd paid more attention.

When dawn came a few hours later, she stood over Lola's sleeping form and chastised herself for being a chicken. What she should do was wake the woman, kiss her and apologize. She should tell Lola she loved her. She should bring her a cup of coffee and some toast and suggest they start over. She should kiss Lola a hundred times and apologize until Lola begged her to stop. She should reassure Lola that she didn't love Janet anymore and that she'd never let anyone get between them again. She should swear that Lola would be safe, both physically and emotionally, if she would just take Del back into her heart. But was that too simple? She was the one who'd done it all wrong, and she was the one who had to do the work to fix it. Why was she trying to push it all off onto Lola? Was she trying to let herself off the hook?

How do I apologize for being in love with my ex? Letting her come in and wreck our life together? How do I apologize for not only letting myself get kidnapped but also letting another psychopath kidnap you and try to kill you?

Del backed carefully away from the bed and escaped to work.

CHAPTER THREE

"You're too close to this," Phan said, leaning across his desk and pointing at Del. They'd both followed up with every contact Mikey might have had and found nothing. No one remembered Mikey, no one had anything to say about him. One group home employee remembered him as polite and quiet, and one guard at the juvenile detention center thought he might have been into Japanese comic books or something. That was about it. "You shouldn't be investigating Mikey's murder."

"It's not like I had a personal relationship with the kid," Del argued. "I met him one time, had a ten-minute interview with him and never saw him again until he was dead. Besides, there isn't anyone else to do it. You and I are it, partner."

"If you say so."

Del offered a curt nod and glanced at her watch: nearly noon. Mikey had been dead for nearly sixty hours.

She knew she'd identified too much with Mikey five years back. He'd been bright and battle-scarred and brave, just a kid and trying to act like an adult. He was only eleven when he shot the man who attacked his mother. How old was that, school-wise? Fourth grade? It seemed like a million years ago, her own fourth grade year. She'd tried to act like an adult at that age too.

Del's fourth grade teacher gave her a book about sea turtles. Del read the book over and over, entranced by the little creatures, struck by how perilous their early lives were, how they had to scramble across the sand past countless predators to the safety of the water. They were clumsy and slow on the sand, but in the water they could glide away from those who would eat them.

All I have to do, she thought day after day in the trailer park of her early years, is make it across the sand. All I have to do is survive until I'm old enough, and then I can glide through the water and be free. Her shell grew tougher and tougher as she endured the neglect and abuse her parents dished out. She didn't cry out when punched in the stomach. She didn't ask for food when she was hungry. She locked the tender, vulnerable parts of herself away for later. Mikey Ocampo had thought he was locked up tight, but Del had known the boy hadn't yet developed the tough shell needed to survive.

Unlike Mikey, Del had. However imperfectly, she had managed to not only survive but also to help some people along the way. She'd poked her head out once or twice, however briefly, with Elise and with Janet and again with Lola. Yeah, she'd retreated into that comfortable old shell more than she liked, but it had kept her alive. Lola's face flashed into Del's mind. Lola had her own little turtle shell, didn't she? And their shells were bumping a lot these days.

"We're getting nowhere right now. We need more information," Phan complained, pulling Del out of her thoughts. "Listen, back to the peeper, where does this behavior even come from?"

"Come on," she stated, "the world is saturated with misogyny. A real man dominates women, uses them, controls them, makes them property. Women are virginal children or oversexed whores. Bitches. Cunts. Conniving, fickle, selfish, inherently sinful and worthless."

"Sick." Phan shook his head. "How are you supposed to raise your daughter to be strong and independent and whole? Kaylee wants to wear makeup, she wants to get a push-up bra and high heels. She's barely a teenager, and she's already sure she's not good enough. We tried so hard, Tina and I made a lousy couple, but she's a good mom. We've both tried really hard to raise Kaylee to be confident and happy and independent, but it seems like the whole world is against us. What are we supposed to do?"

"I can only imagine. But come on," Del put in. "Kaylee's smart, focused, a good kid. She can't wait to get to Caltech so she can take over the world."

"Is that where she wants to go? I thought she was all jazzed about Stanford."

"That was months ago," Del said. "By now she could be looking at Harvard."

Phan shook his head. "Maybe you could keep me in the loop with my kid, huh?"

"Why would she talk to you? You're just her dad." Del rolled her eyes, knowing it would make him smile. Phan's daughter really was a nice kid, and Del kept in her back pocket the hope that of all the nice kids out there Kaylee would be one who got to live the perfect life everyone wanted.

They spent the rest of the day interviewing the other peeping victims again and learning nothing new. By the time they left for the day at nearly nine, Del was as discouraged as Phan looked. The victims all seemed changed by what was, on the surface, a relatively minor crime. And hours of work to identify the peeper were proving nothing but how hard it would be to catch him. Del offered Phan a desultory wave as they trudged out to their respective trucks.

At home she found herself wondering how Lola saw herself, and how she saw their relationship. Del had imagined she could protect herself and anyone who needed help, but she'd failed, hadn't she? From the beginning she'd been unable to protect Lola. Images from James's surveillance cameras, which he'd placed strategically and secretly all over Lola's house, haunted Del: James placing an unconscious Lola on the bed, James touching and fondling her, James tying her to a chair and—Del shut her eyes against the images. Sometimes Del couldn't touch Lola at all without thinking of James. It would make sense if Lola was thinking of her ordeal too.

And what about the terrible night between Del and Lola, when Del was such a monster and treated Lola like nothing? She remembered how she'd looked at Lola and wished it was Janet who lay naked in her bed. She remembered telling Lola she was nothing but the pieces left behind by her ex-husband and by Christopher James. Del knew she wasn't the same as Orrin Beckett or Christopher James, not really, but she didn't exactly feel like she was on the side of the angels either.

Del rose suddenly and started pacing around the room. She felt itchy and restless and worn out, all at the same time. She was on Lola's doorstep a minute later and hesitated only briefly before letting herself in and lightfooting it up to Lola's bedroom. She let out a short bark of a laugh and stifled it at once. After everything, she was sneaking into Lola's? Sure, Lola had snuck into her place, but somehow it felt different. Del snorted quietly then started to slip away, but it was too late. Lola rose sleepily onto one arm.

"You all right?" Her voice was quiet and sweet, her face soft and round in the moonlight. Del crossed over to her and sank onto the floor next to the bed. She laid her head on the mattress, holding on to Lola's arm, crying.

"Shhh. It's okay, it's okay," Lola soothed her.

She climbed into bed next to Lola, who cradled her into her chest. Del let herself be babied and petted, and she cried bitter tears into Lola's soft neck. Lola didn't ask what was wrong, didn't say anything, only made soothing sounds, and Del felt herself cry it all out and then drop into exhausted sleep.

She woke early, still curled tight against Lola's soft warmth, and the doubts and fears of the night before assailed her immediately. Her mouth was sour and dry. Her whole body ached. She felt Lola waking up and hauled herself out of bed. She tried to escape, but Lola grabbed her hand and held it.

"What's going on?"

Del shrugged. She couldn't begin to explain it. Lola got up and stood in front of Del, pulling her down for a kiss.

"Morning breath," Del muttered, resisting.

"Yeah. Me too," Lola whispered, still pulling at Del.

She gave in, then, leaning down to kiss Lola as gently as possible. Her soft lips yielded, her satiny hair tickled Del's cheeks, and Del let Lola guide her back to bed.

"Talk to me." Lola's bright eyes burned into Del's. "What's going on?"

"I'm so sorry," Del said, her voice too loud for the early hour. "I took you for granted. I didn't mean to, I never meant to. You deserved so much better than you got from me. You still do. I've been selfish, I've been such an ingrate, and I'm sorry. Can you forgive me?"

"I think we've both been doing the best we could." Lola scrunched up her nose. "We both have a lot to learn about relationships. I think we both made mistakes."

"You always let me off the hook. I'm not sure that's a good thing, Lola."

Lola seemed hurt by this. She lay on her back and stared at the ceiling. "Maybe you're right," she finally said. "I don't know."

Del lay next to Lola, eyeing the ceiling too. She reached out to hold Lola's cool, soft hand in hers and tried not to squeeze it. "I'd do everything differently if I could get a do-over."

"Everything?"

"Well, I'd make a cleaner break with Janet," Del started. "I'd—"

"Let's not get into all that."

Del bit her lip. She felt cold. Did Lola mean she was giving up on their relationship? Was that why she didn't want to talk about things? But then Lola rolled over and perched on Del, her face only an inch away from Del's, her body's weight on Del's a welcome burden.

"I want you," Lola whispered, her eyes dark and hungry.

Her heart raced as Lola's mouth searched hers. She didn't resist when Lola tenderly kissed her cheek, neck, shoulder, breast. Lola was so gentle, so soft and careful, that Del felt like a fragile thing being nursed to health by whisper-soft kisses. She felt something uncoiling in her. Her skin tingled in anticipation of Lola's lips, and she was breathless.

Lola stroked her curls with loving hands, and Del felt herself relaxing more and more. She could almost forget the world. Lola kissed her mouth again, over and over, so lightly that it felt like a dream. She felt the stirrings of desire again, then her breath caught, and her eyes opened. She didn't deserve to feel this pleasure. She didn't deserve Lola.

"Stop," she said. "Don't."

"Okay," Lola whispered. Her eyes searched Del's. "Are you all right?"

"Yeah, of course."

"Do you remember the first time we met?" Lola smiled and didn't wait for an answer. "I couldn't stop looking at you. It's funny. All the things you hate about yourself are what make you wonderful to me."

Del frowned. "What do you mean?"

"There's who you are inside. You always want to do the right thing. You always want to tell the truth. You always fight for the little guy. It makes life so hard, you work all the time, you never stop to breathe. But I saw you back then, and you were such a warrior woman. So strong, so beautiful. You shine from the inside." Lola's wide eyes were golden in the morning light.

"Come on," Del protested, blushing.

"I mean it. And on top of that, you're incredibly sexy. You have no idea how gorgeous you are. You hate your hair, and it's like this halo. You hate your curves because they get in your way, and they're beautiful to me. Your eyes are so bright and full of life, and you don't seem to see that when you look at yourself. You're tall and strong and golden and gorgeous, and you have no idea."

Del let herself stroke Lola's soft, curved cheek, smiling at the way her finger trembled at the contact. "I remember the first time we met," she said. "Marco and Phil were having that neighborhood safety meeting. You had such long hair. You were so shy and serious."

"Orrin didn't like me to cut my hair," Lola said. She shrugged and sat up, away from Del. "I was a freak. I was a mess."

Del shook her head. "You were beautiful. Especially when you smiled. I was a goner from that second. Then I saw you at the book club and you were even more stunning. You'd cut your hair, you had this little jacket on, but it was you—you were standing tall, you were smiling, and it was like someone had been covering you up and you got out into the light. As time goes by you just become more and more of yourself. I stand back and watch you and can't get over how amazing you are. It's fantastic."

Lola stared at her. "I didn't know you saw me like that."

"I should have found a way to tell you." Del sat up too and watched Lola's shoulders tense as if in defense.

"We're both learning." Lola stood up and eyed Del from across the bed. "Seriously, are you okay?"

Del thought about this for a moment and shrugged. "I think so."

"I know you need to get to work, and I have stuff to do too. You'd said you might want to go to book club together Friday night. Still up for it?"

Del nodded.

"Good." She came around the bed, smiled and kissed Del's hand. "Thank you for coming to see me."

A moment later, the shower started running. Del sat alone listening to the water. She felt her whole body tingling, painfully tender. Her skin felt damp from Lola's mouth. She was dizzy. She wanted more than anything to follow Lola into the shower but felt the weight of their mistakes, disappointments and resentment blocking her path. Del shuddered and skulked down the stairs and back to her own house.

* * *

"So, are you up for book club or not?"

Del hesitated. After a long, fruitless Thursday and tail-chasing Friday, she definitely had to talk herself into keeping her promise to Lola. She'd actually forgotten the event and had just started working on yet another list of people to call in the seemingly Sisyphean task of tracking Mikey's last months, days and hours. "Well," she started. "I—"

"Would you be willing to take me on your bike?"

Del frowned. "What's up? You okay?"

"I'm fine, but—don't you remember—the thing is at a new place, La Boheme? It's by the BART station on Twenty-Fourth. It's a little farther than I want to walk, and there's no parking."

"Why there? What happened? Is the regular place booked?"

"Didn't you hear? It closed," Lola said. "They've been struggling for a while, and they finally had to close a few months ago."

Del was stunned. "How did I not realize that?"

"I don't think you can tell that it's closed when you're driving by, and you haven't had time to do anything but work." Lola cleared her throat. "Anyway, could I get a ride?"

"You bet. I've been meaning to take you on the new bike since I got it."

Minutes later Del was handing Lola her helmet and blinking at the feeling of déjà vu that came over her. "Remember the first time I took you to book club?"

Lola nodded and climbed on behind Del. "It seems like a long time ago, doesn't it?"

Del nodded and started up the bike. When she'd traded in her old Honda Rebel for this larger Suzuki Boulevard, she'd told herself it was so she could take Lola on rides. She'd thought she meant it too, but her actions said otherwise. I got the bike because I wanted it, she told herself as they rode along 18th Street and down Church Street to 24th Street in the Friday evening traffic. She wondered for the hundredth time what it was Lola really saw in her. She found a narrow spot not far from the green awnings that marked their destination and looked around at the strolling, chatting, laughing mix of Mission

District residents. The peeper could be anywhere on this block, in this neighborhood, looking out of his living room window at the passersby. He could be driving that green Ford or that black Toyota. Del pushed away the thought and squeezed into a gap between parked cars. As they started toward the coffee shop, Del again wished she could start over with Lola.

"I'm sorry," she blurted. "I should have taken you for a ride before this. I let it slip away from me. Like the book group, and the house, and everything. I wasn't paying attention to the right things and now I feel like it's all too late."

Lola frowned at her. "Are you really so ready to give up on us? You were talking like this the other morning, and I've been thinking about that. I have regrets too, you know. I think we've been imperfect, but I think that's just how people are."

"There you go," Del said as lightly as she could. "Letting me off the hook again."

Lola shook her head. "That's too simple. I'm just saying, don't wallow in guilt. It's just as bad as self-pity, don't you think? If you don't like what you've done so far, do it differently from now on. If you say it's just too late, then you don't have to do anything to make it better. It's a cop-out. Don't do that unless you're ready to give up on us."

"I keep forgetting," Del said with a smile. "You really are a fighter, aren't you?"

Lola made a face. "What do you mean?"

"Ever since I met you, you've been moving yourself forward, away from bad stuff. You've faced all this crap—you survived Beckett. You survived James. You became a writer. You built a new life in a new city. When I found out you were with Sterling, I was terrified. I thought she'd kill you. But you even got over a serial killer. I don't know many people who could've done that."

Lola shrugged. "It wasn't me. I think she wanted to die. She kept saying she was tired, she wanted to be saved. I think she let me stop her."

Del trailed after Lola, wondering if she realized how blasé she sounded. How close had Lola come to being just another of Sterling's victim's? Sterling had chosen women she considered too damaged or deficient to be worthy of living. The murderer had, according to her defense attorney, considered herself some kind of hero rescuing the victims from the world.

Lola looked small and defenseless, strolling along 24th Street in her usual jeans and sweater, her long, thin neck a stalk and her shorn head a delicate flower. One of Sterling's murder victims, young Paula Wilson, belonged to a book club. Her apartment was overstuffed with novels and textbooks and volumes of poetry. Opal Hernandez, one of the other women Sterling killed, was a web developer and wrote several articles about women in technology and was at the time of her death collaborating with another techie on a book about working as a woman in her male-dominated profession. Sterling followed them, monitored them, judged them and found them guilty of the same thing she'd found Lola guilty of, the capital crime of—what?

"You ever think about the lives you saved?" Too late, Del realized she'd missed whatever Lola had been saying and had interrupted her.

"What do you mean?"

"You stopped Sterling. You survived her. You kept her from killing any other women. Do you think about why you were able to stop her, what it means?"

Lola slowed to a stop and tipped her head to the side. "I survived because I did, that's all. It's like when it rains and the worms scatter on the sidewalk, a lot of them die but some make it. There's no triumph of good over evil. I wanted to live, she didn't. No moral imperatives, no divine intervention. I'm just one of the worms that didn't die."

"There's more to it than that," Del averred. "You outsmarted her. You were the only one who could. Don't ignore that."

Lola glanced at her watch and resumed walking. "I did not outsmart her. I understood her. It creeps me out, actually. She and I were more alike than different."

"You're nothing like her," Del insisted. "You're the kindest person I've ever known."

"But so was she, in her own twisted way." Lola smiled at Del's boggled expression. "I'm not saying she was right to do what she did. Obviously. But she thought she was helping them. Us. She thought she was saving women who needed it."

"You sound like you sympathize with her."

"I know it seems strange, but I do."

They walked in silence while Del tried to figure out how to respond to this. Her first impulse was to argue with Lola, but that never seemed to do any good. Lola would give in to avoid conflict, but she'd go ahead and keep thinking what she was thinking and doing what she was doing.

"Entrenched." Del shook her head.

"What?"

"Janet said I was entrenched. That the only way to get me to listen was, you know—"

"To kidnap you? To drug you and tie you up in that trailer and starve you half to death?"

There was another silence. As they neared the café, Lola put a hand on Del's arm to stop her. "Funny, I'm able to see things from Sterling's point of view but not Janet's. Pretty crazy, huh?"

"Do you think I'm entrenched?"

"Aren't we all?" Lola laughed quietly. "When we believe a thing, no matter whether it's right or not, we hold on to it as hard as we can. Even if it hurts us, we can't let go of something we think without feeling like we'll lose part of ourselves."

Del shrugged off Lola's hand. "That's a horrible thought. Like we're stuck being who we are forever. Like we can't grow."

"I think we can try. That's all we can do."

"Hey, you're here," called out a voice ahead of them.

Del and Lola grinned in response to Tess and Lin, who stood together near the café's entrance and pulled them both in for a long group hug. Their warmth and energy were infectious, and Del's spirits were lifted immediately.

"How's my Del?" Lin nestled into Del's side.

Del smiled down and squeezed Lin's tiny frame. "Glad to see you happy."

Tess grinned at Del, her dark eyes shining, her curls wild. "Remember when you weren't sure I was good enough for her?"

"I'm still trying to decide on that one."

The four stayed interlocked, smiling and catching up for a few minutes. Del had introduced Lin and Tess several years before and was delighted anew every time she saw how good they were for each other. Shy, bookish Lin had come out of her shell, while Tess's cool, polished demeanor had warmed and softened. The safety and security and affection they offered one another seemed to bring out the best in them both. Theirs was, Del realized with a mixture of gladness and pain, the only perfect relationship she'd ever witnessed.

Rachel and Lee arrived then and expanded the circle. Since they were now blocking the front door to the café, they moved inside and broke apart to start claiming seats.

Lola and Lin chatted for a few minutes before the meeting while Tess greeted the other arrivals, and Del thought about her conversation with Lola. They saw things very differently, and she wanted to think about what Lola had said. Was she missing something, or had Lola become a lot deeper? Maybe, she thought, I'm just paying more attention. Maybe I've been missing a lot about who she really is, just like I missed a lot about who Janet really is.

Thoughts about Lola and their conversation carried her along for the first half of the meeting, but her spirits dropped along with her energy, and she fought to focus on the group's lively discussion. The book, a ghost story and mystery, had apparently become a favorite of Lola's, and Del resolved to read it.

"This book is crap," asserted Andrea, Del's least favorite acquaintance. "Whoever picked this, you don't get to pick again. *The Thirteenth Tale* should be burned. I have better things to do on a Friday night than sit around yapping about this piece of crap."

Del watched Lola and Lin exchange glances. Tess, ever the graceful facilitator, tried to direct Andrea toward a productive discussion.

"What specific issue do you have with it? What would you have liked, how could the author have made it better?"

They all listened to Andrea rant until Tess smoothly asked for other input. Every time someone tried to say something, though, Andrea interrupted. She became increasingly sharp-tongued, finally calling Rachel a "stupid bimbo" and scowling. Del leaned forward, trying to decide whether to step in. Rachel shook her head slightly, and Del sat back. She made eye contact with Lee, whose placid face belied the tension in her firefighter's body. Glamorous Rachel, ever composed, leaned only a degree or two closer to her physically imposing girlfriend.

At this point, Tess called for a short break and took Andrea aside. The rest of the group gathered around the coffee and pretended not to watch Tess and Andrea.

"Thanks," Rachel said, smiling at Del and clutching Lee's hand. "I don't take it personally."

Del eyed Lee. "I wasn't sure—"

"We talked about it before." Lee grimaced at Del. "Andrea's been getting quietly nastier over the last few months, especially to Rachel, and we decided to let Tess handle it. No," she added, as if she'd been asked, "I don't like anybody attacking my girlfriend. But it's up to her how we handle it."

Del nodded and once again admired Lee's self-control. She'd have struggled to sit back and let someone mistreat Lola without doing anything about it.

"I'm so sorry." Lin rubbed Rachel's arm. "I don't know what's going on with her. She's always been opinionated, but she's usually not out of control like that."

Lola frowned at Lin. "Will Tess kick her out?"

"Ah." Lin eyed Tess with naked curiosity. "I think—she just did. Whether it's for tonight or forever, I don't know. But we won't let that kind of thing happen again, I promise."

Rachel offered a forced laugh that drew a scowl from Lee.

"I've been called worse, you guys. It's no biggie. I just don't get why she hated the book so much. I loved it!"

"Me too!" Lola blushed when everyone looked at her. "It kept me wondering about so many things, and I just loved her use of imagery."

Del smiled at Lola's enthusiasm.

"Right?" Lin grinned. "It was like a gallery of paintings used to tell a story. And the whole meta-fiction thing was really interesting."

"Storyteller characters," Rachel put in, "I always feel like the author is playing with archetypes, don't you?"

They chatted about the book around the table for a few minutes before noticing Tess's arrival at their little circle.

"Well," she muttered with a grin. "I guess this is the book club that just won't die, huh? I leave you alone for five seconds and you guys have the whole meeting without me!"

"You okay?" Lin reached for her hand. "That couldn't have been fun."

"Listen," Tess said, leaning toward Lin. "Andi's going through a rough time right now, she didn't mean to take it out on everyone. She's gonna skip the next few meetings. I'll keep in touch with her, see about maybe reintroducing her later."

"Does she need help? Is she okay?"

Lola stared at Rachel in naked surprise, and Del again had to smile. Andrea was often abrasive with everyone, but she consistently seemed to be particularly rough on Rachel. After they'd said their goodbyes to the others and ambled toward the waiting bike, Del and Lola talked about it.

"Was she being sarcastic? Or is she really so generous and compassionate? She seemed sincere."

"I think she was."

"I assumed she was selfish," Lola said. "She's pretty and glamorous—designer clothes, perfect makeup, high heels all the time—so I figured she was shallow."

"Well—"

"I saw Janet the same way. I guess I was jealous of Janet too. Maybe I still am."

"I gave you every reason to be." Del shoved her hands in her pockets.

"You still love her," Lola said, as though it were a foregone conclusion. "That's not a thing you chose, it's just how it is."

"But I don't love her anymore. Honestly."

Lola shrugged.

"Don't you believe me?"

"I'm not sure you know how you feel." She turned quickly to take in Del's reaction, and Del stifled an impulse to defend herself. She inclined her head to indicate Lola should go on.

"But I don't think that's unusual. I think most of us have a hard time knowing how we really feel until we do something and can't figure out why. Then we have to choose to take a hard look at ourselves."

"You've gotten pretty philosophical all of a sudden." Del eyed Lola. "Any reason?"

"Well, I don't know." Lola slowed the way she always did when thinking hard. "I take things really personally sometimes, so it helps to think no one's singling me out—we're all the same inside."

"You think so?"

"Yes. And no." Lola laughed. "Does that make any sense?"

"Actually, yeah, I guess it does."

Moments later they were on the Boulevard and zipping home. Del tried to steel herself against noticing, but she couldn't ignore the feel of Lola's arms wrapped around her middle, the warmth that spread from where Lola was snug against her back. She swallowed hard, knowing that if she let herself cry the tears would cloud her vision. She missed physical contact with Lola more than she wanted to acknowledge, but she'd blown it. She drove as slowly as she dared, wanting to extend the ride. She wished she'd thought to ask if Lola wanted to take a detour to the headlands so they could take in the view of the city. Next time, she vowed to herself.

Moments later, Del stayed at the bottom of Lola's steps and watched her ascend and unlock her door. She wanted to follow Lola up the stairs and push her against the wall and kiss her until Lola melted into her. But she didn't deserve to do that. She hadn't earned her way back into Lola's heart. She searched for a way to prolong their contact.

"Hey," she blurted. "You and I have never really toured the city, have we?"

Lola shook her head. "We've talked about it, but something always comes up. I went to Fisherman's Wharf and Pier 39 with Marco and this whole group. The Meetup thing."

Del watched as Lola's expression closed. "That's where you met Sterling."

"Yeah."

"It wasn't your fault," she said on impulse. "Sterling. That was a setup, you know that, right? Janet set you up. It wasn't your fault."

"You make it all sound so simple," Lola said, smiling strangely down at Del with the porch light flickering its inconstant halo behind her. The light was like a hundred things she knew she should have done and hadn't. Now was it too late? She stared up at Lola, unable to speak her feelings. Then Lola was gone behind the door that suddenly seemed like an impenetrable barrier between them. Back in her own house seconds later, she expected to be up all night, worrying it over, but she dropped onto her bed and knew nothing until her alarm.

Just before dawn, Del ran in the thick fog, feeling like the thoughts in her mind were weighing down her body. Each step was a struggle. She had to force herself forward one lunge at a time, and her breath scraped cold through her throat and mouth. She'd forgotten gloves, and her hands were numb.

Why is this all wrong? She slowed to a walk, giving herself a block to rest before starting over. She opened up with a gentle jog for several minutes, keeping it slow and easy until she could feel the tightness in her muscles loosening.

After several minutes, she let her body take off, blindly crashing through the seasonal November fog that hung nearly to the ground. The wildness of it and the feeling that she'd regained control of her body were intoxicating. She laughed aloud, startling a cat that darted across her path from under a nearby car. She went faster and faster, the world around her reduced to a damp cloud of nothingness and dark. She lost track of time and place, nearly falling over a rough spot on the pavement but knowing she would regain her balance in time. She ran until the sun was coming up and she could see the cars and houses and the few early risers around her. Her lungs burned, her thighs and calves were quivering, her still-recovering shoulder felt like a rock at the top of her arm, and her hands were sore and frozen. She didn't care. She was alive and it was Saturday and she could do anything she wanted.

After a long shower she did the housecleaning and bill paying, all the things she'd left up to Lola for months and mostly neglected since she'd left. It took the bulk of the morning. She pulled on her most comfortable jeans and a worn blue oxford, pulling on the low boots she seemed to choose nearly every day. She spent the afternoon at the station, taking another pass at trying to get some movement on Mikey's case. He'd been dead for almost five days.

She was surprised evening was already falling when she headed home and ate a frozen burrito over the sink, thinking of Sofia Gonzalez eating her toaster waffle over her sink in her white, bare kitchen. As if automatically, her gaze went to the window, through which she saw nothing more sinister than her overgrown rhododendron eating the fence. She wandered over to find Lola working in her backyard. The bright day was being slowly smothered by a rolling fogbank, and the diminishing light framed Lola eerily. Del got a chill as she saw Lola straighten up and watch her approach.

"Hey," Del called, "looking good!"

"I think it's crooked. Can you tell from there if it's going wonky?"

Del looked at the low wall of neatly arranged bricks. What, she wondered, had inspired this little project? The whole yard was tidy but mostly undeveloped. The planter border was a finisher, not a place to start. The drainage needed work, and there was paving that needed redoing, and the lawn was a mess. Del stifled the urge to suggest there were more important things to do than make some random little wall along the side. It wasn't her yard.

"Wonky? No, it's perfect. Like you." This she offered with the strongest weapon in her romantic arsenal, her daddy's slow smile.

Lola gave an absent smile and gathered her tools. Del trailed her into the kitchen and watched Lola wash up. Del wondered if maybe she'd already let the relationship die without realizing it. She tried to think of something to say, to bridge the gap she felt widening between them, but she could only stand helplessly by while Lola stood feet away, back turned to her. Out the back window, the fog devoured the last morsels of fading light. Del tried not to flinch when Lola spun around.

"Del?"

"Yeah?"

"I don't know how to say this." Lola's eyes searched her face. "I feel like we're trying, sort of, but we haven't been connecting especially well lately. We talked last night, and I felt like we were really hearing each other, but then I called you twice today and you never called me back."

Del glanced down at the pocket in which she'd stashed her cell phone. "I was busy."

Lola nodded, her lips pursed and her eyes hooded. "I figured."

"Well, I'm sorry. I think I hate the phone because it's the thing I use mostly for work. Plus I want to see your face and know what you're thinking."

"Yes, okay. But you could text to acknowledge my call, right?"

"You're right. I'm sorry. Hey, I'm here now. Doesn't that count for something?"

"Uh-huh." Lola chewed her lip. "I had a therapist, did I tell you that? After Orrin died? The peacock talked me into going."

Del shook her head. "The peacock?"

"The lawyer. My lawyer. I didn't particularly like him."

Lola's late husband had been under investigation at the time of his death, and Del recalled the way the peacock, as Lola called him, had worked to shield Lola from potential accusations of complicity in Orrin Beckett's alleged embezzlement. However obnoxious he may have been, the guy had done his job. He'd apparently sussed out the nature of Beckett's abusive marriage and had tried to lay the groundwork for her defense, should it become necessary. Del considered sharing her perspective on the peacock. Eyeing the closed expression on Lola's face, she decided against doing so.

Del took a long breath. "I'm not thrilled with the idea of going to therapy. We can work things out on our own without some stranger telling us our own business. Please don't ask me to go see some couples' shrink with you."

"I know." Lola looked away. "I figured you wouldn't want to. Actually, I was thinking about some advice she gave me, it might be helpful. Maybe it's stupid. Never mind."

"Just tell me." Del forced a small smile. The little manipulations were definitely getting old. They weren't deliberate, she knew, but they were annoying. She wondered what Lola found irritating about her and realized this was something that should have occurred to her sooner. She also realized she wasn't sure about much of what Lola thought. "Sorry, I really want to know. What did she tell you? What is it you want to tell me?"

"Well, she suggested writing letters. To Orrin, my birth parents. Anyone I couldn't talk to."

"So you want us to write letters to each other?" Del worked her jaw. "Is it really that hard to talk to me? You think I'm like your abusive husband and your parents who dumped you?"

"No!" Lola seemed flustered. "No—that's not—I just, it's hard, sometimes, to say things clearly. When you write, you have time to think about what you really want to say. It's just easier. For me, at least."

"Hmn." Del pushed her hair back. "Well, let's think about it, okay? I don't know, seems like we could just talk."

"But we don't. Not really." Lola's eyes filled with tears, and she rubbed at them. "I've been trying to get you to talk to me since you came back from seeing Janet. And you won't. I don't understand why, I don't even know if you still love Janet, even though you say you don't."

"I—"

"Or if you were ever not in love with her. If we—you and I— are just something you're doing to distract yourself from her. Is that what we are? Del? Or should I say were? I don't even know if we're together. Sometimes I think we are and sometimes—"

"Do you really think I'm just using you? Is that what you think of me?"

"I—no. I'm sorry. That's not what I was trying to say." Lola was looking down, clearly worried she'd pushed a button that would make Del turn into a monster. Would she ever stop worrying about that?

It'd help if I wasn't always snapping at her.

Del took a deep breath and changed tactics. "Hey, how about going out to dinner? Maybe we could talk, like you said. Make a fresh start."

"Really?" Lola's smile was brilliant, though her eyes still shone with tears. "You know we've never gone out on a date, right? Like, out to dinner, to a movie, whatever? I think a dinner date is a great idea. Talk to each other. Listen. Great!"

"Haven't we?" Del shook her head. "Yeah, we just sort of moved in after James—"

"Yes. I was too scared to go home, we got together, that was it. And then Janet—anyway. Yeah, no, we've never been on a date or whatever."

Del was appalled. Had she truly never even taken the woman out for a single meal? She remembered waxing nostalgic about all the fun she and Janet had, once upon a time. She'd wooed Janet, though, hadn't she? And she hadn't bothered with Lola. "Okay, we're long overdue for a romantic evening, aren't we? Let's go someplace really special, my treat."

"Really? Do you want to?"

Lola's excitement was infectious and Del grinned. Now, she thought, please don't let the phone ring. I'd like to actually keep a promise to her for once. As though she'd summoned the sound, the phone's ring sang out. As she listened to the dispatcher's message, Del's grin faded. Now she'd have to deal with Lola's disappointment and resentment and hurt feelings.

"It's okay," Lola said, apparently reading her face. "We'll go another night. It's a bad night for driving, anyway, in this fog."

"I'm sorry. It's not fair, but it's the job. You knew I was a cop when we—shit." Del shook her head. "Listen. I know I'm being touchy. I don't even know why, sometimes it feels like there's been too much bad shit."

"Between us, you mean?"

"I don't know." Del shook her head. "I really don't. Sorry, I gotta go."

"So, dinner tomorrow night?"

"It's hard to plan, with these cases. Let's play it by ear, okay? I don't want to make a promise I'm not sure I can keep."

"Maybe you could make sure you keep it." Lola's voice held an edge.

Del ignored this and leaned forward to give Lola a kiss. Driving away, she realized she'd kissed Lola's forehead instead of her lips. She slapped at the steering wheel.

Pretty much every time things were winding down with a girlfriend, she caught herself doing things like not answering their calls, staying away more and more, and generally withdrawing until she was treating them like houseguests who'd overstayed their welcome. The forehead kiss was usually the death knell. She'd never really dumped anyone, had she? She'd just sort of disappeared, one little step at a time.

She felt heavy and slow, like the laden November air was slowly drowning her. She'd hoped things would be different with Lola. She loved Lola, didn't she? Del watched her little truck's headlights push against the thick mist ahead, thinking about how small and insignificant she felt in the wide, unknowable world. A sea turtle on an endless, danger-strewn beach she might never learn to cross.

CHAPTER FOUR

"He just stared at me." Donette Williams sat shaking in the metal chair.

Del nodded, distracted for a moment by a faint, high sound. It was barely audible, a tiny bell ringing incessantly. Then she placed the source. The victim's tremors were vibrating the chair very gently into the edge of the interview room table.

"Donette, is there anything about his appearance that stood out to you?"

The victim shook her head. She was thirty-five, an attractive African American marketing manager at one of the Silicon Valley startups. It had been an hour since Del had come in to the station to take her complaint. She looked flattened and empty. Her tawny skin was sallow, her dark eyes sunken, her arms crossed protectively over her slender torso.

"Hey, wanna get out of here for a few minutes? I hate this room."

Donette laughed. "God, I thought I was the only one. I feel like a prisoner in here."

Del smiled and nodded. She'd thought as much. Walking in, seeing the victim hunched over at the table, Del had been reminded of Mikey Ocampo and how he'd huddled on the floor. She led the way out of the confines of the small interview room and chucked her chin at her partner.

"We're going to grab a bite, want anything?"

Phan smiled and shook his head, pointing at the paperwork on his desk. He clearly understood what she was doing, softening up the victim before continuing the interview. Del appreciated how frustrating it had to be, getting called into work in the middle of dinner, only to sit and wait while your partner got the victim to relax and remember. When the victim had requested a female detective take her statement, Del had been called. Loyal Phan was here in case she wanted any assistance.

The two women chatted about Donette's job and family as they strolled to the taqueria across the street. Del told her a handful of short, funny stories, the ones she trotted out when she wanted to relax a victim. She also used them to deflect the usual weird questions people wanted to ask in social situations when they found out what she did for a living. It all worked. Fifteen minutes later, Del and the victim were back in the interview room, with Del winding up a silly anecdote about a drunk driver.

"Thanks," Donette said, her huge brown eyes filling. "You made me feel like a human being again."

"Good. That's one of the frustrating things about a guy like this," Del noted. "He takes a whole person—smart, funny, interesting, kind—and he reduces her to body parts. Less than that, images of body parts. Then she feels like she's nothing."

"Exactly!" Donette hesitated then smiled at Del. "You're good at this. Getting people to open up."

Donette had finally started to look like what Del imagined was her real self. The willowy beauty was sitting up straight. There was some light back in her eyes and a square set to her bony shoulders. Her silk blouse and wool trousers looked fresher somehow. Her short, natural hair even seemed springier, her tight curls refreshed. Even her fine features looked revitalized.

It was amazing, Del thought, how the slightest change in emotional state was so clearly reflected in a person's appearance. Was that, she wondered, a chemical thing?

Del waggled her head. "Being scared, being shamed. These things shut people down. Then they can't remember anything, they can't think."

"I feel like I'm overreacting," Donette admitted, her gaze dropping to the scarred surface of the worn interview room table. "All that happened was, this guy looked in my window through the blinds. I almost didn't come here. I was going to call, but then I couldn't make myself do it. What if you didn't believe me? What if you said—I don't know."

"You did the right—"

"I was raped," Donette cut in. "In college. I never reported it. I figured they wouldn't believe me. Or they'd say it was my fault."

Del waited, keeping her expression neutral and receptive.

"I still feel guilty about that. I think I was right, they wouldn't have done anything. But he probably raped other girls. Maybe he wouldn't have, if I'd reported him."

"You were in a tough spot," Del said. "Especially at school, victims tend to get the brush-off. I hope you got some help."

"Well, yes, thanks," Donette said, sitting back and taking a deep breath before meeting Del's eyes again. "I did. I went to the rape crisis center and got counseling. Which really helped a lot, I think. But this guy, just looking at me like that, like I was an animal or something, that brought it all back. I felt like a helpless teenager all over again."

Del nodded. She'd heard the same sort of thing from dozens of victims of rape and other sexual predation, most recently from targets of this particular peeper. Idly she wondered how many had been victims of sexual assault or child sexual abuse or both. Once a victim of sexual violence, she knew, a person was more likely to be victimized again. Why this might be, Del wasn't sure. Again she wondered about body chemistry. Did fear, or posttraumatic stress or some chemical signature of trauma leave a trail that caught the attention of predators? She thought about

Sofia Gonzalez almost not calling in about the peeper because of her bad first experience with SFPD. Was the guy going back to the same women over and over? Was the peeper sniffing out women who were fearful? She pushed the question aside for the moment and asked Donette to walk her through the experience again.

"I was at my mom's all day, helping her organize her garage. She lives in Daly City, and it was actually nice there, not too cold, not too hot. We got done and skipped dinner. I almost stayed the night because it was so foggy. Mom was trying to get me to stay, but I didn't want to have to go to church in the morning." Donette made a rueful face, and Del gave the obligatory smile that let her move forward.

"So I came home. I wanted to take a shower, I was all dusty from the garage."

Del nodded, not wanting to stop the flow of the haltingly told story.

"I'd opened the blinds partway before I left this morning. For the plants." Donette hunched over again, hugging herself. "When I come home from work I always close them. But it's Saturday, and I didn't do that. Which was stupid. I know this guy is out there, you can't miss it on the news. But it's not part of my Saturday routine I guess."

"And—" Del stopped herself.

"And I shouldn't have to lock myself in a vault to feel safe." Donette nodded. "I was in my room, threw my grubby clothes in the hamper. I was just standing there, should I take a bath or a shower? Maybe a shower first and then a bath."

Del waited, staying very still, while Donette took a moment to collect herself.

"I saw something moving through the blinds. I told you, it's a slider, the blinds are the long vertical kind, and I saw something move outside, then there was a little noise. I thought it might be a bird. I put these stickers on the sliding glass doors so the birds won't fly into the glass, but it's the southern exposure side so they're faded. I need to replace them but I keep forgetting. I didn't think, with the fog there's no way a bird would be flinging itself—I didn't even think, I just went over there, and he was standing there, this man—" Donette stopped and swallowed, her eyes wide and dark. "White man. He was standing there, he backed up when I walked over. I screamed. Stupid, but I did, and he ran off. I put on my robe and turned on all the outside lights, but he was gone by then. I wasn't sure what to do, I took a shower and came here. I almost didn't, you know. Because I didn't want to get treated like—so I asked for a woman and they called you." She shrugged. "I dressed like I was going to work, I didn't realize until just now. Like if I was dressed professionally you might treat me better. I didn't even realize I was doing that. Maybe this was a waste of time."

Del shook her head. "I'm glad you came in. What was he wearing?"

"Just regular weekend clothes." She made a face. "Jeans. A Giants cap, black. His shirt was, I don't know, dark. Black or gray, maybe. I didn't notice his shirt that much. I don't know about his shoes. I just didn't—you know, I can't believe how hard it is to remember the details!"

"It's perfectly normal," Del assured her. "You know, when our heart rate goes up a certain amount, like when we're scared or too surprised or whatever, we just don't take anything in. Can't see clearly or hear too much or whatever."

"Like our brain is trying to protect us from whatever's freaking us out."

"Exactly!" Del nodded, guessing Donette would regain her equanimity enough to give a physical description if she had a chance to intellectualize her experience, albeit briefly. "A freakout filter to keep you from going into shock. Then sometimes the details come back to you later when you're less frazzled."

"White guy, I told you that." Donette straightened her spine. "Brown eyes, light. My age or a little younger. My height, about, five-eight or nine." Donette's eyes roved back and forth as she combed her memory. "Light hair, what I could see under the cap. Weak chin, weak mouth. Soft looking, like he lived in a—Boo Radley!"

Del looked a question.

"Like from that book, *To Kill a Mockingbird*."

"Oh!" Del sat back, adjusting her mental picture of the peeper.

"Maybe not that weird. Not that nice or innocent, obviously. But looking at him? He was just totally unlike most of the men I know, my brother and my boyfriend, our friends. He looked like a wimp, I guess. That sounds silly maybe."

"Invisible?"

"Right!" Donette grinned self-consciously. "Casper the Pervy Ghost."

They shared a quiet laugh, and Del wrapped up the interview, promising to follow up with Donette in the following days. She took extensive notes, comparing this interview with the others. She was struck by how destructive peeping was. She'd started to think of it as a relatively minor violation, a precursor to actual personal crimes, but was increasingly aware of how affected the victims were by the violation of their privacy.

Phan tapped his desk to get Del's attention. "Ready to switch gears?"

"And then some."

She and Phan spent a few minutes again going over the files on Mikey's death. Again they came to the same assessment: Mikey was the invisible kid. He had kept his head down and his mouth shut in juvie. He'd completed two years of high school before his release and part of a third before his disappearance from the group home to which he'd been released. His grades were mediocre, his behavior unworthy of documented censure or praise.

"What happened in that group home?"

"What do you mean?" Phan eyed Del over the expanse of files spread over their butted-together desks. "What's on your mind?"

"Okay." Del pointed at the three files spread in front of her. "I know we've been over this before, but it bears repeating: no one knew this kid. The new social worker doesn't even remember him. I get it, she's got a lot of files on a lot of kids. But there's nothing, just his name and case number and placement. The old social worker hasn't returned a single call or email. The supervising case worker at the group home says Mikey was a nice kid, no trouble, ate his veggies and kept his bed made. That's it in the notes. Nothing about school, how he interacted with the staff or the other kids, just little notes about how easy he was before he just disappeared one day."

"They followed procedure," Phan pointed out. "Called in that he was missing an hour after the other kids came home from school—so he must have been attending, right? He must have normally come home right after school. Sometimes these group homes are a little hairy and at this one the kids were mostly post-juvie, so the staff was dealing with a lot. They might've been too busy to take a lot of notes."

"True." Del made a face. "I don't know. I just get the feeling something's missing. Maybe not. Maybe it's perfectly legit and I'm looking at shadows because I want to find something."

"Maybe." Phan looked at his watch. "Listen, I gotta go. Alana's coming over for a late supper, and I owe her. Seems like every time we make plans, I have to come here. You know how that is."

"When we got the call about Donette, Lola was saying, you know, maybe you should make sure you can keep your promises to me."

"Sounds perfectly reasonable."

"But it isn't that easy."

"No," Phan agreed with false cheer. "It's not."

Del went in to the station on Sunday to make yet another attempt to ferret out some usable information from the files on Mikey's death. After several hours, she was no closer to clarity on his last year of life or his death. She considered stopping by Lola's house on the way home, but things were weird between them and she wasn't sure how to change that. Maybe it was time to accept that she and Lola just couldn't work as a couple. How many times should she throw herself at the woman, knowing all she could expect was halfhearted acceptance that only presaged inevitable rejection? And hadn't she earned that rejection by letting Lola down, time after time?

Del listened to Lola's thin voice in a message left that morning.

"Hey. I guess you're busy. Hope you're having a good day." There was a pause. "I feel like I'm always chasing after you."

Del grimaced. Funny, she thought, I feel like I'm always chasing you. She played the next message, left an hour after the first.

"Me again. You're still busy. I guess I'll wait for you to call me."

A few hours later she'd left a third message, and Del hesitated before playing that one, half knowing what she'd hear.

"It doesn't really seem like you're too interested in talking to me, and I don't want to keep bothering you. If you decide you want to see me or talk to me or go to that dinner we talked about, please call me or come by. I miss you. But I don't want to keep treading water like this. Please call me. I love you. Bye."

There was a text too: *I don't want to sit home and not hear from you. Heading out for the evening unless I hear from you by 5.*

Del wondered if maybe she was too hasty, giving up on their relationship. Maybe, if she called Lola back, she could say she wanted to talk. Maybe she should just show up and take Lola in her arms and kiss her passionately. Maybe in twenty years they would look back on this rough patch and shake their heads at how foolish they'd been, thinking things were over between them.

Del tried to put her feelings in a little locker in her mind. They were useless, a distraction. She had Mikey Ocampo's killer to find and a peeper to stop. She tried to remove her emotions from her perceptions of the case. Of course, she'd never managed to be objective where the kid was concerned. She'd made a connection with the boy, telling herself it was for the sake of opening him up and getting him to tell his story. It was the same thing she did with any victim, any witness, but it had been more than that with Mikey. She'd seen herself in the kid and had failed to draw back and analyze his statement and his responses objectively. When Leister had warned her not to get too invested emotionally, she'd dismissed his concerns as sexist nonsense. Had she been too hasty? She'd seen Mikey as an innocent, and she'd taken his word as gospel. Had that been a mistake? What if there was something she missed?

She had seen his mom, Mariposa Ocampo, her face adorned with bruises and abrasions that told a tale of violence. She hadn't seen any recent marks of abuse on Mikey's arms or face back then, but that didn't mean there weren't any. Had there been a medical exam as part of his intake? There must have been, but there was nothing about that in his paperwork from the Department of Juvenile Justice facility in Stockton. Del made a note to follow up on this and decided she needed to get home before it was too late—she'd spent half of Saturday and most of Sunday at the station and was feeling burned out.

Del stopped for a crowd of pedestrians as she was about to turn onto 18th Street. She watched the group of flashy young men jostle and tease and flirt with each other and smiled at their youth and exuberance. The road was clear but she hesitated, trying to decide whether she should pass by home and make a detour for a rare junk food fix. Then as she let off the brakes she saw Lola and dropped her foot harder than necessary on the brake pedal. Luckily she had no one behind her. She pulled over and inched into a tight gap that almost qualified as a parking spot. She tried to talk herself out of spying.

It was creepy, she knew that. It was definitely creepy and inappropriate and not okay to surreptitiously follow Lola on foot. We're not together, not really, Del reminded herself. Single and free, Lola had every right to look pretty and excited and happy, to be lovely with her pink cheeks and sparkling eyes. She looked like she was heading somewhere she couldn't wait to get to, maybe to meet someone she couldn't wait to see. Lola called and texted and didn't hear back from me, Del reminded herself, and then she made other plans. She told me she was making other plans if I didn't get hold of her, and I still didn't bother to call her.

I'm not stalking her. I'm looking out for her. She's a very vulnerable, trusting woman, and she could be putting herself in danger.

Del rolled her eyes. It wasn't even fully dark yet. Lola was two blocks from home and perfectly safe. Del slowed her pace even more. The neighborhood bubbled with people, with voices, with color and sound, and Lola blended perfectly into the liveliness of Castro Street. Even from half a block away, Lola's posture was unmistakably different. She stood tall, her face alight with anticipation and pleasure. She smiled at the same posse of young guys Del had just watched cross the street in front of her. She could have been a movie star in Hollywood or a model in Milan, the way she took in the brightness and energy around her and reflected it back. She looked beautiful and strong and confident. Del couldn't help but compare this Lola to the woman she met at Marco and Phil's house nearly two years back. Today's Lola was a whole new woman, and that new woman didn't seem to need Del.

Del watched Lola wait obediently for the Walk signal at the corner. She'd felt guilty for not returning Lola's calls and texts, an omission she couldn't quite explain to herself. Obviously, Del needn't have castigated herself. The sad little messages had been one big lie. Del had been feeling guilty over forgetting their tentative dinner plans, when Lola had had a backup plan all along. Well, she could stop feeling guilty. Lola was obviously fine.

Del felt a pang in her midsection and took a deep breath to push it away. She left the truck squeezed into its tight little space and walked back the way she'd seen Lola go, toward Castro Street. The sidewalk was crowded, and it was easy to blend in with the dawdlers and follow Lola until she joined the long movie theater line. A pretty young woman with vividly red hair greeted Lola with a squeal and a warm hug, and their faces were immediately animated in conversation. They didn't notice Del or anyone else. Then the woman seemed to be telling a story. She gestured and made faces, and Lola nodded and smiled at the storyteller. Del eased closer and closer, forgetting to stay out of sight. It didn't matter. Lola's eyes were fixed on her companion's expressive face.

Suddenly, Lola laughed out loud and Del found herself smiling. The redhead laughed, too, and the pair went into the theater together. They looked comfortable and relaxed and happy. They looked like old friends, maybe more. Only Lola didn't have any old friends, did she? Beckett wouldn't let her have contact with anyone for all those years. Lola's friends were Del's friends. She knew Marco and Phil, Tess and Lin, the other women from their book club, and that was about it. The one time Lola tried to go out to meet new people was at the Meetup where she met Sterling. Del's smile fell. A part of her still fought against the knowledge that Janet had set Lola up to be murdered by a madwoman. Del had loved Janet. Some part of her always would. She still couldn't reconcile Janet's nefarious deeds with the lover who'd curled up against her and wept over the injustices of the world. Del swallowed hard. She felt a spasm in her belly.

Del's cramping middle propelled her away from the movie theater. Her breath was hot and sour in her mouth, and she stalked back to the truck. In the minutes since she'd gotten out and started following Lola, the clear evening had started yielding to November's creeping fog. The sunlit crowds had started the exodus that damp weather inspired. Pedestrians scurried past Del's vehicle and pulled their coats tighter around them. Del felt the chill hit her through the sweater and chinos and boots that had become her uniform. She escaped to home, cold and blind to the world around her. She was numb with hurt and anger. All that garbage about wanting to talk, about Lola not wanting to chase her—it had all been bull. She heard Daddy's voice in her head and got sucked back to Fresno and fourth grade again.

"Everybody lies."

That's what her daddy told Del when he couldn't find his cigarettes and accused her of stealing them.

"I don't even smoke," Del told him. "I'm nine."

"So what?" He went to slap her but she ducked out of the way. He reached again and managed to smack her mouth.

She gritted her blood-smeared teeth and insisted, "I'm not lying. I'm not a liar."

"Everybody lies," Daddy said. He feinted another slap, punched her in the gut. It was a good move, one Del noted for future reference. He'd shifted his weight, though, and forecast the punch. If she'd been more alert, she'd have been able to avoid his fist handily. This too she noted and put into practice within a few days. Sure enough, watching more closely, she was easily able to shift her own weight nearly in tandem and steer clear of his strike. His being drunk and her being both sober and agile with youth helped, of course.

Maybe, Del thought now, Daddy was right. For all his faults, he was a smart guy before he pickled himself.

Maybe it's not just the bad guys. I lie, everybody lies. Why not Lola too? I wanted to believe she was special. I wanted to think she loved me. But she's just like everybody else, a selfish, manipulative liar who only cares about herself.

Del knew this was unfair. Had she put Lola on a pedestal, one that required her to be absolutely perfect or be disdained? That was obviously unreasonable. Del looked at the mug of vodka in front of her and at the clock. She'd fled her spontaneous Lola surveillance and started drinking, what, two hours earlier? She couldn't really remember deciding to do that. She dumped out the mug and stood at the sink, then shoved her fingers down her throat until she vomited.

"I'm not turning into a drunk over her, I'm not," she told herself. "I'm not turning into Momma and Daddy." She rinsed out her mouth and staggered away from the sink. "I'm better than that."

She looked at the clock, watching the minutes tick away until midnight. It had been six days since Mikey's murder. She'd studied his pictures in the file and wondered if she'd have recognized the little boy in the teenager. She wondered if she'd passed Mikey on the street before his death. His broken nose and some little scars on his ear—these details had stayed with her. But between the first time she saw him at the age of eleven and the time she saw his body when he was sixteen, Mikey had grown nearly a foot and gone from looking like a kid to looking like a young man. She could have walked by him a hundred times and not recognized him. What had he been like, really? She would never know.

* * *

Del hated that she wasn't surprised when a woman was attacked on Dolores Street that Sunday night. Someone grabbed the victim from behind, drugged her with chloroform, and left her naked on the sidewalk not far from the lush green lawns and clustered palm trees of Mission Dolores Park, where an early morning jogger came across the victim and called for help. There appeared to be no vaginal penetration, but she had some minor bruising on her breasts, arms, thighs. Her clothes were gone. The reports read sexual battery. There was nothing much, forensically. No hair, no semen, no fibers, no trace of other drugs in the victim's blood. No witnesses. The last thing the victim could recall was walking to her car after work Sunday evening.

The general assumption seemed to be that this was not an isolated incident, that it was the peeper again and the peeper had escalated. At Monday morning's hastily assembled emergency task force meeting Del tried to address the dangers of such an assumption, but Bradley rolled over her words as though he hadn't heard them. Later Phan commiserated with her but clearly agreed that the peeper was the perpetrator of the assault. Internally vowing to fight that assumption and follow a separate line of inquiry on top of the official one, Del wondered how she would fit that in with solving Mikey's murder. She was failing in every area of her life, not least professionally. She resolved to put aside her personal concerns in light of the more pressing professional ones and tried not to notice how much relief this resolution brought with it.

By Tuesday everyone in the station was alight with frantic activity and earnest inquiry, not least Del and Phan. Alana, Phan's girlfriend, again threatened to walk out on him. She said he worked too much, was too obsessed with his job. It was just like his ex-wife all over again. Kaylee wasn't talking to her dad because he was gone too much. Del offered to fill in so Phan could spend an evening with his daughter, but the kid wasn't done punishing him yet so he turned down the offer. Captain Bradley allocated extra men, extra resources. None of them knew how to use the men or the resources except to do the same useless things over and over. Police work was often a matter of interviewing and reinterviewing, reviewing notes again and again, scouring the same limited pieces of information several times in an effort to find a pattern, or a break in a pattern, or some inconsistency that like a loose thread in a tapestry could be pulled to unravel a crime's cover of secrecy. But they were picking at the same lack of loose ends over and over to no avail. They were zombies. Phan was heartbroken over Alana and Kaylee, and Del was heartbroken over Lola. They talked about drinking it off, but neither of them even wanted to hit the bar.

"Pretty pathetic," Phan commented Tuesday night after another eighteen-hour day. "Too fucked-up to drink?"

Del nodded blearily and trudged off to her truck to drive home. All she wanted to do was sleep. But even when she could manage to doze off, she woke up exhausted. Her stomach hurt all the time. She was caught in a whirling cloud of guilt, frustration and anger. What occupied her mind was that a whole neighborhood was scared. One victim was shaken and scared and humiliated and didn't even remember the attack. Del was unable to do anything to help any of them. She wasn't even able to help herself. She thought about all the victims she'd failed in her two decades as a police officer. And of course so far she'd failed to find Mikey's killer. She kept forgetting about him for minutes at a time, because she was so focused on the peeper-turned-batterer. If, she reminded herself at odd intervals, they were the same man.

When she closed her eyes she could smell the body of Mikey Ocampo. She'd smelled worse, of course, but the metallic tang of blood and sweat and dirt and decay colored her memory of the sweet young kid who'd spent a third of his childhood locked up as a murderer. She'd given him a chocolate bar, and his breath had smelled of chocolate when he'd told her his terrible story. When she thought of chocolate now, she thought of the scent of his body on the Shotwell Street. He was one of her great failures.

Had he been lonely and scared every day and every night of his detention, of his time in the group home, on the streets? If Del had been better able to get his mom to open up, if she'd been able to get one victim to roll on Ernie White, maybe Mikey Ocampo would be alive, trying to graduate high school and find a way to pay for college. Maybe he wouldn't have ended up half-starved and beaten to death, his body dumped like garbage on a street where no one knew or cared about him.

"Why didn't I try harder? What did I miss?" She was plagued by the nagging feeling she'd missed something but no closer to clarity on what that something might be. She'd tried not to get too attached to the kid and failed utterly. She definitely hadn't connected with Mikey's mother. She wondered if this was perhaps the most damning failure, the fatal flaw in her investigation. If Mariposa had been able to open up to Del, maybe Mikey would still be alive. A fog lay over her, thick, blinding and polluted by guilt and inadequacy.

Unable to sleep, Del got on the computer at three in the morning and started typing, realizing only after several minutes that she was writing to Lola.

"You wanted to talk to me," Del told the computer screen. "I should have tried harder to talk to you. I should have tried harder to listen to you."

The letter was a rambling mess, nearly incoherent, and she deleted it when she was done. She felt ridiculous, but she was able to sleep for a couple of hours after that.

On Wednesday Del arrived at the station to learn that another woman had been found naked and drugged on another sidewalk in the Mission. She had suffered bruising and abrasions and had no memory of an attacker. Del's middle cramped at the rapidity with which the attacker had taken another victim. Elizabeth Street was the scene this time, and again the victim remembered only that she'd been walking to her car.

The scene was another forensic desert, which meant the doer was smart enough to employ forensic countermeasures and that he was learning. That didn't bode well for the investigation, and Del considered what she knew of psychopathic behavior patterns. She and Phan went over the reports and tried to piece together some coherent picture of their bad guy.

Del grimaced. "He's ramping up, I think. He'll have to kill one, probably soon."

"The more he gets away with, the more arrogant he'll get." Phan didn't look up from his computer.

"Then sloppy." Del sighed. "Hopefully sooner rather than later."

"How many women'll get terrorized and how many will get killed before he gets sloppy enough to get caught?"

"Too many." Del pursed her lips and returned to her phone work. She'd left so many messages at so many numbers that she was starting to get a sore throat to go along with her seemingly permanent stomachache. She kept careful track of what she'd done and what she still needed to do or should do again, but the notebooks were filling up and her thoughts were no clearer.

The department chugged along like a runaway train, trying to balance the escalating sex crime case and the other crimes that took place with their usual disturbing regularity. Patrols in the Mission District were increased even more. Ever more fervent warnings went out through the media, and citizen watchdog groups took turns questioning the department's ineffectual efforts. The Mission should have been the safest place in the world, Del thought, with all the officers, reporters, and safety patrols on the streets. But with no solid leads, they were busy chasing their bad guy instead of trapping him.

Del told Phan about hunting with her daddy, about the way he would catch a dangerous animal by watching its patterns of behavior and using its predictability against the animal.

"But people are smarter than animals," Phan put in. "Less predictable."

"Are we?" Del rubbed her forehead. "I don't know. Maybe it's just harder for us to see human patterns because we're human too. And we are much more interested in doing harm for the sake of doing harm. Animals usually kill for a reason. They're hungry or scared or competing for resources. Our guy is harming women because he likes to harm women."

Phan waggled his head. "It's the worst kind of case."

She nodded. "No good evidence and a wide pool of victims."

"Don't forget that big, bright spotlight on every move we make."

"God," Del said with a wry smile, "we sound like Tweedledum and Tweedledee."

"Which of us is Dum?" Phan cocked an eyebrow at her.

Del laughed and shook her head. "Both of us."

Examining the extensive database of predators they'd compiled, she played with the data and created a variety of alternate analyses. She teased out discrete sets comprised of men who'd been expensively and well defended and had either been acquitted or not had charges filed, men who'd gotten away with multiple counts of peeping, sexual battery, rape, kidnapping and murder. There were too many of them, and a lot were the same basic type: rich, spoiled, utterly selfish and clever. These sets of names were disturbingly numerous and heavily populated, and there was significant crossover with some of the men.

She created a handwritten list of the names that recurred most often and another of those that stood out for her because their victims were similar to the victims in the current cases. Again the lists were too long. She looked for names that ended up on both of her scrawled lists and saw fourteen. One she recognized immediately—Ernie White. The other thirteen she didn't know, but she wanted to follow up on them.

She'd been systematic but was aware of the potential for her own biases to corrupt her processes. She couldn't be sure of her objectivity. Dissatisfied by the nebulous nature of her interest in these suspects, she wrote a list of the details of the fourteen men she'd isolated. She looked at what they had in common and didn't share. Just before midnight, while examining her lists, Del noted that Mikey Ocampo had been dead for nine days.

Before sunrise on Thursday she was at the station and looking up more extensive and updated information on the fourteen names. Five were incarcerated, five were in the military and stationed elsewhere, and two were dead. They'd managed to live good long lives, though, Del noted with disgust, before keeling over in their nice comfy beds. How many women and children had each victimized in the course of his long life?

That left two names from her list of fourteen: Ronald Teager and Ernest White. She took a quick coffee break, wanting to be clearheaded. She shot Phan an email requesting he look into Ronald Teager and briefly explaining the process by which she'd isolated him as a possible person of interest. After thirty seconds of sitting still and staring at her scummy Snoopy mug, the one she'd been using nearly every day for more years than she cared to count, she got back to work.

Five years after Mikey Ocampo shot him, Ernie White was a multimillionaire. He'd inherited his mother's properties and money and lived in the Sunset District. He drove a black Lexus, nearly identical to the one he'd been driving five years ago. No wife, no kids. A condo on Oahu, a cabin in Tahoe, and several dozen other properties rounded out his real estate portfolio. He owned pieces of several commercial buildings and was a shareholder in several apartment complexes. He maintained a very limited online social profile and virtually nonexistent online professional profile. From what she could see, White lived how, when and where he wanted and did only what he felt like doing. Mikey Ocampo and his mother were dead, and Ernie White was living it up. Del swallowed bile.

He'd kept his nose clean as far as the justice system was concerned, which as Del knew too well was relatively easy for a rich man to do. He'd burned through four black Lexus sedans, one a year, each a little more embellished with luxury features and the latest technology. Del pictured the guy seeing a speck of bird dirt on his car and trading it in on another one, the cars as disposable to him as the women he abused. Del started to feel desperate. She didn't want to confuse her feelings of frustration over letting Mikey's life go down the tubes with certainty that Ernie White needed to be put down like a rabid animal. There was something wrong with White, though, and Del couldn't shake her building tension—Ernie White was a bad guy. She went into law enforcement twenty years ago specifically to protect the innocent from people like Ernie White. What was she, if not a guardian of the thin veneer of civility that kept White from destroying what little was decent about humanity?

Del fairly hummed with impatience. White wasn't even on the department's radar. He'd continue to do whatever he wanted behind the shield his money provided, and there was nothing Del could do about that. How many victims had Ernie White left behind in his years on the planet? How many more would he leave behind before, like the others, he died an old man? Del shook her head. She made a decision that she belatedly realized had been brewing for a while. Without mentioning it to Phan and with more than a few pangs of guilt, she went outside and called an old friend, leaving a message that she guessed was likely to be returned immediately. That was the pattern. That was the way Mac insisted things should be. Del would call one number to leave a message and get a call back on another line.

Del wondered if she would get the expected return call. It had been a long time. Were she and Mac friends? Del wasn't sure. Mac had tried to lure her into leaving local law enforcement for some federal beat, and though she'd refused the offer several times they'd developed a kind of rapport over the years. Mac now worked in Homeland Security and therefore had access to information she was unlikely to get any other way. The phone rang, and Del let out the breath she hadn't realized she was holding.

Mac's greeting was cordial, and she was grateful that Mac didn't give her too hard a time about their years of heated argument over what Del saw as the Patriot Act's overreach and violation of Americans' privacy. They skipped the usual catching up of old friends, as they always did, and Del jumped into the subject at hand with more than a little trepidation.

Mac laughed when Del explained the reason for her call. "You finally ready to come over to the dark side, kiddo?"

"I'm sorry to put you on the spot," she said, her voice subdued. "You have every right to say no, I get that. But I need help."

"Oh. Well. Okay." Mac's tone was neutral.

But then, Del recalled, when hadn't it been? That had been one of Mac's most overriding characteristics, neutrality. Wasn't that one of the things Del had both admired and hated?

* * *

A mysterious stranger called her home phone number. In the mid-nineties, that was how people got in touch with each other.

"Officer Mason, you're wasting your time patrolling the Tenderloin. Probably get yourself knifed before you turn thirty. My name's Mac. I work for Uncle Sam. You're gonna leave the local beat to come work for me," Mac growled, and Del wasn't able to tell if the stranger was joking or serious. She also wasn't able to tell if Mac was a man or a woman. Del wasn't interested in leaving local law enforcement for a federal gig, and she rejected the nebulous offer with a curt negative.

"Not even gonna listen to the deal, huh? Well, I'll be in your neck of the woods," Mac rumbled. "You're not working Sunday night. Meet me at Fiddler's Green—you know it? Seven thirty. I'll be wearing black." Without waiting for a response, Mac hung up.

Too curious to pass up the invitation, Del drove past the San Francisco International Airport—SFO to its many passersby—and found the Irish pub by seven fifteen. It met her every expectation: glossy wooden bar, rows of liquor arranged stadium-style behind the bartender, and sudsy steins at every place. She identified Mac, the only patron sporting a black suit and tie and a brutally short crew cut. Mac was twisted sideways on a barstool, squinting at the doorway and waiting, and Del fought a smile. Was she making some Faustian deal, simply by meeting this federal agent at a bar? She honestly couldn't tell if Mac—no last name, no job title, and no distinct gender markers—was a legitimate federal agent or a criminal. But she slid onto the stool next to the mysterious stranger. They talked about a variety of topics for a good twenty minutes before Del decided Mac was probably a woman. If nothing else, she was definitely curious about the ill-defined job offer Mac was making. Mac's baked skin, squinting gaze, and gravelly voice made her seem otherworldly. Del almost wondered if someone was playing a practical joke on her.

"Why me? How do you even know my name?" Del asked. "What exactly do you want me to do?"

"You're smart. You're wasted on patrol. Even in San Francisco you'll end up working twice as hard as anybody else. You'll kiss the fourth point of contact on a lot of guys with half of your intellect and a third of your drive."

"That's a lot of numbers," Del noted, sipping the dark, smoky-sweet whiskey Mac had ordered for her before her arrival.

Mac ignored this. "In my group you'll work independently most of the time. You'll report directly to me or to my second. Name's Guy. Smart. Smarter than you, almost as smart as me."

Del allowed herself a small smile at this. "Work on what exactly?"

"Depends. Training for a while, mostly cold cases to hone your skills. Your primary source of knowledge about investigation so far has been the library. That's okay, for now, but you'll need to sharpen your skills on a more varied surface. You're too rough around the edges. Too hotheaded. Too inexperienced. Too comfortable relying on your instincts instead of solid investigation."

Del, at that point five years out of college with five years on the force, pushed away defensiveness and examined the stranger's assessment.

"I am inexperienced in too many areas," she admitted. "Mostly I deal with domestics and drunks and bar fights. I've been on nights five years. I'd like to learn more about how people work, why they do what they do." She grimaced. "You know a lot more about me than I do about you and your group. What organization do you belong to? Who would I answer to if you quit or died or whatever? How do I even know you're American? For all I know, you're a KGB recruiter trying to sucker me into treason. Or a criminal. Maybe you work for the Yakuza. Maybe you're—"

Mac's laugh sounded more like a car backfiring than an expression of humor, but it made Del smile anyway.

"You're a cynical kid," Mac opined. "I like that. But I'll tell you what. Go spin your wheels with SFPD for a few more years. The sergeant's exam is in a few months. Take it. Get some experience using your head more than your feet. Call me at this number and leave a message. Don't bother me until you get your stripes." Mac slid a business card across the bar's smooth surface. It was plain white with only a phone number on it. The area code was one Del didn't recognize. Then Mac dropped a five-dollar tip on the bar and sketched a wave before striding purposefully out of the bar's front door. Del sat looking at the card for a minute. She looked at its matte surface and wondered if it held any fingerprints. She tucked it carefully into her shirt pocket.

She didn't find any fingerprints on the card the next day. But she did listen to the stranger who called herself Mac and pass the sergeant's exam. A week after that she called the number on the card.

* * *

Fifteen years later, she wondered where they stood. Did Mac consider them friends? Or was she still grooming Del to join her team? They'd done some investigation together, Del using some of her vacation days once a year for several years to join Mac for what Mac said were practice exercises. Del still wasn't sure if the information in the files they'd pored over had been real or fictional. One case was the kidnapping of a scientist's sixteen-year-old daughter, one the murder of a rugby coach everyone claimed to love, and three were serial murders. After a few of these Mac acknowledged Del's progress as an investigator. It was a few more years before she stopped overtly trying to get Del to quit SFPD and move to wherever Mac worked. They never talked about personal stuff, though Del had come to consider Mac a friend, albeit a strange one. Then came nine-eleven and the changes of the Patriot Act, and the two friends found themselves arguing too much and too angrily to continue their conversation.

"I still think people should have some measure of safety without giving up their civil rights." Del sighed. She was annoyed with herself for persisting as though they were still engaged in the old argument. "Unless they're bad guys. Unless there's a preponderance of evidence that they're bad guys. Under the law."

There was a long silence. Del wondered if maybe Mac was planning her next argument or just irritated. Maybe, she thought, Mac was deciding how to deny her request.

"In principle I agree." Mac was ruminating; Del could hear the short bristles of the familiar high-and-tight haircut as Mac rubbed away a developing headache. It was an old habit, one Del had nearly forgotten. "It's gotten real fuzzy, Mason. Too fuzzy for any thinking person."

Del grimaced. "Do we agree for once?"

"Let's not get carried away." Mac started tapping at a keyboard. "Principles to the side for the moment, since you reached out. You have a particular bad guy in mind. Let's save the philosophical discussion for when I'm in your neck of the woods. I'm sending you some data, subject line 'Rugby' or the name of the rugby coach. Obviously this is under the radar and needs to stay that way. Fruit of the poisoned tree, so it's useless in court unless you can establish contact with the info via another route. I don't exist and neither does the file you're going to open up at home, not work, not on your cell phone, and delete within a few hours. Understood?"

"Understood. Thanks, Mac." Del hesitated. "Listen, I'm sorry. I played all high and mighty, then radio silence until I need a favor. That's not—"

"We're good, kiddo." Mac laughed, a sound like a worn-out motor turning over. "You're a little soft in the head, but I like you."

The rest of Thursday was a blur as Del worked with Phan on the peeper case. He asked about Teager, and she mentioned her following up on White as another possible perv but kept him in the dark about her conversation with Mac. If anything came of it, she'd tell him what she needed to. If she didn't have to tell him about breaching her own code of ethics, she would let him stay clean. Wearied by the weight of her secret, she cut out early, claiming tiredness.

"You all right?" Phan frowned and examined her with his usual frankness. "I don't think you've ever wanted to leave before me."

"Just tired," Del claimed, looking at his shoulder to avoid eye contact. Lying had become second nature on the job, but lying to her partner, a good partner at that, felt dirty. She let her discomfort show, figuring he wouldn't ask too many questions if he saw she didn't want to talk. "See you tomorrow."

Mac came through. By seven that night Del was at home on her computer. She followed Mac's instructions before sifting through the files and realizing just how much data the Feds had compiled on Ernie White. While it was clear someone had at least occasionally been keeping an eye on his comings and goings, it was just as clear from the state of the data that no one had gone through it. Doggedly taking notes from the files, Del found herself collating hundreds of disparate tidbits of information. It was overwhelming and tedious at once. At one point she stopped to look over her dozens of pages of notes, spread out like fallen leaves on the dining room table.

She printed everything Mac had sent her, sorting data into discrete categories that she hoped made sense. Soon her table was covered with neat stacks of printouts, and the walls were decorated with giant sticky notes sporting theories, questions and timelines. She was glad to have so much data to work with, despite the unmanageable size of the data pool, but she was also horrified there was so much intrusion into the private life of a man who hadn't actually been convicted of a single crime. Her head ached with cognitive dissonance: she couldn't comfortably maintain outrage over the invasiveness of federal law enforcement agencies and use their data at the same time.

She noted White's regular trips overseas, not only to the usual tourist destinations but also to a variety of countries where it was relatively easy to buy and rent women. And, Del realized with dawning horror, children. Was that what she'd been missing? She'd assumed Mikey's story was true, that his mom was White's victim. Had Mikey been White's target? Boys and men underreported rape and sexual abuse even more than girls and women, a thing Del figured she should have recalled back when she was interviewing Mikey. Had Ernie White raped or tried to rape Mikey? Had he raped both mother and son? Or was she grasping at straws?

On Friday morning she put out a formal request for information regarding ongoing investigations into Ernest White to state, federal and other local law enforcement agencies and called to ask Jones, her favorite computer expert in the department, to create a bot that would track Ernie White's presence in any investigative nets. It was technically legal but could be challenged by a decent defense attorney, and Del heard Jones's hesitation when she asked. She was bypassing procedural channels with this particular request, and they both knew she was asking him to go out on a shaky limb with her. She could only hope she'd built enough trust and good faith between them to compel him to help her.

"He's a really bad guy," she said lamely. "I have to know."

Jones talked for a few minutes about the nature of curiosity and its role in learning. Then he discussed its possible neurological correlations with memory formation and retrieval. Through this lecture Del kept her tongue. Jones was brilliant. When he turned pedantic it was because he was buying time to decide how to respond to something, and Del wondered how aware he was of this. Finally Jones was ready to render his verdict. He laughingly demanded payment in the form of chocolate-covered pretzels and a giant bag of gummy spiders, to which Del agreed, knowing this was his way of expressing his discomfort with her request. She felt a pang of guilt. She was calling in all of her favors for this case.

"Sounds fair," she said, keeping her tone light. "And thank you. I know I'm putting you on the spot."

"Yes," he said. "You are. I'm not going to—"

"Of course not," Del rushed to say. "I don't want you to do anything unethical or illegal, but if there's stuff out there in the public domain, information that's just floating out there and it can help us—"

"Yeah, yeah." Jones scratched the stubble on his cheek. "Got it. Infospace, the final frontier."

* * *

They tried to anticipate the perv's next move. That he was heading toward murder seemed inevitable, and the slow, sure force of that inevitability appeared to paralyze their thinking. In the coming days Del took to driving around and around the Mission at night, looking at each house and apartment and wondering if he was right there in that house, or there in that car, planning his next move. Had he taken pictures of the victims? Was he looking at them right now?

Janet had conducted an in-depth investigation into the ways predators sometimes used cameras as weapons, often violating the privacy of their victims without their knowledge. That was part of how she'd connected with Sterling, the serial killer who'd come after Lola. Sterling had used her camera in part of her hunting process, following and photographing her potential victims for weeks before kidnapping and killing them.

Before she got derailed into her strange relationship with Sterling, Janet had been developing an interesting set of theories about photography and film as weapons. Del wished she'd asked more about it. Would Janet have some special insight into peepers? She had, after all, studied the subject in some depth. Del played with the idea of going to visit Janet and see if she could gain any insight. Shaking her head at her own folly, Del pushed this thought away.

Captain Bradley called each team of investigators into his office, demanding answers they didn't have. When it was Del and Phan's turn, they exchanged warning glances, each telling the other not to rise to whatever bait Bradley threw their way. After haranguing the pair for several minutes, their captain sat back and rubbed his thinning hair.

"We need to get this asshole. What's our next step?"

"Come on, sir," Del said. "You know the next step."

Bradley frowned as if in confusion.

Del shook her head. "He takes another one. Maybe he moves her and someone sees it, maybe he rapes her, maybe he kills her, maybe he leaves something behind. Maybe she lives, remembers enough to tell us something about him. Maybe he takes two more, or three, or seven. He's escalating, that's what we know. And he's smart and careful. We don't have enough to stop him for now. At this point, we're just hoping to get lucky."

"That's not good enough. Your plan is to what, sit and wait for him to victimize another woman?" Bradley's thundering voice rang out and his face was bright red. Del almost felt sorry for him. "You're fucking this up. Maybe we need better guys who actually know what the fuck to do."

Del blinked at Bradley, refusing to rise to the bait.

"Sir." Phan shook his head. "Captain, put whoever you want on the case, but it won't make a difference. We need more evidence. We need some way to narrow down the pool of suspects. We don't want another victim, of course. But the odds are, that is what's gonna happen. You know that as well as we do."

"Shit." Bradley rubbed his mouth. He sat back and shook his head. "Maybe I need a new team on this."

Del cleared her throat. "If the next one, assuming there is a next one, gets classified as a kidnapping, the Feds will take it. Until or unless, we'd like to keep it. If that's what you decide, if you let us, we'd like to keep it."

She felt the heat of Phan's gaze and ignored her partner as they left Bradley's office a few minutes later. She wasn't sure why she even wanted to stay on this, especially since it pulled her time away from Mikey's murder. It didn't matter, anyway, and they all knew it. The disposition of the case was hardly up to anyone in the station.

"You think we might get to keep it?"

Phan shook his head. "I think it's kidnapping and high profile, which will make it the Feds' new pet project. It's too high-profile for them to sit on their hands, you know that. In the meantime, I'm looking at Ronald Teager but not finding a lot on him so far. I'll get back to you on that soon. Let's move off those two for the rest of the day and come back to White and Teager tomorrow."

By lunchtime on Friday, the attacks had indeed been classified as kidnappings and the Feds had taken over. Del and Phan, along with the rest of SFPD, would be allowed to pursue leads, but those leads would be turned over to the supervising Fed, who would not be obliged to reciprocate. Del tried to tell herself she was relieved, because she'd be able to focus on Mikey. It was a lie, but she decided to believe it for the time being.

CHAPTER FIVE

Friday afternoon was split between working Mikey's murder and hunting for the predator. Del and Phan again reached out to everyone who might have encountered a homeless teenage runaway in Mikey's last year. They also continued to dig through the mountain of files of convicted and suspected sexual predators in the area.

Del's stomach roiled. None of the rapists or batterers or peepers they interviewd admitted they were guilty. None of them had ever done anything wrong, none of them would admit he'd ever hurt anyone. One creep, convicted of raping a blind eighty-seven-year-old woman, looked right at Del and swore up and down that he had been celibate his entire life. Del laughed and it tasted sour.

"You don't remember me, do you?"

The rapist shook his head.

"I'm the one who arrested you, asshole. I'm the one who found the video you made of yourself raping somebody's old, blind granny, you—" She heard her voice rising and saw Phan's narrowed gaze.

She stood abruptly and left, waiting outside for Phan to finish up. Twenty feet away, a group of kids played on the sidewalk. Great, she thought, perfect. Maybe he can start raping kids instead of little old ladies. It was getting dark and Del wondered where the kids' parents were. She shook her head.

"I'm done for the day," Phan said, joining her at the car. "We'll work on Mikey tomorrow."

"We haven't gotten anywhere," Del retorted. "Or doesn't that matter anymore?"

"Don't pull that shit with me, Mason." Phan tossed her the keys. "Kaylee's actually willing to spend some time with me, and I'm not letting her down. Especially since tomorrow's Saturday, and neither of us even considered taking the weekend off. Or doesn't that matter? I think it does."

Del flushed with shame and nodded her agreement. "Sorry. I guess I'm just frustrated. Which I know you are too. Say hey to Kaylee for me."

As she headed to her empty house for the night, her stomach roiled. She was going to have to go to the doctor soon. Her gut was churning day and night, and the pain was getting worse. She was downing antacids like candy. She walked into her dining room and was surrounded by the evidence of White's self-indulgent life. She sat wearily in front of the neatly organized documentation of an American citizen's private life and felt soulless. After a while she started slogging through her list of questions and worked on a timeline of White's life.

"What would a timeline of my life look like?" she wondered. "Who's keeping track of what I spend my money on and where I travel to and who I spend time with?"

She wasn't sure if she was paranoid to even wonder about these questions. White was under suspicion because he behaved suspiciously. Resolutely she pushed aside her qualms and focused again on tracking White's movements over the last several years. By three in the morning she was blind with exhaustion. She staggered up to bed and wished Lola was in it.

"I miss you," she whispered, only half awake. "I miss you every day."

On Saturday, Del and Phan were at the station by midmorning despite being off duty. Milner and his current partner, a relative newcomer named Doyle, were already on a call, so Del and Phan were pressed into service on a homicide only a few blocks from the station. They spent an oddly satisfying weekend solving the new case. Their killer was a young man who believed that the victim, a seminary student named Victor Gutierrez, had insulted him. The incident had been initiated by a misunderstanding that took place in front of a Mission Street grocery. The store was one of a row of small, locally owned commercial businesses not far from the station near the other end of the colorful gallery of murals known as Clarion Alley. The shooter had seen Gutierrez standing outside with his sister and her infant son. The seminary student had apparently made some kind of gesture the shooter interpreted as an insult or a challenge.

"He was praying," the victim's sister wailed when Del took her statement. "He made the Sign of the Cross!"

Apparently unfamiliar with that particular ritualistic display, the killer had followed Gutierrez to his mother's home and lay in wait outside. He stuck around until the victim, holding his infant nephew, went outside to feed the family dog. The killer used a semi automatic and fired six rounds, killing the seminary student and the dog, and wounding the six-month-old nephew and an elderly neighbor who came outside at the sounds of the shots. They arrested the shooter after his ex-girlfriend turned him in by way of a surreptitious phone call.

"We got three kids," Esperanza, the teenage girlfriend, had mumbled. "He don't pay nothing to me. Now he gone and kilt a priest? Oh, hell no. He can go to jail. Fuck that piece of shit."

"Thank you, ma'am," Del said.

"They got a reward for me?"

"I'll check on that. Thank you for helping us."

Over the weekend the victim's family and friends organized a fundraising website and gave Esperanza Cortez, the nineteen-year-old mother of three small children, just over six thousand dollars as thanks for coming forward.

On Monday morning, it was Captain Bradley, flanked by members of the Gutierrez family, who handed the young woman the check and smiled for the cameras. After the brief ceremonial meeting, Phan thanked the witness. He bit his lip. Del knew what he was trying not to say: put it in the bank for your kids instead of giving it to your new boyfriend. They watched the couple race out of the station, the three youngsters trailing behind them. Del and Phan exchanged a hard glance. The paramour was Sal Jameson, a parolee with a penchant for beating up his girlfriends and their kids.

"How long," Del wondered in an aside to Phan, "before those kids are in foster care because Jameson kills their mom?"

Phan shook his head. "Or he kills her or one of the kids because she spent a single dime on her babies?"

They reinterviewed the residents and business owners around the Shotwell Street crime scene. Del wished she knew where the primary crime scene was and whether she would ever know. Mikey had bled a lot at the site of his beating.

As they wrapped up their interviews, Del stopped on the sidewalk and looked at a group of kids playing in front of yet another worn, gray apartment building decorated only with graffiti. Too young to be outside unsupervised, to Del's mind, they sounded like happy little children anywhere, shouting, laughing, making silly noises. But the oldest two, maybe seven and nine, kept a wary eye on the surroundings. What did it cost a child to be on guard from such a young age? How old, Del couldn't help but wonder, had Mikey Ocampo been when he'd first sported that guarded, careworn look?

"Anything wrong?"

Del heard the undercurrent of alarm in Phan's voice and met his eyes.

"No, sorry."

"Let's head back." In the car, he flicked a finger at her. "Where'd you go?"

"Nowhere." She shook her head. "Do those kids have any chance?"

Phan looked around and shrugged a question.

"They deserve a hell of a lot better than this."

"Agreed."

They headed back for the station at a slow crawl along 17th Street. Del was itchy. When it was Phan's turn to drive, she had too much time to think. She pushed her hair back off of her forehead.

"What's goin' on, Mason?"

She blew out hot breath. "Maybe Mikey was doomed from the start. I want to find his killer, but maybe he wouldn't have been able to make a decent life for himself no matter what. It could have been some desperate kid just like Mikey who killed him. Another kid, and Mikey had five bucks on him and the kid needed it."

"Maybe." Phan made a face. "But growing up in poverty doesn't make it okay to kill people, or mean you're necessarily going to—"

"Obviously."

"And look at that seminary student. He grew up in a crappy neighborhood too, and by all accounts he was a decent guy. So maybe they do have a chance. Some of them."

"Of course." Del nodded. "I'm not saying people are doomed. I just think we allow people to be set up for failure."

"I know. But what can we do? We try to keep people from getting away with killing each other. A guy kills his wife, we try to keep him from killing another one. What else are we supposed to do?"

Del shrugged.

"Besides," Phan added, "with the gentrification, in five years the Mission will be completely different and we'll be reduced to busting hipsters and tech nerds for drugs and domestics."

"You think?" Del wondered at his conversational left turn. Was he suggesting, however indirectly, that gentrification was contributing to the neighborhood's tension and exacerbating decades-old problems? Or was he trying to distract her?

Phan chucked his chin at a group of twenty-something yuppies lounging outside a coffee shop on 24th Street. Del realized how familiar a sight they'd become, the ironically grungy youngsters and their fixie bikes clustering on parking lots and on street corners.

"I don't know," Del said, her gaze on a pair of red-clad Norteños up the block. "Culture clash and class warfare seem more likely."

"The guns and knives'll only slow things down," Phan claimed. "Money always wins, in the end. You can't stay in a neighborhood you can't afford, and the computer guys are coming in and driving up the prices. The gangs'll have to head out."

"Maybe the engineers will need less policing."

"Worried about job security? Nah." Phan laughed. "People are still people, and people like to kill each other."

Silenced by the sound of her own cynical thought in Phan's voice, Del wondered how much longer either of them would be able to stay in the job and still be decent human beings. And what then? Del couldn't imagine doing anything else for a living and couldn't imagine still being on the job in ten years.

They headed in to the station to fill out more of the seemingly endless paperwork that comprised far too much of their jobs. It was necessary, of course, but Del had to force herself to do it without complaint. She looked over at one point and saw Phan frowning down at his own block letters. It looked like he was trying to read what he'd written to see if it made sense. She'd gotten lucky. She had a partner who was smart and a decent human being. Hopefully she wouldn't fuck this up the way she'd fucked up everything else. Her stomach cramped, and she chomped another trio of antacids.

Del's stomach hurt so much and so often, she thought she would rather die than feel that pain for one more day. After work she did her usual cruising and wrote another unsent letter to Lola. After that she made a toaster waffle, thinking about Sofia Gonzalez standing over her sink. She caught herself looking at the kitchen window as if she half expected the peeper to be there. Sudden pain drew her mind away from that weird imagining. She looked at a large, sharp kitchen knife and wondered if it would hurt less if she cut her stomach out.

"That's crazy talk," she told herself. "Time to do something really crazy like go to the doctor." She broke into a ragged laugh. "I'm talking to myself now. About being crazy. I must really be sick."

She looked in on the dining room, which she'd transformed into a strange, angry shrine to Ernie White, and couldn't face it. She lay in bed unsleeping and stared at the red numbers of her ancient clock radio, which she rarely used for waking up or for listening to music.

"Mikey's been dead for two weeks," she whispered into the darkness. She didn't say the rest but couldn't stop thinking—she'd let Mikey down again. Hot tears ran down the sides of her face and into her hair until she curled up on her side with her hands wrapped protectively over her burning middle.

She finally gave in and went to see Dr. Philipps, her general practitioner, on Tuesday afternoon. By then she was doubled over in pain. Philipps, shaking her oversized head, ran a few tests and pending definitive results gave a preliminary diagnosis: she had an ulcer. After lecturing Del on her eating habits and blood pressure, Philipps relented and gave a strained smile. Her dark brown eyes shone with concern.

"Try eating an actual meal once in a while. Sleep for more than a couple of hours. You can't do a good job on anything if you don't take care of yourself." Dr. Philipps was tiny, just under five feet tall, and she peered up at Del with a stern expression on her elfin face. "I don't want to see you work yourself into an early grave."

Del nodded contritely. "You're right. I know you are. You say this every time I see you."

"Have you considered listening to me?"

At home an hour later, Del examined the prescriptions she'd picked up at the drugstore: antibiotics for two weeks, some kind of liquid medicine and another set of pills. Super, she thought, now I'm an old lady with a bag full of pills. It was just like after she got shot. Her body was letting her down again, only this time she was on her own with no Lola to take care of her. She read the instructions from the pharmacist and took two teaspoons of the liquid. She decided she'd start with the rest of the treatment tomorrow. Tonight it was time to go out and have fun, blow off some steam. This would apparently be her last hurrah before turning into Nana and echoing her slow descent back into dust.

As she passed Lola's house, Del noticed all the lights were off. *Is she out at a party? Maybe she and that redhead are making love right now.*

She walked the two miles down to The Wild Side West on Cortland Avenue. The walk gave her time to think about the dozens of times she'd haunted the Bernal Heights bar before she'd met Lola. There was always something going on at Wild Side, and Del grinned at its saloon façade as she approached. Light and music and women's voices reached out to invite her in. Wild Side was packed, even though it was a weeknight. There'd been some kind of trivia game earlier in the evening, according to a posted sign, and Trivia Night always drew a crowd. Del ordered a beer and looked over the pulsing throng of chatting, flirting, dancing women.

Who would she approach? Definitely not the redhead, even though she looked nothing like Lola's new lover. The woman with the blue ponytail was too young. The cute Latina with the purple hair was too drunk. She felt like a shopper, looking over the goods. Like the perv choosing a new victim.

One of the women he'd kidnapped had previously reported being raped, though no one had been arrested. Four peeping victims had confided that they'd been raped but hadn't reported the assaults when they occurred. How many other victims had also been victims of sexual violence and not brought it up when reporting the peeper? Not one of the men who'd abused or raped any of their peeper's victims had ever been arrested or jailed.

Of course, Del reflected, something like ninety-seven percent of rapists never faced a single day in jail, so the failure of the justice system in any particular case wasn't too surprising. And with a female victim, being a survivor of prior rape or sexual abuse wasn't usually uncommon enough to serve as an effective differentiating feature. Still, the fact that so many of the reporting victims were self-identified survivors could be a pattern worth documenting and analyzing. Were the women targeted because of their prior experiences as victims? One of the kidnapped women had asked if she was wearing a target on her back, and the officer interviewing her had rushed to assure her, talking about coincidence and happenstance. But Del wasn't so sure. Did the peeper—the man Del was still not entirely convinced was also the kidnapper—somehow sense some psychic scarring on victims? Was that what drew him to one woman and not another?

Del thought about Ernie White. She'd bet he was the peeper and that he had a good eye for which women would make good victims. Was he born with that sensibility, or had he honed it over years of predatory practice?

Del pushed the thought aside and tried to focus on the scene before her. It was hard to tease apart the practice of selecting a potential lover and doing a predatory survey. What did that say about her? Did guys, straight guys, look at a roomful of women and assess the best candidates for seduction? Did they worry that this was predatory?

She scanned the roomful of women again, draining her beer and imagining herself a bad guy. Whom would she target? Looking at the room that way, she could clearly see the best victims. It was remarkably easy. That little brunette with the glassy eyes and ravaged fingernails, she was a good one. Del pushed away thoughts of Janet and her chewed-up nails and cuticles.

There was a youngster, probably barely old enough to be in a bar, a slightly overweight girl with dark eyes and dyed pink hair. She sported fading fingertip bruises on the backs of her upper arms and wore double the recommended daily allowance of makeup. Was it to hide scars, or to cover fading bruises on her face or throat? Either way, the bruising and the tentative way she tried to strut marked her as a good victim. How long before Del was standing over her body? If the girl dated women exclusively, she might last a little longer—women were much less likely to kill than men, but there was no guarantee. Del shook her head. The girl might as well be wearing concentric circles on her forehead and a toe tag inside her obviously uncomfortable high heels.

Is this how the predator feels, Del wondered again, walking around the Mission? Does he walk by each woman and assess her as a victim? Does he walk past every house, thinking, I'll check this one tonight? That one tomorrow? Does he case them ahead of time, so he knows which ones are females living alone? Does he choose the women when he passes them on the street, or does he watch their homes and pick them that way?

Unable to leave the case behind, Del had decided to abandon the bar for the night when a waitress walked up and handed her a whiskey.

"Ah, I didn't order this, ma'am."

"No, sweetie, she did." The overworked server pointed vaguely at the crowded dance floor. "You have an admirer. Tight dress, red hair dye. And cutie, if it turns out you're not into her, I admire you too."

Del sketched a wave, not sure at whom, and looked at the overfilled glass. She pulled out her wallet to offer a tip but the waitress was already gone. She didn't usually drink hard liquor except at home, but it had been a long day. A long week. A long month. A long lifetime. Del eyed her watch. Almost midnight. Mikey had been dead for fifteen days. She upended the whiskey and remembered the first time she met Mac. She smiled and shook her head again, not sure she wanted to clear it. She'd just started wondering belatedly whether the booze would mix well with her ulcer medication, when a woman with teased auburn hair approached and stood uncomfortably close.

"Hi," she whispered, and Del had to lean close to hear her. "I'm sorry to just walk up to you like this, but, um, your gun is showing."

"What?" Del looked down. Sure enough, her weapon was poking out of her waistband. It could hardly have been visible from anywhere more than a foot away, but she adjusted her holster anyway. "Hey, thanks."

The woman sported the tight little black dress to which the waitress had referred and bright, sparkling brown eyes. Not a victim, Del thought. Insecure enough to wear too much makeup but self-assured enough to stand up for herself if pushed. Maybe.

"Do I owe you a thanks?" Del waggled the empty tumbler, and a different passing waitress snagged it without a backward glance.

"I wanted a reason to approach you."

"You could approach me with or without a drink, but thanks. Can I return the favor?"

"I think I've had enough to drink. Now I'm looking for something else."

Del nodded, breaking eye contact. She looked for a graceful exit but was forestalled by an outstretched hand.

"I'm Sara."

"Del."

Sara's skin was soft and cool, and Del held her hand for a fraction of a second longer than necessary. Was this a good idea? Hadn't she just been about to go home and really focus on the case?

She's just another badge bunny. This is dumb. I have work to do.

"You have nice hands." Sara kept hold of Del's palm, turned it up and ran lotion-smoothed fingertips along the sensitive skin of Del's wrist.

"And you're alive!" She giggled and held a red-tipped digit to Del's artery and pretended to count. "It's speeding up. I wonder why?" She wrinkled her nose and winked.

I could have her for the night. Take my mind off things.

Sara was smiling up at her, licking her lips. Her abundant bosom spilled out of the black polyester sheath stretched over her spray-tanned skin. Four-inch heels brought her up to Del's nose. Oddly, she smelled like Del's Nana.

"Are you wearing Shalimar?"

"Wow, you have a sensitive sniffer." Sara's eyes widened. "You like it?"

Del gestured, and Sara leaned even closer, tiptoeing to expose her neck to Del. She also exposed even more cleavage and a lacy, beribboned red bra. The women were interrupted by the waitress returning with another whiskey, which Del drank in one swallow.

"Sure I can't get you—?"

"I'd prefer a dance, if you're offering gifts." Sara looked down, as if modestly.

Del offered her daddy's slow smile, and Sara reddened all the way down to her porn-star bra. It was too easy. Maybe choosing a lover wasn't so different from choosing a victim. Sara looked confident but was easily manipulated.

Del had seen it a hundred times. Little girls learned to please early on. Mothers taught the lessons without even realizing: smile, flirt, lean in, touch someone in just the right way, and you can get what you want. Attention, approval, an extra cookie, whatever—the best and sometimes only way for girls and women to get what they want was by pleasing someone more powerful than they. That was the lesson. What else did they know? It was part of what made them such great victims.

Convince women they are only as important as they make someone else feel, and they are ripe for the plucking, whether that's exploitation or oppression or seduction or violence or murder or some cocktail of those things.

Or was that too simple? It was Sara who'd approached Del, bought her a drink, offered another, pointed out her weapon. Who was seducing whom? Del let her smile fade. Janet had approached Del in this very bar a few years ago. She'd been feisty, overconfident, aggressive. Del had found it enchanting. Of course, Sara was no Janet, was she? Janet really was one of a kind. Del tried to imagine Lola walking into a bar in a fuck-me outfit and buying drinks for strangers she wanted to sleep with. It was cartoonish, ridiculous. Del felt her blood slamming around her body and pushed thoughts of Lola away.

"So?" Sara smiled, tossing her carefully careless hair.

"I'm waiting for a slow song," Del said with an easy grin that belied her inner tension. "I'd like to get another whiff or two of you and that Shalimar."

"I think that can be arranged."

They danced, and Sara rubbed up against Del, who was trying to decide. Should she sleep with this girl or go home? It suddenly seemed like too much work, pretending to like this woman for more than her desirability. But Del was already entangled, wasn't she? Or was she? Lola was tumbling around with that grinning idiotic ginger-haired woman, doing God knew what, and Del was supposed to just wait for her to get over whatever bee had flown into her bonnet? She knew the whiskey was making her mean-spirited, but she slugged down another when the waitress cruised by, this one a double.

It was an hour later, in an expensively furnished, extraordinarily messy apartment on Ellsworth Street, that Del found herself making out with cute little badge bunny Sara and wishing she'd just gone home. There was nothing wrong with Sara. Sara was fine. She was bright and attractive and sexy. She was into Del or at least into being with a police officer, but Del couldn't focus on her. Somehow, the pretty, responsive, soft-skinned woman came up short. Despite or maybe because of the Shalimar she didn't smell right. Who wants to sleep with her grandmother? The night just didn't feel right. Sara's perfectly toned body was the wrong shape, somehow. Her hair wasn't Lola's, her skin wasn't Lola's, her lips weren't Lola's. While they were both still fully dressed, Del excused herself and escaped to the bathroom.

How do I get out of here, she wondered, without hurting this chick's feelings?

"Sara, I'm sorry," Del called in a regretful tone, striding quickly from the bathroom to the front door. She felt like a jerk, but she couldn't sleep with this woman. "I got a call. I have to go."

"Oh, my God!" Sara was trailing after her, her eyes bright, her expression mixed. "Do you have to go right now? We were just—"

"Yeah, it sucks, but that's the job. I'm sorry to run out on you."

She rushed out, ignoring Sara's requests for a phone number, a rain check.

"Good night, now. Lock this door behind me, Sara."

Del walked home in the bracing cold. She looked up at the stars, wondering where Lola was, if she was safe, happy. Was she with the moronically happy redhead? Was she gone from Del's life forever?

"Good night, honey, wherever you are."

CHAPTER SIX

When she saw finally checked her personal email after getting home and showering, Del saw a series of digital missives from Lola. She ignored them, spending an hour working on White's timeline before she stopped to make a cup of tea. Finally unable to keep her curiosity at bay any longer, she stared at her inbox on the computer's glowing screen. What if she was announcing her intentions to move in with that woman? What if she wanted to get back together with Del?

Instead, Lola explained that she'd had a burst of inspiration and produced her new collection of stories. She wanted to send some of the stories to Del, and she mentioned again her preference for writing over talking. Del realized Lola had sent her each of several stories as attachments to several individual email messages. She wondered why Lola had sent those and not communicated directly. Was it really so hard for Lola to talk to her? Del made a face before opening the attachment, not entirely sure she wanted to read these stories.

Half drowsing at a diner in Chicago, Lola stared at a woman in another undersized booth. She was in her fifties, maybe, and a bit overweight. Her coat obviously didn't close over her massive chest. But her hair was carefully styled and her makeup flawless. Lola leaned to the side to peek at the woman's feet. She wore beautiful and undoubtedly expensive shoes, but there was a gigantic run in her stockings. Closer examination revealed a smudge in her too-bright lipstick, along with a faint line near her jaw where the makeup ended and her paler, pinker skin was revealed.

Lola sneaked glances at the woman as she chatted on her cell phone, as she pulled out a mirror to refresh her fuchsia lipstick and cleaned up the smudge, as she sipped her coffee and left a bright new lip print on the white stoneware mug. Lola tried to imagine what the woman was thinking, what was important to her, what she hoped for and feared.

Lola was almost as surprised as the stranger to find herself standing over her table, asking if she could sit down. The woman narrowed her eyes and nodded a grudging yes.

"I'm a travel writer, looking for an insider's take on things," Lola fibbed. She couldn't believe she'd lied like that, and she was further surprised when the woman seemed to believe her. They spoke for over an hour about what Chicago offered its visitors, and Lola took copious notes on restaurants and theaters and parks and shops. Then the woman began to tell Lola her story.

Her name was Helen Rollins. She was fifty-two, divorced. She had been married at nineteen to a man far above her in status, she said, a handsome doctor in his thirties.

"I was pretty then," Helen asserted in a matter-of-fact voice. "Thin as a rail and pretty. Bright, too, or so I thought. Back then I was an innocent. Trusting, you know? Sweet. But mostly I was pretty."

Lola believed this. The woman carried herself with the confidence of someone who has been admired for her beauty. Helen waved her hand, adorned with heavy rings, her nails displaying a French manicure. It was a graceful hand, small and long-fingered and dainty. It was a delicate pink rosebud of a hand and seemed to hold all of Helen's former beauty in its tapered digits and curved palm.

Helen continued her story, her ironic tone a thin veneer of indifference over what seemed to be great pain and loss. The doctor,

Gary, came from a rich family. A good catch, her mother told her, and her family was in awe of him. Yes, Helen was pretty, but was she really pretty enough to snag a doctor?

Lola smiled faintly when Helen repeated the question, in her nasal, ironic voice.

"As a matter of fact, I was," she declared, her slight jowls wobbling. "I was more than pretty enough. I knew that. But what I didn't know, at first," she whispered, her other graceful hand held up in a warning, "is that my good catch was a goddamn rutting dog. Slept with everything in a skirt. Gave me a social disease. Knocked me around. Flirted with other women right in front of me."

Lola shook her head.

"I put up with all of it. He's rich, he's a doctor, that's what I told myself. It's part of the deal. But then I couldn't get pregnant. Oh, boy, that was that. He had to have a son. Had to. Made me go through all these goddamn clinic visits and shots and he didn't do anything to test himself. He didn't care when I cried, when I gained weight from the shots, when I had one miscarriage after another. He just had to have a kid and it had to be a son. So I finally get pregnant and manage to carry it, after all those years. Well, it's a girl, and that's that—he leaves me. Right then, the day I had her! Our daughter. I had to move in with my mother, can you imagine? All she could say was, what did I do wrong? What did I do to make him leave like that?" She rubbed her ring-laden hands together so roughly the skin reddened.

"How did you get by?"

"Got a job, counter girl at the drugstore. After a few years I got a ratty little apartment, let my mother tell me I was garbage so she'd watch my daughter while I was at work. I did what I had to, to take care of my daughter. Gary? He married a twenty-two-year-old nurse. Had three kids with her. All three of 'em are goddamn girls, can you believe that? Ha! Lived in a fancy house in Orland Park. Drove a Hummer. Bastard never paid a dime in child support. Never even bothered with my daughter until she graduated college, which I paid for. She asked him to walk her down the aisle. After all that. Here I paid for the kid's roof and food and clothes and shoes, walked her to school, took her to the dentist. Paid for the wedding too! And that smug bastard walked her up the aisle like it was his right. While I just sat *there like an idiot, wishing my girl had an ounce of self-respect. Only she don't, and you know why? She learned it from me."*

Lola made a questioning face, loath to interrupt.

"It's true! I still loved him and she knew it and so did he. Never stopped loving him, not for a minute. If he'd a crooked his little finger, I woulda come running, even after all those years."

Lola made a sympathetic face.

"Don't worry," Helen assured her. "I got my revenge. Second wife left him for a younger man! Ha, ha! And that's not all. My Gary, he's dead now. Heart attack, three years ago. Bastard thought he was God. He never expected to die, never changed his will. I got a pile of money." She smiled, but then her face collapsed. "I still love him," she muttered, her hands covering her face, muffling her voice. "Can you believe that shit?"

Lola held Helen's soft, pretty hand, ignoring the rings that were cutting into her fingers. "I'm sorry for your loss."

"Thank you, honey." Helen blew her nose into a beautifully embroidered handkerchief. "I tell you what, I never told anybody all that. Honest." Helen shook her head. "Everybody figures I hate him and Lord knows I have good reason. But I've loved that man since I was a teenager, and I'll love him till the day I die. What can I say, I'm a hopeless romantic!"

Del sat watching her tea cool as she tried to figure out what Lola was trying to tell her. Or was she reading too much into this? Maybe Lola had just experienced a creative flood and was excited to share it with Del. With anyone. For all Del knew, Lola had sent the same email to ten other people. Had she sent it to Marco? The redhead? Pushing her questions aside, Del opened the next email, which had no content but the attachment.

"It's a damn shame," the withered old man sputtered, staring at the Grand Canyon.

Lola turned away from the awe-inspiring view to look questioningly at her fellow tourist. When she asked if he was okay, the old man introduced himself as Stanley.

"You must think I'm a loony bird."

"*No. But you do sound like you could use someone to talk to.*"

Stanley poured out to her his grief and loneliness and despair. He told her about despising his son when he was a child, almost hating the boy for his weakness and softness. He went on to detail how, thirty years later, he now adored and admired the same son for his open heart and kindness and courage. But he admitted that he couldn't seem to tell his son about the change of heart or apologize for his harshness and disapproval.

"*Why not?*" *Lola asked him.* "*Why can't you just say it?*"

Stanley shook his fragile-looking, blue-veined head. His cataractous eyes stared into the distance. "*I don't know. I honestly don't. I just can't.*"

He lurched away from her as if she might infect him with a disease, and Lola watched as he shuffled slowly toward the parking lot. She wondered what had made him open up to a stranger and whether he would ever tell his son how he really felt.

Turning back around, Lola gazed out over one of the Wonders of the World and saw only a big hole carved from rocks. What occupied her thoughts, even when she used her phone to take a dozen pictures of the sight before her, was the story of the old man. Stanley loved his son, admired him, wished to connect with him before death took away his chance to do so. As though helpless to change things, he'd admitted that he would say nothing. He'd told Lola he could predict exactly what he'd do on the visit: comment on the dryness of the perennial birthday roast beef, criticize his son's driving, grouse about taxes and the government. He already knew he would not for one minute let down his guard enough to tell the truth.

Del again questioned Lola's motive in sending these stories to her. Was she supposed to be the old man? Was Lola? Or was it egocentric, thinking everything was about her and Lola? This story was set in yet another geographical location. Did that mean Lola was traveling?

Del made a fresh cup of tea before opening the next email, then poured out the tea and filled the mug with vodka. She remembered a dream she had right before Janet kidnapped her. In the dream, Janet made tea in her funny, impatient way and then drank vodka from the mug instead. Was it a dream? Del looked at the vodka. She couldn't remember.

Del trudged back upstairs to the computer, hesitating before opening the next message. Her hands were sweating and she decided to wait. Should she reply to the emails she'd already opened?

No, she decided. Not until she'd read everything.

Del eyed the clock on her computer screen. It was three thirty in the morning, well past time to get to bed so she could go to work in a few hours. Too late, she decided, for decoding Lola's wandering missives.

CHAPTER SEVEN

Wednesday morning dawned with dazzling brightness for November, and Del groaned as her body fought waking up. An hour after dragging herself to the shower, Del stood at her front door and saw a couple walking up Lola's front steps. There was a sign that claimed Lola's house was for sale, and Del dragged herself across the street to check it out.

A woman in a green tweed suit stood on the small front porch with a phone pressed to her ear. She was promising someone, a co-worker maybe, a quick sale, and with a friendly wave nodded at the open front door, continuing her conversation in a low voice.

"It'll go in a week. It's crazy, right? Only in this city can you hold an open house on a weekday and attract a dozen buyers before nine in the morning."

Del nodded at the realtor, her face tight with shock and hurt. She walked through Lola's place, noting small changes the realtor had made. It wasn't Lola's home anymore. It was a showplace, designed to seduce buyers. She was gazing out at the backyard when she felt a hand at her elbow and looked up to see the familiar face of her longtime friend and neighbor.

"Marco?" She searched his eyes, wondering if her friend had chosen Lola in their breakup. That was how it worked, wasn't it? The friends had to choose between the exes. But Marco pulled her in for a long hug.

"Haven't seen much of you, Del."

"Yeah." Del smiled wryly. "I miss our talks. Remember when we tried to make Christmas dinner for Phil?"

"Hey," Marco said in mock protest. "My biscuits were delicious!"

"Your biscuits were too heavy to lift. But your turkey was a thing of beauty."

Marco made a face. "What's going on?"

"I'm sorry I've been out to lunch. How have you been? Is everything all right with you two?"

"We're fine. Phil works a million hours a week like you. I can't paint for shit anymore, so I think I'm going to kill myself." Marco smiled at his own hyperbole. "You know how it is, up and down and all around. And now I need you to tell me about you and Lola. Talk to me. I miss you."

"I know, I'm sorry. It's just this case. Cases, actually—"

"I watch the news, honey. I'm asking about you." He released her, and they stood side-by-side looking at the yard. Someone had laid sod, an awkward rectangle of green, and stuck rigid rows of colorful flowers in the narrow twin planting beds on either side of the grass. Lola had made one of them, and Del wondered if someone had been hired to duplicate it on the other side, even though that side didn't get enough light to sustain a flowerbed. The tiny yard looked like a little kid's drawing of a backyard, and Del shook her head. She doubted the underlying issues, the drainage and leveling, had been addressed. The realtor had arranged to make things look good and done no more.

Del shrugged. "There's not much to say."

Marco shook his head and stared at her with his big dark eyes. "If you don't want to tell me what's going on between you two, say so. But I can't understand how things could have gone so wrong so quick. I don't want to pry, but you've shut me out. I've been polite for as long as I could. What happened?"

"I—listen, I don't know. It seemed like we were a million miles apart after all the shit with Janet and Sterling. You had a stalker, she had a stalker." Del colored. "It was my fault. All that other stuff was crappy, but the real issue is that I cheated—did Lola tell you? With Janet."

She glanced at Marco's expressionless face. "You knew?"

He waggled his hand. "I guessed. Janet saw you and Lola were happy together, and she couldn't leave it alone until she ruined things. I was here when she ruined your life the first time, remember? She's a succubus."

Del laughed in spite of herself. Then she sobered. "I was the one who cheated. I—"

"Right. I get that. But Janet had her hooks deep in you from the first day. Don't you think she still does?"

Del bit back a reflexive denial. "I don't know. I can't see any of it clearly. After I found out Janet was trying to get Lola killed, I just went numb. Then after everything, I should have been there for Lola but I wasn't."

"Well, you were kidnapped."

"Ha." Del snorted. "By Janet. Come on, it's not like she's some kind of monster. She only got over on me by drugging me and tying me up."

"Okay, Patty Hearst. Tell me all about your trip to Sweden."

Again Del laughed in spite of herself. "You think? Yeah, I don't know, it doesn't matter anyhow. Lola was the one kidnapped by the serial killer, and she saved the day. Then I just went off to see Janet in prison like it was nothing. Lola wanted to talk about it, and I wouldn't. I fucked it all up."

"So tell her that." Marco nudged Del with his shoulder. "Call the woman you love and tell her you're sorry and you miss her and you'd do anything to get her back."

"Oh, please. She's too busy with her girlfriend."

"Girlfriend?" Marco frowned at Del with obvious confusion.

"The redhead? Young? Pretty? Makes Lola smile like a kid on Christmas?"

Marco's laughter burst from him. "You don't mean Emily?"

"I don't know her name, Marco. I just saw them together."

He rolled his eyes. "I love you, honey, but you're a jealous idiot."

Del shrugged, annoyed.

"Emily was just a friend, a straight lady with a boyfriend. They met volunteering at the food bank. They were friends for about five minutes until the boyfriend didn't like it."

"Did the boyfriend—what happened? Is Lola okay?"

"Lola's jetting around the country trying to avoid the woman who broke her heart."

"Oh, God." Del had seen a dozen friends lose their hearts to straight women who'd ultimately gone back to husbands and boyfriends and left only pain, humiliation and bitterness in their wake. "Poor Lola! She—"

"Sugar, Emily's not the one who broke Lola's heart."

"Oh." Del felt a bubble of defensiveness rising and collapsing. "I don't know if I believe that."

"Do you really not—why can't you see how much she loves you?"

Del swallowed hard. "Is there any chance she'd take me back?"

"Not if you don't call her." Marco held her gaze. "Ask. Maybe she'll say yes."

I wouldn't. If I were Lola, I'd tell me to go to hell.

Del stepped back. Tears pricked at her eyes and she turned from Marco.

"I gotta go," she muttered. "See you around."

Fleeing home, Del skirted the realtor's sign. Lola had put her house up for sale. She'd never said a word about it. She'd never given Del a chance to ask her to stay. Had her remaining emails included a warning that she wasn't coming back? Del couldn't force herself to open them and find out.

* * *

Uncertainty made Del's stomach hurt. She was faithfully taking the medicine, but it was taking its time working. She absently rubbed her aching forehead. Her body was falling apart without Lola. Everything was falling apart without Lola. She pushed the thought away. What if Lola never came back from her travels? What if she came back but didn't want Del?

"Focus on work," she told herself. "Just forget about everything but work."

Despite the abundance of FBI resources in San Francisco, including a huge building on nearby Golden Gate Avenue, the Fed contingent had commandeered SFPD's Mission station's largest conference room and two interrogation rooms, and the Feds swaggered around with unmistakable arrogance.

Fine, Del thought, watching a young agent shoulder his way past a group of seasoned SFPD patrol officers, be the biggest assholes in the world. Just catch the bad guy. But hours and days slid by, and the Fed party shrank as no new victims came forward.

Captain Bradley quietly broke up what was left of the task force, and the department was focused on new and more pressing cases. Violent crime was down, the budget was cut and the station seemed almost somnolent. Del was certain she and Phan were the only ones who remembered the murder of Mikey Ocampo, who'd been dead for over two weeks and whose case was sliding precipitously, inexorably into the cold case category.

"And just like that, it's no big deal."

"Sucks," Phan agreed. "But it's natural, isn't it? Bigger things come along, the Feds take over, what do you expect?"

"I expect you to tell me about Ronald Jeremy Teager."

Phan rolled his eyes. "I emailed you all about him, remember?"

Del nodded and recited from memory. "Teager's a web developer, works from home. He's never been arrested or charged. Never even been booked. But he's been questioned about seven different incidents over the last ten years. He's hinky. Guy's nobody, he's invisible. Like Sofia Gonzalez said.

Like Donette Williams said. She talked about him being like Boo Radley, did I tell you? You don't even know he's there."

Phan made a face. "Okay. Is he some predatory super genius? I mean, if he was really a peeper, wouldn't there be some actionable evidence? Does he have a Harry Potter cloak?"

Del rolled her eyes, knowing Phan was trying to make her laugh. "Ronald Teager, invisible peeper. Thirty-two. Five-eight, one-seventy, White, brown and brown. Only reason he pings is that there were two clusters of incidents and because of the persistence of the lead investigator on those first ones. John Garibaldi, do you know him?"

"Never met him."

"Garibaldi retired eight years ago, but for a while he kept tabs on Teager, thought there was something there but couldn't get anything on him."

"You talked to Garibaldi?" Phan made a face. "Let me guess, he was full of insights."

"Listen, I know what you're thinking."

Phan wouldn't be derailed. "These guys, you know how it is, they retire and they wanna keep a hand in. You call about anything, they think there was something there. The guy's sitting home, the wife's driving him crazy, nobody wants to listen to his stories. Somebody calls him, treats him like one of the boys in blue again, he perks right up."

"It wasn't like that, Phan. Garibaldi's a security consultant for some big company in Cupertino, he's not sitting around twiddling his thumbs."

Phan shrugged.

"Anyway, I poked around a little, and Teager really is pretty hinky. He never married, lived with his mother until her death a couple months ago from a heart attack. Just before our peeper problem started."

"What makes you—do we have anything on this guy, Mason?"

"Not really." She sighed, frustrated. "Teager inherited a house on Capp Street. Mom's death could be the trigger, maybe.

Guy's squirrelly, Phan. And smart. Could be smart enough to employ forensic countermeasures."

"Yeah." Phan rolled his eyes. "I'm convinced. Let's round him up right now. Who needs evidence? Not me."

"Ha, ha." Del sat back, pursing her lips. She noticed how automatically Phan mirrored her expression and posture. "I know it's thin. Practically transparent. But there isn't anybody else who stands out as a repeat as often as he does, other than Ernie White. Teager is a guy I'd look at and think, invisible. He's one of those guys, you look at him and there's something really off about him. Probably always has been. We need something on him, or on somebody, and he's the only one I've noticed. The one who seems least likely to have a normal relationship with other humans."

Phan shrugged. "We can't get anywhere with anybody else. Might as well poke around, see if we find anything."

That was the best she'd get, Del knew, and she was lucky to get that much cooperation on so little good data. She asked Angela Carter from sex crimes to look at her file on Teager and got only a short email in reply saying that nothing about the guy jumped out at her.

"Great, thanks," Del snapped at the screen. "Sorry to fucking bother you."

She did a photo array with Sofia Gonzalez, who couldn't place Teager or any of the distractors as the peeper. She did the same with Donette Williams.

"Maybe him," Donette said, pointing at Teager. But then she pointed at a photo of one of the distractors, a sergeant who looked rather like Teager. "Or maybe him."

Del did photo arrays with each of the other complainants. None of the other witnesses were sure either. But Del was. And she couldn't explain it. The guy pinged for her. It was the Boo Radley reference she couldn't let go of. Not the innocence or sweetness, but the oddness.

She talked Phan into helping her tail Teager, and she smiled at him that afternoon while they cruised Teager's neighborhood.

"Thanks for doing this."

"Yeah, well, at this point, I'll follow any suspect just to feel like I'm doing something, you know?" It was her turn to drive, and Phan slouched next to her. "Maybe we'll catch somebody doing something."

They were seven houses down from Teager's. Capp Street was experiencing another upswing in prostitution and its related crimes, but it was still a mostly residential street that during the day sported more strollers with sippy cups than johns holding dime bags.

A group of high school girls sashayed past Teager's house and he came outside. Del forced herself to stay still. Teager stepped onto the sidewalk maybe ten feet behind the girls and they didn't seem to notice him. A mother with three kids and a baby in a stroller passed going the opposite way and returned his nod of greeting.

"He fits right in," Del noted. "No mom radar goes off when they see him."

"The girls aren't nervous either."

The teens veered into a house a block down from Teager's. He continued on without pausing and turned at the next corner. Del started the car and glided slowly down the street. Following a pedestrian in a car was less than ideal, but they had to consider the possibility that he would get in his personal vehicle or take the bus. Trailing Teager, they made a slow, rambling tour of Capp Street, 21st Street, Mission Street, cruising in a parade of impatient, distracted drivers and a swirling stream of cyclists and pedestrians.

He went to a bodega and bought a soda, browsed in a hardware store, rented a video from a vending machine, went to a bakery, spent some time nursing a hot chocolate and bought a cookie on his way out. He looked for all the world like a relaxed, casual nobody, wandering the streets of his beleaguered neighborhood aimlessly and harmlessly. There were many colorful characters on the streets—a homeless veteran pushing a wheelchair crowded with small dogs, several couples strolling hand in hand, two sets of gangster kids jostling each other, a few working girls getting an early start—and unremarkable Teager faded into the background.

"Either he's made us," Phan asserted as the afternoon turned to evening and the evening turned darker and colder, "or this guy is on some good meds."

"Yeah." Del rolled her stiff shoulder at a stoplight. "If I wanted to watch girls, maybe grab them, I'd want to be such a familiar face that no one even sees me anymore. Teager goes from street to street, store to store, wastes all this time. Why? Maybe it's so the moms walking the kids home, the teenagers, the prostitutes—all the women think of him as part of the scenery. I don't think he's made us. I think we should stick with him. Maybe he gets off on just walking around and watching everyone. I think it's foreplay. The hookers are starting to outnumber the citizens, and I wonder how he'll respond to them. How they'll respond to him. Let's stay on him for a little while, okay?"

"Why not?" Phan shrugged and offered a bitter smile. "I like to celebrate the week with a little creepstalking. Hey, it's not like I have a life anyway, right?"

"What's up? Alana's mad at you? Still?"

"Same as the ex-wife. 'You work too much, you're never home,' blah, blah, blah. What exactly am I supposed to do?"

"Bitter much?"

"Nice." Phan snorted. "You make up with Lola yet?"

Del raised her eyebrows in acknowledgment and was silent. It was dark now, and Teager was walking slowly down 21st Street. There were a few shops, most of them closing for the night, among the private residences. After dark, prostitution stained the neighborhood like sour wine.

What are you looking for? Do you already have someone in mind?

"How about a decoy?"

Phan smirked in response to her question. "Feds are already doing it."

"Really? Where? And how do you know about it?"

"Bathroom."

"What?"

"It's a boys' club, darlin'. Or have you forgotten?"

Del made a face.

"Two of them came in yakking about decoy this, locals that. Like any good boy I eavesdropped. They're putting her on Dolores tonight, Valencia after that."

"But our guy hasn't been to Dolores yet. And why on Valencia? Nothing's happened there. The station's right there. Who would do something down the street from us?"

"They're Feds. Who knows how they think? Anyway, the night is young. And he's skewing later now."

As if responding to their words, Teager headed past Mission Street toward Valencia Street. Del and Phan backed off, not wanting to take any chance on interfering in the Feds' trap.

"Weird," Del noted. "All he does is walk around and drink soda and eat sweets. All he does is hang out. Who eats that kinda diet except teenage boys and serial killers?"

"They do like their sugar, don't they?"

"Too much. One after another, nothing but candy and sodas and all that crap." Del shook her head. "Makes you wonder, doesn't it? Is it poor impulse control, as in, I'm having what I want regardless of the consequences, or was that old Dan White Twinkie defense a legit thing?"

"What it really makes me wonder about is all the little kids who grow up eating nothing but crap. What kind of adults will they turn out to be?" Phan shook his head. "Okay, enough philosophy. We don't have to save the world tonight. We have to catch one creepy, escalating asshole. Isn't that enough?"

"I don't know," Del responded. "I hope so."

"Maybe Teager is just a lonely, weird little dude. Mason, sorry, but I'm done for the night. We can't just wander around. It's been too long anyway. The guy'd have to be blind not to know we're following him at this point."

At home finally a while later, Del tried not to think about Lola but couldn't stop. Lola made herself invisible whenever she felt threatened. It was one of the first things Del had noticed about her. She thought of Mikey, who disappeared one day and became invisible. Teager was good at being invisible too.

Pervs see what they want to see. Impose their fantasies on the victims. Is that sort of what I did to Lola, try to make her into someone else?

She'd put it off as long as she could. Del went to face the next installment in Lola's email series. Would there be a direct message? She skimmed the first paragraph—no, it was another story. She settled in to read.

* * *

"Too much thinking, too much drinking, sit down too hard, lose your card." Lola heard a woman's voice and realized it was her own.

An arm pulled her up. Someone told her she was fine, she was almost there and just needed to put one foot in front of the other. She pointed at the floor and a hand came near with the hotel room key card and gave it to her. She peered up at a friendly looking face belonging to a woman in dark clothes. She tried to smile but felt her stomach do a wild, acrobatic flip. Suddenly, unable to stop herself, she vomited on her good Samaritan.

"Oh," Lola gasped between heaves. "Oh, no!" The world shimmied like an incandescent, amateur belly dancer. Then the black curtain went down.

When she awoke, it was afternoon. Her head felt like it had been smashed open and glued together with kindergarten paste. Her mouth was crackling with dryness and her stomach felt torn. She smelled vomit and sweat and the sickly sweetness of champagne and groaned aloud. She was in her hotel room and couldn't remember getting there. She crawled to the tub, turned on the taps and climbed in, adjusting the water so it dripped warmth over her. Finally, she could stand up, using the smooth, slippery marble of the shower wall as a nearly worthless ladder. She took a proper shower, stripping off the encrusted black dress and underwear that she decided would go into the trash bin. Her shoes, where were they? Oh, who cares, she thought, rinsing her mouth in the shower. Those things hurt, anyway. She stepped out to get her toothbrush and toothpaste and got back in, letting the water restore some of her body's sense of normalcy.

Lola ordered coffee and toast, unsure what else to brave in her treacherous stomach. She straightened up the room and found a business card on the nightstand. Her rescuer had apparently been an NYPD cop named Jude Meeker. Lola tried to conjure the woman's face in her memory, but she mostly remembered trying to wipe frothy vomit off a jacket.

When the knock on the door sounded, Lola assumed it was room service and opened the door. She saw a young woman holding a leather jacket and scowling at Lola. She had big, dark eyes, dark, smooth skin and perfect posture. A cop, not a civilian—she could see that, even with the nondescript sweater and jeans the woman wore. Her hair was very short, and her face seemed naked because of this. Lola could only gape at her beauty.

"Miss Bannon, I'm Jude Meeker. Ma'am, this is New York City. Please check your peephole before you open your door."

"Oh. Right. Please, come in."

Her visitor gave a crisp nod, took a few steps in and surveyed the room as another knock hit the door. Lola self-consciously peered through the peephole and saw a waiter.

After he'd left, she offered coffee and toast to her guest, who declined. "You need it more than I do, Miss Bannon."

"Please call me Lola." She sweetened her coffee and hesitated. Was it rude to eat the toast? Her stomach rumbled and she decided to risk it.

"I hope you don't mind me coming by. I just wanted to make sure you were okay."

"Of course not, Officer Meeker, I just left you a message to thank you and apologize and offer to pay for your dry cleaning. I'm so embarrassed and so sorry. I can't believe I threw up on you like that, it was so gross."

"Yes, it was." The cop laughed. Her big eyes sparkled with good humor in the late afternoon sunlight streaming in through the open blinds.

"Sadly, you were the not the first person to hurl on me last night. Or the last."

"That's terrible! I'm even more sorry. I don't normally drink like that. I guess I just got caught up in the moment."

"*Well, you were nursing a broken heart.*"

Lola stared at her. "*How do you know?*"

"*You were chatty.*" The police officer slightly relaxed her upright posture.

"*I'm so embarrassed.*"

"*You don't seem like somebody who makes a habit of wandering around strange cities late at night drunk off your behind.*"

"*No.*" Lola smiled and shook her head, wincing at the pain. "*And I don't intend to do it again.*" She sipped at her coffee, again offering a cup to the officer, who accepted this time and shook away offers of cream and sugar.

The sun was already slipping behind tall buildings, and the sky began to blaze with the rich, rosy colors of evening. The light was different here. It had been a little different in each city, most noticeably at morning and evening, a thing Lola had come to appreciate. New York's sky seemed overlaid with a soft filter of gold.

"*Well, I'm gonna take off. I just wanted to make sure you were okay.*"

"*Wait!*" Lola followed her to the door. "*Please. You've been very kind and I really appreciate it. You could have arrested me and you didn't. You made sure I got back safe, and you didn't even get mad at me for getting sick on you. Apparently while I talked your ear off the whole time. Thank you for being so nice to me.*" She was again struck by how beautiful the officer was. "*I'm sure you had better things to do on your day off than check up on a drunken lunatic.*"

"*Sadly, no.*"

Lola realized Officer Meeker was attracted to her. She cleared her throat to speak up. "*Uh, this might not be entirely appropriate, but I don't know anyone here and I'd like to thank you, and if you're not busy I'd like to take you out to dinner.*"

There. She'd done it. Whether the answer was yes or no, Lola had actually asked someone on a date. Sort of. What if the woman wasn't really attracted to her? What if she didn't think of it as a date? Well, it didn't really matter. She asked someone on a date, whether it came across as such or not. She smiled proudly.

"*Yeah.*" Officer Meeker smiled back. "*Sure. What kind of food?*"

"*Oh, gosh.*" Lola considered. "*Something unique. Something I couldn't make at home. That won't make me vomit on you. Again.*"

"Got it." She nodded. *"Wanna go now?"*

"Lemme grab my jacket."

The restaurant was homey and warm, with copper cookware and pop-art posters brightening the beige wall on one side of the narrow space and brick on the other. Their casual conversation flowed and soothed her. Meeker talked about her childhood in the Louisiana countryside, where she was raised by her grandmother until her death and then was sent to live in Brooklyn with a great-aunt she'd never met before. She told several anecdotes about the academy and different people she'd encountered on the job.

In the soft candlelight, the broad planes of Meeker's face looked soft and round, and Lola glanced at her wide, generous mouth. She would be a good kisser, Lola thought, and blushed. Meeker looked at her questioningly, interrupting her own story about a mugger with a speech impediment.

Lola shook her head.

"No, what?"

"You're so pretty. I'm sorry. I don't mean to embarrass you. It's rude and I'm sorry."

Meeker made a face. "I don't get called pretty a lot."

"You are, though."

Meeker shrugged. "I'm not dumb enough to argue with flattery twice, so thank you. As long as we're talking about it, you look beautiful."

"It's the candlelight."

For the second time, Meeker threw back her head and laughed. "I thought I was bad at taking compliments."

Lola smiled. The food had been delicious and the conversation delightful, but dinner was over and she wasn't sure how to end the evening. She cleared her throat. "I need to say something to you." She smiled at Jude's raised eyebrows. "I've had a wonderful time and I'd like to see you again. But I don't live here. I'm not planning to stay in New York for more than a few days. And I don't kiss or make out with or sleep with people I barely know." She considered how to continue, but Meeker put her hands up.

"Hey don't worry." Jude leaned forward and smiled. "I'm glad you're straightforward. I know you're leaving soon and I don't sleep

around either. So, let's get you safely back to your nice hotel, and maybe you'll let me take you out to a mediocre dinner tomorrow. Sound good?"

Lola smiled and nodded, too pleased to speak. She paid the check, waving away mild protests, and they walked back. The street was icy and Lola's chest hurt from the cold air, and she was having trouble keeping her balance. Meeker put one arm around her and held her steady as they walked, and the warmth between them was welcome. Meeker's body was shapelier than Del's, Lola realized, her waist smaller and her hips and breasts larger. She was built more like Lola, only an inch or two taller and more muscular. Lola wondered what Meeker would look like naked. Would she look as beautiful as she felt? She stumbled, her focus broken, and giggled as her hip bumped Meeker's. She'd never been so keenly aware of another woman's body before, except for Del's, and she felt like Meeker could read her mind. The silence between them should have been awkward but wasn't.

Too soon, they were back at the hotel lobby. They made plans for the following evening, and Lola rode up to her room feeling alone and lonely. The door had barely closed behind her when there was a knock. Mindful of the late hour, she used the peephole.

She opened the door and was enveloped in Meeker's firm arms, crushed against her soft lips, smelling her cologne and tasting curry and sweet tea. The kiss made her dizzy with sensation and longing, and she melted against the generous curves. Meeker broke off the kiss suddenly and whirled around, escaping the room without a word. Lola stood in the doorway, her body shaking and her heart pounding, a small smile playing at the corner of her tingling lips.

It was strange, kissing someone who wasn't Del. At the thought of Del, Lola's smile faded. Had Del really ever loved her? Did she miss Lola even a little? Who was she kissing these days? Del was too attractive to be alone for long. Lola felt a sudden chill. She wished Del's arms were wrapped around her, Del's voice was whispering in her ear, Del's lips were kissing hers.

CHAPTER EIGHT

Del stalked away from the computer as if covered in stings by the words on its screen. She'd been trying to figure out what Lola wanted her to read in the stories she was sending, and at least that mystery was solved. She'd moved on. She'd traipsed off to New York City to have a fling and had had the audacity to throw it in Del's face.

Del took a long pull from the emergency vodka bottle she kept in the freezer and rubbed her aching gut. Wandering toward the dining room, she stood in the doorway and examined the stacks of data she'd violated her principles to obtain. To follow her guy, she'd asked a favor she hadn't earned from Mac. She'd dived into Ernie White's disgustingly privileged and destructive life. She'd invaded his privacy to at least as great an extent as the peeper violated the privacy of his victims. She'd done all that and accomplished exactly nothing.

If he turned up dead, Del mused, she'd be a great suspect: her walls were covered with giant sticky notes detailing the man's life, his whereabouts, his interests, his habits. She knew how he liked his coffee—extra sweet and extra hot—where he went on vacation, how much he spent on his cell phone service. But she couldn't find out what his criminal activities were and she couldn't connect him to Mikey's murder. She felt powerless to do her job effectively and powerless to manage her personal life. It was midnight, and Del glared at the clock. Mikey had been dead for sixteen days.

The house felt empty without Lola in it, so she took off on her motorcycle. Usually a ride helped Del relax and get away from her worries, but her wandering began to feel more like patrolling after only moments. Cutting through the dystopian landscape of the Tenderloin, she saw gleaming high-rises and late night streets populated almost exclusively by the homeless and the desperate. She zipped toward the tourist spots around the wharves and saw too many drunken, restless pedestrians for midnight on a weekday. Most were probably tourists and college students, each group over-represented in the categories of both victim and perpetrator of personal and property crimes.

Nearly every section of Hyde Street she passed featured at least one transient, most cloaked in featureless squalor that erased individuality, age, gender, race and background. When she'd first moved to the city, she had been shocked by the number of raggedy wanderers she'd seen in doorways and alleys and parks. Now, twenty years later, Del smirked at her own last-millennium naiveté. There had to be at least three times as many street people now. Each of them, she knew too well, had a story. Each of them carried around hopes and losses and wishes and regrets and hurts. She'd had to harden herself to their stories and their personal difficulties long ago, and she wondered about the cost of that.

Stopped at a light, Del watched a couple of young boys in fatigues, stringy arms around each other's necks, looking for sex or fights or maybe their car. They seemed too young and scrawny to be soldiers, but then more and more people looked young and scrawny to her. She dragged her gaze away to continue along the grim pathway through the most dehumanized part of the city. Mikey had probably spent the last year of his life like the drifting castaways she passed, unwanted and unseen.

Hyde Street led her from the post-civilization world of the Tenderloin to the more livable neighborhoods she had seen but spent little time in—Nob Hill and Russian Hill. Nice houses, fewer street people, the city as people liked to see it. There was character here, but it was the kind of character people liked to experience: fun and quirkiness buffered by money and safety. Del thought she'd feel soothed by the more affluent air, but she still bristled with restlessness. She was turned off by the shops, restaurants and clubs that drew the discontented with bright lights and inviting music and colorful displays. As she headed toward Aquatic Park, her itchiness was only increased by the disconnect between her mood and her surroundings. Despite leaving them behind, she still smelled the denizens of late night streets. She felt their loneliness and desperation and blind blankness as a viral infection that chased her through the nighttime façade of the city. Each of those transients was Mikey and he haunted her. Del gulped the cold night air and tried to push away her ennui. She'd been planning to ride along the marina but no longer wanted to do so.

Del reversed course and headed back toward the Mission District. She took a short tour of the livelier Mission late night streets, feeling cheered by the colorful murals and variety of languages and people she saw. A pair of moms pushed a blanket-laden stroller, probably taking a colicky infant out for cool air. They passed an elderly couple wearing tweeds and following cocker spaniels on well-worn leads. She smiled at a group of well-heeled, middle-aged revelers doing the Electric Slide in front of a French restaurant where the house wine was twenty dollars a bottle and where Janet once got into a loud argument in French with the Armenian restauranteur over the proper way to caramelize an onion.

A few minutes later Del stood outside The Lex, debating whether or not to go in. Outside the air was cold, and the neon Lexington Club sign looked like a beacon from a lighthouse. A few couples stood clustered on the sidewalk, chatting and smoking. Inside the music was soft and mellow, and the heat from the dancers was steaming up the stained glass window by the front door. A flash of long hair went by, a misty wraith, and

Del could almost smell the dancers' sweat and perfumes from the sidewalk.

"Welcome to Elysium," she muttered to herself, her smile a bitter twist. She'd found refuge and companionship and comfort at The Lex more often than she would ever care to admit, but she had the distinct feeling her depressed mood would sour even this favorite place. I should bring Lola here, she thought, as she strode the last few steps to the entrance. But it was too late. She should have brought Lola here back when Lola was still interested in going places with her.

She pulled open the familiar door and made her serpentine way over to the bar. The Lex's Whiskey Wednesday drew a younger, more adventurous lesbian crowd. These ladies were on the make. Wasn't that, she asked herself as she surveyed the room, why she'd come here instead of somewhere else? Del felt like she was playing a role: butch on the prowl. Hadn't she done this once already? She'd scooped up a badge bunny in an hour and then gone rabbit on the poor girl.

Why am I here? Why the hell did Lola send me that stupid story? Is this her way of telling me to fuck off?

A squadron of young studs stood shoulder to shoulder a few feet from her. Their brutally shorn hair, their lean, muscular bodies, their arrogant posturing—all were designed to signal prowess.

As Del watched the youngsters pose and preen, she recalled her own years of strutting with carefully cultivated indifference. Their naked desire for validation and acceptance made Del smile and left her feeling maudlin at the same time. They looked unbearably young and vulnerable to her, which was not, she knew, the image they wanted to project. She avoided their eyes, not wanting them to see her condescension. She could remember all too well how it felt to be a lonely twenty-something woman in men's trousers and loafers, breasts bound and shoes shined. She remembered feeling like a kid wanting to be chosen for the team, desperate to project strength and confidence and to woo that most elusive object of desire, the femme. It had been scary and exciting and titillating. Of course, like anything, as it became easier to pull off, it got boring.

Again Del was reminded of the way predators needed ever more stimulation. Why was it so hard for her to tease apart the mating dance and the hunt? Was that normal? Or was she as twisted as the perverts and monsters she chased? Had the chase changed her in ways she would continue to have more and more difficulty differentiating between?

Determined to push aside the contamination of her job, Del got a beer and scanned the room. The studs had naturally attracted the attention of a group of girls dancing in a colorful cluster several feet away. Each wore the requisite femme uniform: high heels, layers of makeup, short skirts. The two groups of young clubbers were living stereotypes playing out in front of her. The femmes flirted, giggled, tossed their hair. They coyly cut their eyes away from the butches, and then glanced back through their false lashes.

She usually enjoyed watching the alcohol-fueled opera, but tonight she felt the players' desperation and loneliness more than their excitement and hopefulness. She was tired for them. Dating was too much work. Being young was too much work.

I'm too old for this. I don't wanna flirt and play games. I wanna go home and cook dinner and talk about nothing and snuggle and make love with a woman who loves me. I want Lola.

She scanned the room again. There were eight, no, nine, women in their thirties and forties with long dark hair. Only, she reminded herself, Lola cut off her long hair. Now she's different and she doesn't want me anymore. She looked around again. There were seven women about Lola's age with very short brown hair. Del let her gaze slide off each of them.

I'm profiling, just like the fucking predators.

Hadn't she had this same thought in the last bar? She laughed quietly to herself but kept scoping out the room. Two of the brunettes were pseudo-hippie chicks and clearly a couple. Three were fairly androgynous, which was fine with her. But none of them looked especially interested in a blond Amazon.

Del recalled the motel where she and Janet had first made love and how they'd met at Wild Side West, the other bar she'd been into hundreds of times, and she quickly and resolutely ignored the memories and the nostalgia. She eyed two women she'd seen notice her. One was so heavily made-up she looked like a caricature, even in the variable light of the bar. The other looked a little uncomfortable, shy, maybe bookish. She sat alone at a table in the corner, her pretty eyes wide as she took in the scene. Was she even out? Del had seen more than one straight or bi or curious or whatever chick show up and sit down to watch the bar's patrons with the same wide-eyed look.

Del ordered a dirty martini and shrugged away from the bar, noting the untouched white wine in front of the woman she thought might be playing tourist in the lesbian bar. She took her beer and the martini over to the quiet table.

"Hi."

"Hi." The woman's gaze was clouded, her voice muted.

"I don't want to bother you, but it's pretty crowded." Del waved a hand around the room. "I can't find a seat anywhere. Mind if I sit here?"

Del flashed a shy, brief smile. She was reasonably sure her target would be too polite to decline unless she felt encroached upon. The woman nodded her head. She licked her lips nervously, and Del offered a reassuring smile.

"Kinda like a circus, huh?" She gestured with her beer at the flirtation show.

"Kinda." The woman's nervous laughter was quiet. "It's not so different from a regular bar." Her dark eyes widened. "That came out wrong."

"No worries." Del pushed the martini halfway across the small table.

"They just seem very, very—"

"Young."

The woman's laugh tinkled out, and she covered her mouth. It was so like Lola, that little surprised laugh, that shy gesture. Del looked away from the woman. They sat in silence for a few minutes, watching a particularly flashy young femme sashay up to Stud Row and choose. The stud selected played it too cool, though, and the red-clad young blonde tossed her hair and chose another dance partner.

"I don't think I was ever that young." The woman next to Del spoke so softly, it hardly seemed like she'd uttered the words aloud.

Was it too soon for the obvious compliment? Del considered. Yes, definitely. She simply smiled and raised her eyebrows in agreement. She pushed the martini a bit closer to her table companion.

"Ever tried one of these?"

"A martini? No." The woman shook her head, and her hair fell into her face. She tucked it behind her ears and smiled uncertainly.

"Take it if you want. I ordered it for a friend, but she just texted to cancel. I don't like martinis, and I don't want to waste it. Why don't you try it? If you don't like it, no problem. But sometimes it's fun to try new things, right?" Del leaned close. "I promise and swear, it's not spiked or drugged or anything, but if you're not comfortable drinking from a stranger's glass I completely understand. No hard feelings."

Del looked away again, giving the woman time to consider without feeling scrutinized.

Nothing's changed. The same lines, the same games. It never changes. We just get a tiny bit more subtle, a little less overt. Or do we only think we do?

"Right," the woman said, smiling bravely, and sipped at the drink. She made a face and Del laughed with her as she set down the glass and pushed it away.

"Well, at least you tried it," she said and saluted with her beer. "To trying new things. My name's Del."

"Tracy," the woman replied. "My name's Tracy."

"Nice to meet you, Tracy." Del sat back, crossing her legs. Tracy was not her real name. Tracy was too scared this little adventure would taint her real life to use her real name, but she wasn't a good enough liar to be convincing. She was looking for something that didn't fit into her life, some temporary fix to the problem of her sexual orientation and the heterosexual marriage it threatened. That was okay. That was better. Tracy, whoever she really was, had a tan line on her left ring finger. Probably, Del figured, she has the ring in her purse, wrapped in tissue paper or a hankie to protect it.

Hubby's out of town, kids are at sleepovers. What'd she tell her mom, her friends? Maybe said she would be at a spa? Whatever.

"I'm guessing you've never been in a bar like this before."

Never say lesbian to the tourists. It scares them.

Tracy shook her head, biting her lip. "It's that obvious?"

"My guess is, a lady like you doesn't frequent any kind of bar." Del made a face at her own too-obvious flattery and saw Tracy's answering smile. Self-deprecation worked wonders. When had she learned that? Not soon enough and too long ago, her daddy would have said.

Her gaze slid to the butch squad. They would learn the same lesson eventually. They'd find it easier and easier to talk a woman into bed. Then, having mastered the game of seduction, they would end up finding it unsatisfying. Not all of them, of course. But the smart ones, the ones not addicted to drama and conquest and ego, would get tired of it. Del dragged her attention back to her smiling quarry, wondering if she was blind her to own hubris.

"True. And thank you." Tracy was relaxed, enjoying the ever-bewitching combination of feeling both safe and attracted, charming and charmed. She took a long sip of her white wine, pushing the martini a few more inches away.

"Tracy, can I ask what brings you here tonight?" Del widened her eyes in a none-too-subtle signal. *Trust me, little bambi, I'm just the harmless hunter you're looking for.* "Or is that too personal a question?"

Tracy blushed and laughed, leaning forward. Del caught a peripheral flash of impressively generous cleavage and pinned her eyes on Tracy's face. She listened to a rambling explanation. She already knew the words to the familiar story—good girl marries good boy and realizes later it wasn't a boy but a girl she wanted. She found it easy to respond effectively, making the right faces, the right noises, waiting the perfect amount of time to reach over and pat Tracy's forearm. She nodded and laughed and shook her head and let Tracy lead herself along the path of seduction. How many times had she played this particular part in this little psychodrama? *Twenty minutes of sympathetic attention and she's yours for the taking.*

How many toaster ovens had she earned? Too many. Sometimes she worried she fell too easily into stereotyping people, particularly women. It seemed like they all wanted to be the princess in the fairy tale. Gay, straight, bi, trans—none of that mattered. It was the unmet needs of their early lives that dictated what women craved, and it was appallingly easy to figure out what those were. Del was getting bored.

She almost called it off twenty minutes later when she found herself back at home with tipsy Tracy, whose real name would be Brenda or Camille or Elizabeth or whatever. Mrs. Somebody, doting mommy of two or three darling little kids and devoted wife of some clueless guy. He'd come home from his business trip and be delighted because his pretty wife was always particularly amorous after he'd been out of town for a few days.

Del went through the rest of the seduction by rote: candles, more wine, soft music, let the girl make the first move, take your time, let her think this whole evening's a fairy tale, that the pickup at the bar was true love's first dance at the ball in the castle and she was wearing a glass slipper. It was almost painfully predictable. Del had known Tracy would sleep with her from the moment she'd leaned forward at the table in the bar. There was little satisfaction in such an easy victory, and Del was disappointed. It would have been nice to have to try.

Tracy would have her fun, and she would think she felt something for Del, but she would be ashamed of her one-night stand. She'd go back to her husband with only the slightest twinge of guilt. Her infidelity wouldn't count, because she'd only fooled around with a woman, and she'd figure that wasn't really cheating. By noon tomorrow, Tracy would have convinced herself that the whole evening had never happened.

Del had her own twinges of guilt. She was helping this woman cheat on her husband, hardly an ethical thing to do. Of course, Del told herself, Tracy would have cheated with someone else if Del hadn't taken the hook. But wasn't that the way drug dealers and pimps and other criminals justified their actions—if I didn't do it, someone else would?

Leading Tracy through the house toward the bedroom, Del felt a tug of resistance.

"My gosh," Tracy said, sounding nervous. "What's all this?"

Del looked at the dining room, where she still had all her data on Ernie White printed out in stacks and on a dozen poster-sized sticky notes on the walls. It looked like a stalker's war room, and for the first time Del wondered if her ongoing study of White's movements might border on obsession.

She caught Tracy's eye and faked a laugh.

"My roommate's writing a play." Del hastened to add, "She's not here tonight. Out of town."

The lie worked, and Tracy let herself be ushered up the stairs. In bed Tracy was sweet and shy and uncertain. A perfect pillow princess, thought Del, running her hands gently over Tracy's sumptuous hips and breasts. She was responsive and suggestible. She was perfumed and lotioned and waxed and toned. She was perfectly prepared for infidelity. Del pushed aside this observation and instead played with Tracy, teased her, brought her to gasping, groaning, shuddering orgasm twice, and then watched her sleep. She'd done well; Tracy was exhausted and satisfied. But Del was still restless.

She'd hoped sex would satisfy the longing she'd been feeling. She'd hoped to wear herself out and feel the tired contentment that a one-night stand would have given her just a few years ago. But she felt nothing. She rolled over, wishing Tracy would just disappear, wishing she hadn't gone to the bar, and wishing it weren't so damned easy. Her body ached. She felt like she would explode. After tossing and turning for hours, she finally gave up on sleep. She left a note for Tracy and pulled on her running clothes and shoes, desperate to burn some energy.

The air was cold enough to chap her skin as she tried to keep a steady pace. She had to fight the urge to sprint. Her body was like a spring coiled too tightly, and she felt a frantic need for some kind of release. Her stomach hurt and that made running hard. She turned back. This was unbearable. She couldn't think, couldn't sleep, couldn't do anything but obsess about Lola. Every woman she met she compared to Lola. Every day she wondered what Lola was thinking, was feeling. Was she happy, safe, fulfilled? Was she lonely? Did Lola miss her? Did Lola still love her? Was her short story autobiographical? Or was it a warning—get it together or I'll replace you?

Del slowed to a walk as she neared her street. It was nearly five, and the sun would be up before too long. God only knew where Lola was, what she was doing, what time it might be where she was. They hadn't spoken in weeks, but Del couldn't stand it. She pulled her cell out of her sock and dialed.

"Hello?" Lola's voice sounded sleepy. Del rounded the corner and saw the light go on in Lola's bedroom.

She's home? She's home! Del's heart leapt. She stammered a hello and fought to catch her breath. Lola was right there, less than a hundred yards away! What now?

"Del?"

"Uh, hi." She didn't know what to say. She stood in front of Lola's house, thinking of Romeo and Juliet, knowing how ridiculous that was but still wanting to declare her love like some stupid, heartsick kid.

"Are you okay?" Lola sounded more worried than sleepy now.

"I'm just outside."

"Oh." A curtain opened, and Del saw Lola standing at the window. Lola's white hockey jersey, ridiculously oversized, glowed in the moonlight.

"Can I come in?"

"Now?" Lola hesitated. "Okay. I'll be right down."

Del bounded up the stairs, fidgeting until Lola opened the door.

"Want some coffee?"

"Please." Del tried to smile, but Lola was already on her way to the kitchen.

"I'd offer you toast, but there's no food. I just got back."

"Yeah, no. Of course."

Now, steaming coffee in front of her, Lola three feet away across the table, her eyes ringed with tiredness. Del looked at her and was mute. She'd followed an impulse, calling Lola. She'd been so surprised to see her light on, she'd followed another impulse and asked to come in. Now she didn't know what to say. Lola didn't seem all that excited to see her.

What did I expect? She sipped at the coffee to buy time.

"Uh, sorry for the early hour."

"No problem." Lola's face was impassive.

"When did you get back?" It felt strange, making polite conversation. Like they were strangers.

"Last night. Late." Lola sweetened her coffee and seemed to hesitate. "You know, I was thinking of trying to sell the house."

"I saw that."

"But the housing market has gone down a lot." She cleared her throat. "I overbought, and now I'm sort of tied to the house until it regains its value. I can't afford to sell it at a loss."

"No," Del responded, too quickly. "Of course not."

"So I guess I'm staying for now." Lola rubbed the rim of her coffee cup as if to clean an invisible smudge. "I hope that won't be a problem for you."

"No," Del repeated. "Of course not." Why couldn't she just talk to the woman? Why couldn't she just say she loved Lola and that she was sorry for her behavior? Instead, she took another sip of coffee and offered a bland smile. She thought about Lola's story of the man who couldn't really talk to his son.

"Well, okay, then." Lola examined her coffee, bit her lip, nodded.

"How was your trip?"

"Fine, thank you." Lola looked away. She got up and started rearranging things on the counter. Finally, she faced Del. "What are you doing here?"

"What?" Del felt helpless. "I don't know."

"You left me, remember? I don't understand!" She flicked at an imaginary crumb on her jersey. "How can you just show up here like nothing's happened? What do you want?"

"What do I want?" Del felt the tumble of words and tried to stop it but couldn't. "I love you. I'm sorry. I'm so sorry. I blew it. I want you back. I want to be with you again. I can't be without you. I can't take it. I won't ever fuck up again, I swear it. I—"

Lola was shaking her head.

"Look, I know I messed up. Okay? But I love you."

Lola snorted, and Del almost laughed at the unexpected sound.

"Yeah, okay, maybe for today," Lola said bitterly. "Until you decide I've done something wrong, or Janet needs you, or some case takes up every single minute of your life, and then you'll leave me again and not even say anything."

Del sat back.

"I deserve better than that," Lola told her. "I deserve to be loved by somebody who would never, ever walk away or cheat or come up with excuses to ignore me. I trusted you!" Her voice broke, and Del watched her fight for control. "I love you but I don't trust you anymore."

"I love you too. You can, I swear, you can trust me."

"No." Lola whirled and stalked to the front door. Del followed. "I thought going to see Janet would clean it all out of you, you'd come back ready to put the past behind you and really focus on our relationship. But you copped out. You didn't deal with any of it, not your parents and definitely not Janet. She's still here in your head, and I'm just the woman who's not her."

"What?" Del gaped.

"Really?" Lola shook her head, scattering tears. "I hope you find someone. I hope you figure out why you keep sabotaging your relationships. I want you to be happy. But I need a grownup. I need someone who won't leave me if I gain five pounds, or get mad if I can't read her mind, or flip out if I get the wrong kind of shower curtain. I need someone who knows what she wants, and it doesn't change with her mood. Someone who can talk to me. Who's the same person every day. Please leave. Please."

Del shook her head again.

What was that about, gaining five pounds? The wrong kind of curtains? What was she even talking about? Del wanted to defend herself, to convince Lola that she could be what Lola wanted, but she didn't know how to do that. She stood by the door, wanting to find a way to explain things, and couldn't do it.

"Is Meeker real?"

Lola reeled backward. "You read my emails? Why didn't you—?"

"Is she?"

"Yes." Lola crossed her arms. "I—"

"Why would you send me that? How could you?" Del sputtered with outrage. Suddenly she remembered the woman she'd taken home. Tracy, was that her name? And she looked away.

"Did you just remember the woman in your bed?"

Del gaped at the acid in Lola's tone.

"Come on, you smell like sex and somebody else's perfume, it's all over you. You come into my house reeking of another woman and have the audacity to play victim because I told you about Jude Meeker? Who, in case you missed it, I didn't sleep with because of you."

Del backed away and slunk out of the door. She felt her face with both her hands, and it was wet and cold with tears. A sob caught in her throat, and she struggled to contain it. She walked slowly home in the pale dawn, fighting the urge to turn back. Her stomach hurt.

Go home, make coffee, shower and dress, get whatever-her-real-name-is back to her car. It's probably parked at the bar. Or get her a cab if that's how she got to the bar last night. Whatever. Get rid of her. Take a damn shower. Go to work.

She did all of those things, starting with a long, hot shower that left her skin tender from scrubbing. Tracy was dressing when Del came out of the bathroom. She didn't meet Del's eyes and refused the offer of coffee but not the offer of a ride, and thanked her for the ride back to the bar, sliding out of the truck and trotting over to a beige station wagon festooned with a parking ticket. She snagged the ticket and ducked into her

Volvo without a backward glance. Shame had overcome passion, just like Del had known it would. She made sure Tracy's wagon started before heading to the nearly empty station.

The place looked more like a weekend than a Thursday morning. Phan was out, was taking his daughter to the orthodontist. Bradley was at a meeting downtown. Everybody seemed to have scheduled something somewhere else. The weeks without progress, the lack of recent incident, meant people had started living their lives again. As much, Del thought, as we ever actually do. No one on the job seemed to successfully manage a personal life.

She flipped through the case files and tried to concentrate on work, but she couldn't stop seeing Lola's face, hearing Lola's words. If only she could have said something to turn it all around. Lola still loves me, she thought. She said so. I just wasn't prepared. I wasn't ready. I hadn't figured out what to say to get her back. She pulled out one of her notebooks, writing down all the things she needed to say—and do—to win back the love of her life. After nearly an hour she examined the scribbled list and blinked.

"Time to get to work."

CHAPTER NINE

After outlining her plan for wooing Lola, she focused on her job, leaving messages for people who'd ignored her previous messages and reinterviewing those who'd already responded to her previous calls. She combed through Mikey's case file, hoping she'd find something, anything new. She spent a couple of hours traversing her handwritten notes on miles of data on Ernie White, whose activities were littered with red flags but who seemed smart enough to leave only hints of impropriety and not clear evidence of lawbreaking. If he was, as Del suspected, a dangerous predator, he was really clever at getting away with it. As was, Del noted, the kidnapper. But she couldn't connect White or Teager to the kidnappings. There just wasn't any evidence. Phan called to say he was taking the day off.

She felt like she and the bad guy were stuck on parallel tracks, barreling along some Sisyphean cycle—she chased him, he chased his victims and the victims ran away over and over. She'd gone to Disneyland once, back when she still dated women with kids, and seen a fake pirate chase a fake wench, the animatronic figures stuck on a track that pulled them in an endless circle of uselessness. That's what she was doing.

She gave up and drove home, pointedly not letting herself look at Lola's house. She'd never been the world's best girlfriend to anyone. But she'd never cheated before. She'd never imagined herself a cheater, not like that. Sure, she'd slept with married women before, but only if she was not committed to anyone herself and if she was sure they were committed to cheating with someone anyway. Somehow she'd decided, twenty years earlier, this was okay. Still she didn't feel guilty about sleeping with Tracy—not after Lola's absconding and sending her that stupid story about not-quite-sleeping with that cop in New York.

But until Janet had come storming back into her life, Del had never deliberately made love to one woman while in a committed relationship with another. She wasn't sure how to live with that. She and Lola hadn't even really talked about it. Was it even possible to have that conversation at this point, or was it just too late to retrieve their relationship? She felt reluctance warring with impatience as she carefully picked her way upstairs and to the computer. Was she punishing herself for cheating? Maybe so. Maybe she deserved some punishment. Lola had been pretty angry. But would she be so angry if she didn't still care about Del?

"Time to read the next one," she commanded herself. It was another untitled story:

Lola and Del were walking on a beach, sun-warmed and smiling. A soft breeze lifted Del's curls and made them dance around her head. Lola's hair was long and it tickled her bare arms. They were barefoot, but the sand wasn't rough on their toes.

Lola smelled flowers and saw that there were baskets of them nearby. She could smell the clean scent of the sea and something else, perfume? She could hear the surf, the distant call of a bird. There was music, soft music, not far away. There were other people there, too, but she didn't look at them. She looked only at Del, whose eyes sparkled and shone. She looked so happy! Lola felt tears cool her sun-pinked cheeks and knew that they were tears of happiness. She heard the call of the bird again, closer this time, and flicked her gaze up to catch movement overhead. She let her gaze return to Del's face.

Del reached out her hand and Lola took it. She could feel Del's warm fingers wrapped in hers. She could feel that Del was shaking, and that she was too. They looked at each other and Lola felt her breath catch in her throat. The bird circled over them, calling loudly, but she ignored it. I love you, Del, she thought. I love you more than anything or anyone. I will spend the rest of my life loving you and wanting you and making a life with you. I will never leave you. I will never stop loving you. Del's smile grew even broader. Had she heard Lola's thoughts? Or had Lola spoken aloud? Del whispered something, and Lola had to lean close to hear.

"What?"

She wanted to hear what Del was saying, but she could only hear the bird, cawing. It was coming closer and closer, its flat black eyes growing larger and shinier. Its sharp beak grew enormous and gaped hungrily open. Its talons flexed menacingly. Lola could feel the wind from its beating wings. How, she wondered, was that even possible? She tried to catch Del's eyes but couldn't seem to. Was this really happening? Was this crazy bird really interrupting their romantic moment?

"Caw! Caw!" The giant black bird screamed at them, circling lower, diving toward them. Del seemed not to see or hear it. She just kept whispering. Lola tried to warn her, but her mouth wouldn't work. Instead, it stretched into a grotesque parody of a smile, and she couldn't stop it. She tried to hold her face together with her hands, but the bird hovered over her.

Its wings beat the air with a fluttering thud like a sickened heartbeat, and it pried her lips open with its talons. It hurt, it ripped her skin and spread her face open and left only emptiness inside. The bird dived into the emptiness and took her voice, her face, her body. It made them disappear.

Lola could see Del, could see that she was still whispering, that Del still thought Lola was there, holding her hand. No! She felt herself being lifted up and away. She could see Del standing there, holding nothing, smiling at nothing, whispering words no one could hear. Lola *was being lifted higher and higher, and Del was getting smaller and smaller, farther and farther away.*

Del!

Lola screamed with no voice and flailed with no limbs, trying to get back. Water sprayed up from the now-turbulent sea, drenching her, though she had no body. The bird's claws held her firmly, and its hard, glossy feathers scratched her. The bird lifted her up, up into the cold sky, and Del was a tiny black dot on the wide surface of the coast.

Lola woke up then, on the floor, drenched in sweat, her hair wild. She was alone, always alone—she'd let the bird take her away from the one person she loved most in the world, and she didn't know how to get back to her.

I'm nothing, she thought, and we're nothing.

Del walked away from the computer. Her hands were shaking as she changed her sheets, loaded up the dishwasher, checked the mail. There was one more email, and Del didn't think she wanted to read it. She called Tess and wasn't sure why she'd called. What would Tess think of her if she knew she had cheated on Lola? She recalled Tess's coming to spell Lola after the shooting, how Tess had gently remonstrated with Del and suggested ways to show Lola how much she appreciated her round-the-clock caregiving. How nasty had she been, exactly, that Tess had felt compelled to intervene on Lola's behalf? Shame tied Del's tongue, and she regretted calling Tess.

"How are you really?" Tess asked, after they had made arrangements to go to the shooting range the following weekend.

"Fine." Del tried not to sound like she was rushing off the phone. "You?"

"Good." Tess seemed to hesitate. "It was nice, seeing you and Lola together."

"At the book thing?" Del's mouth tightened. "Yeah. Listen, I gotta go. See you Saturday, huh?"

"Yeah, okay, take care."

"You too. Uh, say howdy to Lin for me."

Del fell asleep thinking about Lola's strange bird story and dreamed. The sun was shining, and all of their friends were there to wish them well. Even her parents had come. They stood with beaming faces among Del and Lola's friends, her father restored to his former handsomeness, only a little older. Her mother looked happier than Del had ever seen her. They held hands, and Del felt a hiccup of happiness. Lola's mother was there too. Del had found her, and she was pretty, an older version of Lola. She smiled at them with warm hazel eyes so much like Lola's that Del could hardly look away from them. Del gazed around at their friends, all smiling and watching her and Lola. And finally she let herself look at Lola, who gazed up at her in adoration. She was smiling so sweetly! She looked lit up with happiness.

I did that, Del thought. I made her happy. I am making her happy. She'll be my wife now and she will be mine forever. I'll make her happy. And I'll be happy.

She felt her own face—she was smiling too. The sea was a mild blue, and a gentle breeze made their hair dance around their faces like halos. The moment was enchanted. Del was afraid to do anything to ruin it. She just stood still and looked around. Lola's eyes were fixed on her face, and Del reached out to touch her. But Lola didn't move. Her skin was rubbery and too smooth.

Del shook her head. She looked down to see she held a pin in her hand, an old-fashioned hatpin, like Nana kept in her purse as a tiny weapon against what she called mashers. Del stuck Lola with the pin, doing it before she'd thought about it, immediately horrified by her act. But Lola didn't react.

She wasn't real! Del stepped back. She tried again, but Lola didn't even blink.

"Lola? Lola!" She screamed at her, but Lola's fixed gaze was that of a mannequin, a robot. A thing. Del tried to take her hand, but it wasn't real either. She could make the hand rest in hers, she could force the fingers to curl around hers, but they didn't move easily on their own. *Lola, please! Wake up!* But Lola wasn't in there. No one was.

Sickened, Del tried to pull her hand away from the Lola-thing, but she was stuck. She yanked her hand and pulled the thing over and watched it fall stiffly to the ground. It lay still for several minutes before it slowly and clumsily struggled to regain its feet. Del backed away from it in disgust.

She looked around. The others were all still watching her, their hair blown by the wind. They blinked, they shifted their feet. One of them even coughed, but they weren't real. They were things too. Horrified, Del stepped back.

"No! No!" Again she looked down at her own hands. They were smooth, like Lola's. There were no pores, no lines, no scar from that time her mother burned her. No little hairs, no shiny fingernails. The hands were dummy hands. She felt her face.

I'm a thing? I'm a thing, like the rest of them? She screamed then, a guttural cry of fear and rage and grief, and the scream woke her up.

She was tangled in the sheet, and she flailed desperately, trying to get free. She staggered from the bed and caught herself on the dresser.

"What the hell?" She was shaking, her body covered in sweat. She felt her stomach flip, and raced to the bathroom to vomit. Several minutes later, she flipped on the light. The vomit was bloody. *Oh, crap.* She'd forgotten to take her ulcer medicine the last few days, and her stomach was burning with acid. Her throat, her mouth, her lips were on fire. She shook with pain and shock.

It's fine, she told herself. It's nothing. It's just an ulcer. People don't die from ulcers. But she wasn't at all sure dying would be such a bad thing. She flushed away the blood and scrubbed at her mouth and rinsed and rinsed it. She drank water, popped a handful of antacids, and went to take her medicine. Her whole body ached. She was freezing.

The phone rang. She answered with a hoarse hello. There'd been an attack, Phan told her. It might be their guy, and Bradley wanted them to beat the Feds to the initial victim interview. Phan offered to pick her up.

"My turn to drive," he asserted. Del wasn't sure that was true, but she was shaky and glad, for once, not to have to drive. They'd meet the victim at the hospital.

By the time Phan showed up, Del was ready. She'd tried to clean up, but she knew she still looked rough. Phan gave her a long look when she stepped through a white wall of damp, heavy fog into the car but said nothing.

"Anything?"

"Nothing good," Phan muttered. He offered her a cup of coffee.

"Teager?" She asked hopefully about her best suspect. She accepted the cup, wondering how her stomach would respond.

"He's not our guy." Phan shook his head. "World's best alibi. He was in the station."

"Arrested for what?"

"Nope. Filing a nuisance complaint. Somebody threw a rock through his window."

"You're shitting me."

"I wish. I called, I knew you'd ask about your pet weirdo. Phil Sutter was on the desk, said Teager wouldn't shut up about the neighborhood going downhill. Brought up the sex criminal, the vandalism, the prostitution, the gangs. Stayed almost an hour."

"So Teager just happens to have an alibi for the exact right time? How solid is the timing on the attack?"

"Fuck if I know."

"Shit." Del sipped her coffee, wincing as it burned its way down her tender esophagus. "Press'll have a fucking field day. Bradley's gonna shit a brick."

"All over our fucking heads."

"Glad the Feds took over." Del pushed her hair back.

"'Cause they're doing such a great job."

"Which is why Bradley wants us to get there first."

"Right." Phan shrugged. "If they're already there, we'll have to wait."

"Funny."

"What?" Phan rubbed his jaw.

"I liked White and he has an alibi. I liked Teager and he has an alibi."

"You're losing your touch."

"Apparently."

By the time they reached the hospital mere minutes after the phone call, the victim had been pronounced dead. Del and Phan stayed in a waiting room and wondered where the Feds were. The body would now go through the series of photographs and the lengthy forensic exam and the autopsy. They could maybe get an initial lead, though, if they hung around for a bit. Besides, Bradley would be pissed about the victim's death, and it was better to wait for that dust to settle. As daylight approached, more officers would show up at the station to take the captain's wrath.

The victim's body would be processed in stages. The hair had to be combed through, the nails cut, every inch of skin examined. The woman was now just a body, a field of evidence that belonged to doctors and police and forensic scientists. The victim had been young, healthy. Twenty-two, according to her driver's license. Leslie Thorne, a student at Stanford University in Palo Alto. Five-two, one-oh-nine. Tiny. Pretty, her photo indicated. Long, straight brown hair. Big brown eyes. She looked like everybody's daughter or niece or neighbor, a nice young woman who would have lived a productive life and been a decent human being and done who-knew-what with her time on the planet but would never have that chance because somebody wanted to get off on using her body and defiling her personhood.

Del had hated working sex crimes, hated dealing with victims. They needed kindness, compassion, reassurance. What she wanted to do was go bust the head of the bad guy, not hold hands with the victim. A body was much better, a thing she could work with. A thing she could look at as a resource for evidence. But that didn't mean she could accept a victim's death as a lucky break. She'd sit through a million lousy interviews before she'd comfortably accept a victim's death. She hated that Leslie Thorne—this nice kid, this bright young college student, somebody's precious daughter—was dead.

A young doctor, male, Indian, maybe thirty at the outside, came out and met with them. Leslie Thorne had died in the ambulance. Cardiac arrhythmia. Probably caused by something the doctor referred to as an "external agent" and which Del inferred was a drug or chemical reaction. She squinted at the tall, skinny medic who didn't look much older than Mikey Ocampo.

"Special K? Roofie? GHB?"

"Possibly. No jaundice, though. No foaming." The doctor shook his head. "Your forensic people will be able to tell you more. No obvious markers for the usual things."

Del considered this. No jaundice probably meant it wasn't a ketamine overdose. No foaming probably meant no seizure, so it likely wasn't a rohypnol overdose. "Chloroform?"

"Maybe. Maybe not. Hard to tell for sure," the young doctor said, his smooth forehead creased by a frown. "Chloroform disappears rather quickly and can be tricky to administer. It's easy to kill someone by accident with it."

"Takes a while though, right? To dose somebody? Would it be easy to just miscalculate how long?"

The doctor again frowned. "Not my area of expertise, I'm afraid."

Del nodded, exchanged a glance with Phan.

The rape kit was negative. No semen or hair left behind. No statement from the victim, the doctor said, but Del and Phan would follow up with the EMT to make sure.

The doctor seemed tired. Caring, Del thought, but tired. She thanked him and watched him approach a family. Del looked away. She could tell by the doctor's shoulders that he had bad news to deliver, and she didn't need to see that.

He wasn't doing the notification to Leslie Thorne's family. That would be a police matter, a Fed probably, given the high profile of the case. So the doctor had to talk to police about a dead girl he'd already turned over to the medical examiner, and then he had to talk to a family about another dead person. Had this day been what the guy had pictured, slogging through medical school? Almost certainly not. Del tried to console herself with the thought that she wasn't the only one with a shitty job. She remembered the nurse, Sofia Gonzalez, talking about the difficulties of putting her job aside at the end of the day. They all struggled with the same thing, didn't they?

Del and Phan rode back to the station to compare notes with the responding officers. Del tuned in to catch the details but felt removed from the discussion, as if there was a veil between her and the others, even Phan. Why was that? She'd been connecting well with Phan for months. She'd even managed to regain some of the rapport she'd worked so hard to develop with the other officers after the mess with Janet. These men were the closest facsimile she had to a band of brothers.

Still she felt apart from them. Was it because she was the only woman? Of all of them, was she the only one who'd ever had to walk down the street with one eye open for rapists? Was she the only one who'd had to monitor the respect, the attentiveness of her fellow officers, her superiors, her trainers and trainees, her witnesses, her suspects, everyone?

What did it cost a woman, holding that lifelong need to assess every man around her as a potential attacker? Men were not, she knew, free from fears. They could be mugged, carjacked, murdered, and also raped. But in most circumstances, men were relatively free from such concerns. And a man who was assaulted was unlikely to be shamed and humiliated by not only his attackers but also the police and his own family, told he must have done something wicked or dirty or immoral to deserve being attacked.

Leslie Thorne was dead. That the other victims had survived was obviously a good thing, but now what were they facing, what would they face for the rest of their lives? They had been slandered in social media in a wide variety of ways: as hapless children who should have been supervised by real adults, as promiscuous slatterns who therefore deserved sexual predation, as careless idiots whose victimization was their own fault, as fakers who'd made up their attacks. They would have to live with the devastation and confusion and loss of privacy their attacks had engendered, and there was nothing they could do to change this. They didn't even remember what had happened. And the peeping victims—what were they going to feel when news broke of the death caused by the man everyone seemed to assume, because of a similarity in appearance, was culpable in both sets of crimes?

Del looked around at her brother officers and wondered how much any of them could comprehend of what the victims had experienced, were experiencing. Phan was a devoted dad to Kaylee, and he seemed to run his perception of every female victim through the filter of how he would feel if she were his daughter. Still, Del wondered, how much could he really empathize? Had societal disdain for women permeated even his consciousness? It sometimes seemed that the other officers had to fight at least some ingrained misogyny during at least one stage of nearly every investigation.

Del pushed her hair off her forehead and at the same time pushed away her dark thoughts. It was time to focus on Leslie Thorne.

A group of students out for pizza had been walking back home together Thursday night and had stumbled over Leslie Thorne on a section of Frederick Street sidewalk that bordered Golden Gate Park. She'd been naked and unconscious. They'd called nine-one-one, but they hadn't seen anyone else around. Not, they asserted, that they would have. They'd almost stepped on the victim, unable to see her in the fog. An ambulance had picked her up, and the students who'd found her had been taken to the station for statements. That was all. It was remarkably little to go on, and Del fought despair as the team spent endless hours canvassing the park environs and chasing down every possible lead. The guy would only get more confident and more skillful. There was no time to waste and yet every investigative lead felt like a waste of time and energy.

Lola's words came to Del's mind. This was another case that would take all her time and attention until it was solved, or until another, worse one came along. Mikey's murder had occupied her mind and her time until Leslie Thorne's death. Now she was prepared to put it aside entirely because the case had gone nowhere and she felt nearly as guilty as she felt about letting the kid down way back when.

The murder—conveniently reported in time for Friday news deadlines—made the oft-frothing media mad with gleeful outrage. Leslie Thorne's killer had been dubbed The

Grabber, the nomenclature struck Del as disrespectfully glib. The community churned with chaos and fear. Captain Bradley again second-guessed their every move. Officers recanvassed the neighborhood, scouring the community for clues. Feds were tripping all over themselves, trying to regain control of the investigation and fighting public perception that they were just as ineffectual as the lowly local cops.

There was one usable fingerprint, a partial, on the roof of Leslie Thorne's car. Of course it had been run through every database, but there hadn't been any hits. It might not even be his. He seemed too careful to leave a print. It could be some homeless guy or jogger or would-be car thief had touched the car at some point. But it was the only print on the car that wasn't from Leslie or her boyfriend or her mom. The boyfriend had an alibi. The mom's boyfriend had an alibi, and so did Leslie's dad. Leslie's ex had an alibi, as did the creepy guy who'd followed her around in high school and the sister's ex-husband who'd been accused of sexual harassment by a co-worker some years before.

With no good witness information and no meaningful forensic evidence, victimology was all they had. They re-interviewed all of the surviving peeping and kidnapping victims and the families and friends of all the victims. They learned nothing of obvious significance. Del watched the victims for the inconsistencies in affect and tone and body language. She also watched them from inside her new perspective. She saw Lola in their hesitant voices, their shaking hands, their lowered gazes. She saw Lola in the shame and pain and guilt and uncertainty in their posture and words. She couldn't help remembering when Christopher James had been stalking Lola, how he'd rendered her frightened and powerless and humiliated with a few sharp words and hard blows and unknown threats. Again she pushed away her thoughts, wanting to analyze the evidence without the taint of emotion.

"Okay," Del said to Phan, consulting her notes, "the kidnapping victims are brunette, White, female, pretty. Middle or upper middle class, dressed fairly conservatively. Average weight except for Leslie, but she was wearing a bulky jacket.

Average height, except for Leslie, but she was wearing platform shoes, could have looked taller. All three were high risk, likely to be taken out in the open, to be missed fairly quickly. All three were alone at night. Leslie was walking to her car, the other two were walking home. The first two were taken in the Mission and dumped in the Mission." She pointed to a printed map. "Leslie was taken in the Mission and dumped by Golden Gate Park."

"Right." Phan spoke without notes. "No pattern in the days of the week. Nighttime. No defensive wounds on any of them. Let's guess chloroform, until we get the forensics back, it's not Special K, no roofie, none of the usual narcotics. So let's say he's using something that doesn't show up, fine. Chloroform, you asked that doc about it. If he is using chloroform, why? It's not exactly high tech. And how's he getting it? Do you have to have a license to sell it, buy it? Who uses chloroform?"

"I did a little research for a case several years back," Del put in. "It's used for all kinds of things. He could be a painter, a dry cleaner, a mechanic, something medical. A chemist, a pharmacist. There are a lot of choices."

"Can people make it themselves?"

"I don't remember that, but I don't know." Del made a note to research this. "What's the delivery system, old-timey, movie-style hankie? Or something more sophisticated? A respirator of some kind?"

"He works a regular job? I don't know. Maybe he's in the medical field?" Phan shook his head. He seemed as removed as Del felt. "Was Leslie's death an accident, and if so, why? And did he give them all the same amount? Leslie weighed less than the others by almost thirty pounds. Maybe he gave her the same and she died because she's littler."

"Could be." Del rubbed her stomach. "It seems too random, too unplanned. Maybe Leslie isn't connected to the other two."

"Any update on your profile?"

Del shook her head. "I'm not qualified as a profiler, you know that."

"Still." Phan smiled. "You have a picture of this guy. Boo Radley's evil cousin, right?"

"You've seen the guy," Del said. "Roll with me for a minute. Teager could have grabbed Leslie Thorne, drugged her, and been driving her around. Something happens, maybe there's some interruption, maybe he thinks she's dead or he realizes he messed up. He dumps her by the park, maybe while she's still alive. He comes here to alibi himself. She could have been lying there dying for an hour before she was found."

"Hmmn." Phan frowned. "That's a lot of maybes. You gotta consider the possibility it was someone else. Teager's print doesn't match the one on her car. He does have an alibi, and until we have a time of death, there's no denying it. That print's the only physical lead, we gotta go with it."

"Sure. Though the print could have been left there days before. A jogger, a would-be car thief, anyone. I know it might not be Teager, but how many escalating creeps could one little area have at one time?"

"Leslie Thorne was a comparatively high-risk victim, as was the dump site. Out on the street by Golden Gate Park?"

"Even when it's foggy, there's always a chance someone could come along. And these three women aren't invisible. They're not hookers or homeless or runaways. They're attractive, middle class, visible. When they don't show up at home, someone starts worrying."

"If she was still alive when Teager came in, her time of death could be during or even after he was in here filing a complaint."

"Until now, activity has been all over the Mission but stayed pretty neatly within the neighborhood. Golden Gate Park is way outside that comfort zone. It's strange. I get that it's a good dumping ground because it's so big, but he didn't exactly hide the body. He put her where someone was sure to find her. And he left her over a mile from her car. Is he a different guy? Or is he getting more confident and therefore expanding his territory?"

Phan shook his head. "Was this an escalation to murder, or was it an accident? That's the fundamental question, as I see it. If he's escalating, we have a very different animal to cage."

Del rubbed her stomach. "And if it was an accident, how did he respond to that? Did it excite or horrify him? He didn't cover her face, but he didn't pose her provocatively either."

"We don't know enough about this guy." Phan ran his fingers through his surfer's mane. "He's smart or lucky or both."

They eyed each other for a moment, and Del smacked the desk, groaning. "What was the weather when each of the victims was taken?"

"Ah, shit. Shit. Shit." Phan started typing.

Del stood and paced. She couldn't believe she'd missed it. "We are so damned fucking stupid. It was foggy every time, wasn't it?"

"Maybe it's a coincidence," Phan muttered, banging on the keyboard. "It's always foggy here in November."

"No, I think this is actually something. It wasn't regular foggy. Really, really foggy. Right? The other victims talked about it. How they couldn't see, how it was hard to see anything. The students who found Leslie Thorne said they almost tripped over her. The guy is using fog as a cover."

"Maybe, or maybe it's a trigger and it's coincidentally useful." Phan sat back. "Right?"

"Either way, what do we do, put decoys out when it's foggy? How foggy is foggy enough? You wanna put a bunch of brunettes out on overcast days?" Del grimaced when Phan nodded. "Oh, come on! How many? Huh? In the fog? We wouldn't be able to see the decoys ourselves. And if he's got a car, which seems likely, the territory is too large, especially now that he's expanding. We'd need the whole fucking department in on it. It would be a logistical nightmare. And the Feds own it, remember? Hey!"

Her partner was already striding toward Captain Bradley's office. Del had serious reservations about the plan she'd seen working in his mind. She trailed after Phan.

She listened as the captain directed the team he gathered to pull off Operation Foghead, as someone laughingly named it. Del vaguely remembered hearing about a radio station whose fans used that term. She noted Bradley's excitement, the delight of the whole station at having something they could do. They slapped each other on the back, they joked about it, they got wound up like kids on Christmas morning. Del sat back and listened to their energetic brainstorming. They could borrow Vice officers, personnel from everywhere. Hell, they could put male cops in dresses if they ran short.

Del tried to suggest alternatives. She tried to slow the momentum of what seemed like a reckless plan. All she could picture was a bunch of wig-wearing young, testosterone-riddled cops wired for sound, armed to the teeth and wandering the Mission on the next foggy night.

It's ridiculous. Dangerous. Monty Python meets the Keystone Kops. After her concerns were pointedly ignored, Del focused on minimizing the dangers inherent in the trap they were setting. Del looked at the officers around her. Everyone was pissed. Everyone wanted the bad guy. Now all they had to do was make sure nobody shot an innocent bystander or fellow officer. She had to hope the officers involved would remember their training. Playing decoy was far more dangerous than most officers understood. Del had long wondered if the downplaying of the danger was a result of some sexist dismissal of women's contributions and experiences or a natural outgrowth of the job's overwhelming dangers. She also wondered whether the operation's risks and payoff would be increased or decreased by the distinct possibility of the Feds' parallel operation. Because SFPD was obliged to share information and strategy with the Feds but could not expect the same courtesy in return, the Feds could do whatever they wanted. Sitting in the middle of the station, awash in doubt and uncertainty and surrounded by brother officers and the swirling storm of their excitement and relief at finally having something to do, Del felt entirely, painfully alone.

For twenty years she'd inhabited the role of an outsider in her law enforcement family. She'd learned not to let people bait her with sexist, homophobic taunts. She'd developed the thick skin necessary for surviving the clubby blue fraternity of each station, each division, each team. Her first decade with SFPD showed her the value of cultivating friends on the fringes.

SFPD's overt attempts to hire and promote a more reflective pool of officers arose from a federal mandate in place from the early 1970s until the end of the 1990s: the department was required to demonstrate due diligence in diversifying its force. Del and her fellow outsiders were hired under a cloud of resentment over the federal mandate and its fallout.

When, per Mac's advice, she took her sergeant's exam fifteen years back, she scored in the top ten percent of the hundreds of SFPD officers who took the written component and in the top five percent of those who completed the verbal component and interview. Scores were posted internally, and there was a lot of chatter about the patterns in the results. Some officers who'd scored well on the written exam found that their scores plummeted after the interview and verbal component. Other officers reflected the opposite trend: lower scores on the written exam and higher on the verbal test and interview. There was, some officers claimed, a scoring penalty for officers who didn't fulfill one or more of the city's mandated diversity requirements. The long-overdue implementation of mandated inclusiveness exposed the worst of the department's old guard—bitter and clubby, the white boys in blue didn't seem to want anybody new in their fraternity.

When Del was made sergeant she faced a wall of resentment and a general assumption that she hadn't earned the promotion. She soon found that attempts to prove her right to wear the stripes only earned her more resentment and exclusion. At one point, Del heard herself referred to from around corners as "Sergeant Quota" because SFPD's federal mandate required it to hire and promote a certain quota of female officers within a certain number of years. She struggled with how to respond to this disrespect. At first she tried to reason with her brother officers. Then she realized the futility of this. Occasionally she let herself get pulled into heated arguments with the mouthiest jerks on the force. Twice she allowed things to escalate into shoving matches that were quickly ended by quick-thinking officers and that could easily have curtailed her plodding rise through the ranks. At one point she felt herself tensing up every time someone looked at her crosswise and realized she had to make a change in how she responded to her detractors.

"Cool it, kid." This had been the constant refrain from her first training officer, Jack Halloran, way back in her long-ago rookie year in the era of acid-washed jeans and regrettable mullets. Long after his retirement she still struggled to take his advice. As a kid she'd used her fists to deal with would-be bullies; as an adult she decided to use her wits. She focused on the worst offenders and monitored them surreptitiously. She tracked their behavior patterns and relationships with other officers. There were always power plays between clusters of friends, and she exploited those by quietly befriending the most discontented of the cronies. The leaders of the loudest groups of swaggerers were her easiest targets. She was careful to minimize her teasing, but she could make one joke over their vulnerabilities and weaknesses, and their buddies would run with the theme for days. She sharpened her wit on their failed marriages and sloppy investigative practices and burgeoning beer bellies. Mostly she kept her eyes and ears open and her big mouth shut, as her daddy used to say, and this served her well. She found that often the biggest talkers were the worst performers and would almost inevitably self-sabotage without any help from her.

She continued to forge alliances with other outsiders, creating a network of other undesirables who helped each other get their jobs done effectively without relying on the goodwill of the good old boys. Over time, the department came somewhat closer to reflecting the communities it policed, though the end of the federal mandate at the end of the last century slowed this progress.

Due as much to her maturing emotional self-control as her ongoing dedication to the development of her other professional skills, she eventually earned her promotion to Inspector, and she became still more adept at identifying who she could work with effectively and who would only ever see her as an interloper who'd taken a job away from a more deserving male officer. As the former increasingly outnumbered the latter, Del wondered if this resulted from a change in departmental culture or her ability to read people more quickly and effectively.

Now she sat listening to her brother officers enthusing about their awesome new plan to dress in drag and skulk around the neighborhood in the fog. Well aware that her misgivings were unwelcome intrusions on the planning party, Del offered some suggestions for minimizing potential problems. Then she gladly retreated to the bathroom. On the way she looked out one of the wide windows that looked onto Valencia Street and saw that for now the sky was reasonably clear. If her theory was on target, the women of the Mission were safe for this Friday night, from one bad guy at least.

She stared at her reflection in the bathroom mirror and wondered how clearly she saw herself. Was she completely blind to her own character? Maybe she was losing the ability to know herself because she spent so much time examining the world from other people's perspectives. She often looked at things from a bad guy's point of view, but she rarely wondered what it was like to stand in the victim's place. Would doing so help her get out of her thinking rut? She tried to imagine herself as Leslie Thorne, nice young college student, heading home and looking forward to her evening routine, a sensible snack and extended study session.

Del could picture herself walking down the street and could even try to shrink down to Leslie Thorne's diminutive stature, but she couldn't forget she was armed and able to defend herself. Was she a coward, pushing away the vulnerability inherent in being a smaller, unarmed, untrained woman? If she walked down the sidewalk exactly as she was now, even wearing a dress and makeup, a bad guy would have to be blind to pick her as a victim. Del shook her head.

"What if he has some kind of vision impairment?" Del asked this of her mineral-spotted reflection. It was something to consider. Maybe the fog made his glasses spotty with mist. She'd have to ask somebody who wore glasses how much the fog messed with them.

"One last try. Okay. I'm a regular, average woman, coming home from work or a friend's house. Say my car breaks down and my cell battery is dead. I decide to walk home and I'm scared. It's foggy and dark, and I'm not sure if I'm going the right way, because I can't see anything. So I'm walking fast and then slowing down 'cause I'm not sure, I'm clutching a ten-pound purse." Alone in the ladies' room in the station, Del widened her eyes and hunched her shoulders. She stared at the mirror. "I'm looking around, and I'm taking little tiny steps in stupid high-heeled shoes that slow me down, and off I go."

Her pantomime looked ridiculous in the mirror. She was like a cartoon character, hunched over and tiptoeing. I can't do it, she thought, recalling the night she went to Lola's house and tried to behave in a stereotypically feminine manner to entice Lola's stalker into coming after her. Del could mimic the girly stuff, but she couldn't stop being who she was. She'd been able to put herself in the shoes of a killer, a rapist, a robber, a kidnapper, and any number of other bad guys, but she couldn't seem to really put herself in the place of a victim. She knew Lola thought it was hard for her, walking around in the larger world as an obviously butch lesbian. But for her money, walking around as herself was easy. From her point of view, being a girly girl seemed outrageously dangerous.

Didn't they get frustrated, spending hard-earned money and precious time on hairstyles and makeup designed to titillate? Not that Del didn't appreciate the efforts of the femmes of the world. She just wasn't sure why they were willing to spend all their time and money on the work it required. Viewed through a hyper-sexualized lens, disrespected and demeaned on a sometimes daily basis, women like Lola, like Leslie Thorne, like half the population of the city, were constant targets. Poor women, lacking the insulation provided by money and social support, were often especially vulnerable to exploitation and disrespect. Del's years as a patrol officer had been blanketed in exposure to the indignities to which the unprotected were subjected. She would be a different person, she thought, if she had to walk through the world unable to defend both herself and others.

Del let go of the thought. It was a distraction. She glanced at her watch as she headed back to the team, knowing that it didn't help Mikey but still completing the new ritual: midnight meant Mikey had been dead for eighteen days. As soon as she decently could, she headed home to spend the next few hours detailing the life of Ernie White and wishing her efforts were worthwhile.

* * *

Saturday morning Del was leaving for work when Lola came tearing out of her front door. She raced toward Del's truck, reaching the driver's side door just ahead of her.

"I know you're busy, and I assume you're working," she said, breathless and flushed. "I wanted to apologize. I was a little cold to you when you showed up that morning. I was surprised and pretty tired. And—anyway, I just wanted you to know I love you. I still love you. That's all." She turned as if to go.

"I love you too," Del said, her voice catching. "I still love you too."

Lola responded with the same dazzling smile that had caught at her heart the first time they met.

"You're so amazing," Del whispered, feeling an answering smile form on her face. "I can't even breathe when you smile at me."

Their grins deepened into a shared laugh, and they stepped closer together. She could smell the coffee on Lola's breath, the shampoo in her sleep-tousled hair, the clean and fresh and sweet smell that was uniquely Lola. She closed the narrowing gap between them and kissed Lola's soft lips as gently as she could. She felt Lola trembling and broke the kiss, wishing she could spend the next forty or fifty years exploring that warm, sweet mouth.

"Listen, I'm sorry, I gotta go. Phan's waiting for me. I'll call you later, okay?"

Lola nodded mutely, and Del hesitated.

"Hey. Listen." Del leaned against the truck. "You said we'd never been on a date, you've never been on a date with anyone."

"It's weird." Lola rolled her eyes. "I know it is. Would you have gotten involved with me if you'd realized how backward I am?"

Del rubbed her stomach absently. "You don't talk about your marriage, but I get the notion Beckett wasn't exactly sweet to you. Or romantic or whatever. Then you got together with me, and I didn't romance you either. I thought about that, a beautiful girl with no romance or sweetness in her life."

"You think I'm beautiful?"

"Of-of course," Del sputtered, her eyes wide. "Don't you know—?"

Lola's frown darkened her eyes. "Do you hate that I was married to a man?"

"What? No." Del made a face. "I hate that you were married to an asshole who hurt you and scared you. I hate how he made you think you were nothing."

"Just like I hate," Lola responded slowly, "the way Janet treated you."

There was a long pause, and the two shared wry smiles.

"You know what I hate the most?" Del blew out a gust of hot air. "I hate talking."

"Me too." Lola laughed.

"Really?"

"It's awful. Talking about your feelings means having to think about them. It sucks."

"Ha." Del snorted a laugh. "I don't think I've ever heard you say that before."

"What? 'Sucks?'" Lola smiled. "I got it from you."

"Yeah?" Del reached out to take Lola's hand.

"Yeah."

Del rubbed her thumb in Lola's soft, curved palm. "I don't mean that I don't want to, or that it isn't worth trying. I want to work things out. If you're willing."

"Yeah." Lola nodded. "Okay."

"Good. Good."

"It's not going to be easy." Lola pulled away and hugged herself. "We don't trust each other right now. I need to know that you'll be able to actually trust me someday. I need you willing to be as vulnerable as I am."

"Vulnerable." It was Del's turn to nod. "Right. Got it."

"But I want to try."

"Okay." Del smiled. "Can I kiss you again?"

"Do you want to?" Lola asked coyly, grinning.

Del answered so thoroughly they were both left breathless and laughing, clinging to each other there in the street next to the truck.

"Come over for dinner tonight?"

Del agreed and watched Lola trot over to her house.

At the station, she ordered roses to be delivered to Lola at four that afternoon—along with never taking her out to dinner, Del had also failed to ever get her flowers. How, she wondered, had she managed to hold on to the woman for as long as she had? And was it really not too late? She felt hope bubbling up inside her and fought the urge to tamp it down before she really started to believe in it and count on it. What if it didn't work out? What if it was too late? What if she did everything perfectly—and what were the odds of that—and it still didn't work out? Del took a deep breath and counted herself lucky she had her work, where at least she understood the rules.

CHAPTER TEN

By five thirty Saturday evening, San Francisco was adorned in November's most audaciously foggy weather. Everything beautiful in the city was hidden behind a veil of obscurity. Del couldn't stop picturing the fog as an evil, insidious predator attacking the very life force of the colorful, magical city and its inhabitants.

Nor could she block out thoughts of tiny, vulnerable, painfully young Leslie Thorne. She and Phan had spent a good part of the day taking their turn going through the victim's apartment. They'd noted the evidence of a young life lived well, for too short a time. There'd been plenty of evidence of loving parents and nice friends and a devoted boyfriend and a sensible car. They'd seen the organic food and the vitamins and the carefully compiled lecture notes sitting alongside the selectively highlighted textbooks. They'd exchanged glances over the neatly folded clothing and the tidy closet and the expiration dates written in permanent ink on her refrigerated food and the neatly arranged rows of her favorite canned foods—turkey chili and lentil soup and black olives and albacore tuna—in the pantry. Their victim had been careful, conscientious, deliberate, organized. A nice kid, just like they'd both thought right from the start. She'd done everything she could to make her life orderly and productive and safe.

All of that had been useless when young Leslie had been heading home on a foggy November night, probably shivering even in her oversized coat, maybe working not to twist an ankle in the platform heels designed to make her appear taller. Had she been afraid? Had she been thinking about a hot cup of tea and a warm bath and a steaming bowl of her favorite lentil soup? Had she been distracted, thinking about the essays she needed to write for her history and sociology classes? She'd been in a lab for her biology class just that morning. Had she been worrying about her lab notes? Leslie Thorne had been detail-oriented. She'd rewritten her notes two or three times, getting them neater and clearer and more cogent each time but keeping the older versions, presumably just in case she'd missed something. Del hoped she'd been thinking about her class notes, too distracted to be scared of a madman lunging at her from out of the unreadable nothing that was the foggy nighttime world.

The Feds had initially laughed off Del's suggestion that the kidnapper was attacking during heavy fog. No one had been surprised, though, when they subsequently agreed to a new program of sending out decoys on particularly foggy nights. They only shared their plans insofar as was necessary to keep local officers from blundering into the way. SFPD's parallel effort, Operation Foghead, was taken from the municipal Mission station and put under the purview of a Special Investigations team. Once again they had been sidelined.

Left out in the cold, Del and Phan decided to take a little field trip before going home. They'd tried to develop insight based on victimology and now wanted to further develop their understanding of the geographical profile of the bad guy's territory. They cruised around the neighborhood with some vague hope they would stumble across some insight. It was Phan's turn to drive, and Del examined a series of crime maps to look for patterns.

"Okay, let's review it again. He dumped her in Golden Gate Park," Phan noted as they drove slowly past Mission Dolores Park. "This one would have been more central to his comfort zone."

"Agreed." Del tried to peer through the wall of droplets that hid the park from view. "We think he's smart. Maybe he wanted to cross jurisdictions. Which worked. Now it's in the hands of two new teams that haven't been on it from the first. I wonder if he could have any law enforcement background."

"I don't even want to consider it without a good reason," Phan murmured. "We don't have any evidence of that."

"I know." Del peered at the blankness. "What if there are two guys, Phan? What if the peeper, Teager or someone else, lives in the Mission, and the kidnapper lives somewhere else, maybe north of the Mission? Closer to where he dumped Leslie Thorne?"

"Could be, I guess. We don't have a lot of hard evidence of anything."

"Yeah. Hey, let me out here," she hissed, hushed by the world of white that surrounded the car. As soon as the car was stopped she ducked out. "Be right back. I just want to see what it feels like."

"Don't go far," he warned.

She waved her agreement, realizing too late he probably hadn't been able to see it.

Mere seconds later, Del stood encased in invisibility. The fog was more than blinding. It was disorienting, nauseating. Del felt almost drunk. The air was heavy with water. She couldn't see the ground beneath her. She couldn't even see her own feet. The voices of the city were muffled and impossible to place. The only smell was dankness. She heard a dog bark, and the sound could have come from ten feet or a block away. She looked into the blankness that covered the world. It was an enemy dangerous in and of itself. It was a monster trying to drown her and pull her down. Del suddenly remembered the feeling of being drugged by Janet, the sensation of falling into unconsciousness. She had to hold herself very still, momentarily convinced that moving would mean dissolving.

"Done playing around, Mason?"

With a shake of her head, Del recalled herself to the moment. Phan couldn't have been more than a dozen feet away, but she couldn't see him or determine where his voice had come from. She took a few seconds to clear her mind and headed back to the car, eleven feet to her right, three steps left. Of course she'd counted, without even realizing she was doing so. Tracking her location was the habit of a lifetime.

"It's just fog, you idiot."

"You say something, Mason?"

Del tried not to grab at the door handle like a drowning victim. She opened the car door with mindful care and watched the darkness swallow the feeble light from the domed fixture inside the department vehicle. She shook her head as she sat. "I'm spooked. It's ridiculous. Not by the asshole. By the fog."

"Any insights?"

"They weren't wearing shoes," she murmured. "They were naked. I don't remember seeing abrasions on their feet, though."

"What?"

"I was wondering if he scared them, got them to run in the direction he wanted. Hunters will work together. One of them will scare the prey so it runs toward the other hunter. But the victims didn't have damage to their feet or twisted ankles or anything like that."

"We'll get him," Phan muttered with a distinct lack of conviction. "Does this feel as useless to you as it does to me?"

"At least."

* * *

"Sorry for showing up so late," Del offered lamely. She wished she'd taken the time to change out of her damp clothes. She felt stiff and heavy in her fog-speckled brown chinos and blue oxford. She ran a stiff hand through her clammy, messy curls. They were tickling her ears and neck, and she needed a haircut.

Lola smiled. "No problem. Thank you for the roses, by the way. They came this afternoon. They were a nice surprise."

"You said once no one had ever—"

"It was very thoughtful—"

"It was nothing. Long overdue. I wish—"

"I really appreciate—"

They both stopped, smiling lamely at each other.

"You look lovely."

Lola looked down at the flattering blue wrap dress she wore. "Thanks. It's a nice shape, isn't it? Marco picked it. He keeps telling me to wear blue, and I think he's right. I never know what looks good on me. I'm babbling, aren't I?"

Del grinned. "We're nervous."

"Well, this feels important, doesn't it? We're trying to—God, I'm going to keep babbling if you let me. Please say something so I'll shut up."

"I like how your dress is so feminine and your hair is so short. I've always thought that was a particularly fetching look. Sexy. And on you—"

Lola flushed, waving away Del's words. "Oh, no, you're embarrassing me, please stop. I mean, thank you, I appreciate it, but I'm already so self-conscious and—"

"All right." Del wanted to touch Lola's soft skin and silky dress and smooth cap of hair, but she wasn't sure Lola would welcome such overtures.

Lola waved vaguely at the stove.

"Are you hungry?"

Del shook her head. But she was, she realized. She nodded, and again they smiled awkwardly.

They sat at the table, and Del chewed on pasta she didn't taste. She had the feeling something had gone wrong between their kisses that morning and her late evening arrival. The vase of flowers stood between them, and Lola eased it to the side, nearly toppling the display. Del reached out to right the vase, and their hands touched. Lola pulled her hand back and Del grimaced. The smell of the roses was oppressive rather than perfumed, and Del regretted making the silly gesture. What did sending the flowers mean, if she wasn't any good at showing her love for Lola in ways that actually changed anything?

She shook her head. "I wish I knew how to do this."

"I don't know how either." Lola picked up a petal that had fallen to the table and rubbed it against her cheek. The deep red made her pale skin look even lighter, almost ghostly. Her smile was wistful.

Del looked away. "What if we went to therapy?"

"You said you didn't want to." Lola held the petal in her open palm and gazed at her with wide, unreadable eyes.

"We could try it."

"Really?" Lola almost seemed more surprised than pleased, and Del wondered what this meant.

"Okay." Del reached out and almost took Lola's other hand but didn't. "Just tell me the door's not closed. Just tell me there's a chance?"

"I'll set it up."

"If you're not sure you want to—I just think we should try before we give up on each other, you know?"

"Yes."

"If you still want to. Something—can you tell me what you're thinking?"

Lola sat back, her shoulders slumped and her eyes heavy-lidded. "I almost wish I could just walk away from you. Because I think we're going to end up back together. And I'll start to feel safe and trust you and let myself feel happy. Like today. This morning we were kissing and laughing, and I felt so close to you. You got me flowers! I was so excited. Then I called to thank you for the flowers, and you never called me back. I texted you. Nothing. You didn't tell me when you'd come over for dinner. You just showed up, expecting me to be ready whenever. No consideration of what else I might want or need to do besides wait for you. So my feelings were hurt, but I told myself I was being too sensitive. I didn't want to complain or make demands on you, because you're already halfway ready to give up on us. And, as usual, even when you're here you're focused on a case."

Del blinked.

"This is what always happens, Del. I tell myself your work is really important and that it's selfish to want more of you than I have. I ignore things that hurt my feelings and hope you'll return my love when you can. When you do, it's amazing. But I spend a lot of time waiting for that. Then, every time we're getting really close, something happens that I don't even understand. You just drift away and leave me more and more alone until you're all the way gone. I don't know where I stand with you. I don't know how you feel about me. I'm not sure you know how you feel about me. You wander in and out of my life like I'm a way station, and I deserve better than that. So I cut ties with you and then I'm even more lonely. One of these days we'll just be all the way apart for good, and I won't be able to live without you. It'll kill me."

She stood up, her chair scraping the floor. Del felt helpless, watching her.

"That's what I think is gonna happen."

She walked out and plodded noisily up the stairs, and Del sat alone at the table for a few minutes trying to think of a response. Another petal dropped to the table, and Del thought about how strange a practice it was, buying moribund plants and forcing the woman you loved to watch them die and decompose.

CHAPTER ELEVEN

It was Sunday and theoretically the weekend, but Del and Phan were working. They used much of the day to follow up again on every detail of Mikey's life and death, and each was still going nowhere.

Del watched her partner cross out a dozen items on a handwritten list. He pressed the pen so hard that it tore through the paper in places. She that saw his face was bright red and that his whole body was tense. She'd been working on her own list of follow-up calls and emails and hadn't noticed Phan's silent distress. She watched him slam closed a file, shove a pile of papers into a folder, and jam a pen into a drawer.

"What's up?"

"Nothing."

Del tried to lighten the mood with a teasing tone. "Don't try to bullshit me, partner."

"I'm tired of watching you play hide-and-seek with this guy, partner," Phan blurted.

"You're lying."

This pronouncement prompted a long, silent impasse, and the pair sat staring silently at each other for two full minutes.

Del raised her good shoulder. "Spill."

Phan rolled his eyes and crossed his arms over his barrel chest. "Kaylee had a physical a few weeks ago."

Del leaned forward, alarmed. "She okay? Something wrong? Is she sick? Why haven't you said anything?"

"No, she's fine. Perfectly, perfectly healthy." Phan sighed heavily. "She's five-two, one-oh-nine."

"Oh."

Now Del understood. Phan was freaked out because his daughter was exactly the same height and weight as Leslie Thorne. Del wanted to say something about how Kaylee wasn't in their bad guy's target age range or neighborhood. Phan and his ex-wife both lived in the Sunset District. She wanted to remind him that lots of girls and women were that size and were not targets. But it all rang false in her head. If she had a kid Kaylee's age, she'd be afraid for that kid every day. Working the job was bad enough. Coming across a victim with the same stats as your only child had to feel like a punch to the throat. There was nothing Del could say that wouldn't either dismiss Phan's feelings or sound patronizing or both.

"That's disturbing." She knew Phan would hate any gesture of comfort. "I can't imagine how that feels."

"Yeah." Phan scrubbed at his scalp, messing up his expensively cut, surfer-boy hair. For the first time Del noticed a few strands of silver. "I know it doesn't mean anything. I just don't like it."

"Yeah, neither do I. Let's get this clear: anybody lays a hand on your girl, you and I take care of it privately. We don't leave behind pieces of him big enough to find."

"Deal." Phan allowed himself a small smile. "She isn't even dating yet. I can't imagine letting her go out with some idiot boy. Or," he continued, "some idiot girl, for that matter."

"When she starts dating we'll follow her. Discreetly."

"Obviously." Phan nodded. "Listen, this being Sunday and all, let's go home."

"Deal." Del led the way into the station. "Unless we get snagged."

"Now you've done it."

"You know what really sucks?" Del eyed her partner.

"I know. I'm doing it, too—waiting for the next victim to show up so we have something to work with."

"What's wrong with us, Phan?"

"The job. That's what's wrong with us."

CHAPTER TWELVE

Del spent most of Sunday night poring over the data Mac had sent her, refining her timelines for Ernie White's movements and expenditures over the last several years. It was clear that no one else had ever gone through the mountains of undifferentiated data. Was there, she wondered, a roomful of data on every single American? Or only those who met certain criteria? If so, what were the criteria? She was drowning in information on the guy, struggling to separate the important from the unimportant. For the first time she was truly aware of how useless information was without some system of screening and organizing. The Feds' data collection was like fishing with a net wider than the Pacific Ocean. She resolved to choose the fifty most important facts about White and see if that told her anything. It was slow going, and close to dawn she fell asleep with her head on a stack of reports on his travels.

In the morning Del was only too glad to go to work. She walked in to find that the Feds had abandoned the station, leaving behind only displaced furniture and boxes of neatly collated paperwork detailing the fine work of the federal investigators, focused in particular on how carefully they had covered their asses.

Captain Bradley was unable to explain why the Feds had suddenly left Mission Station or whether they'd set up a new base camp in their own building on Golden Gate Avenue. They were, Bradley said, still investigating the kidnappings. When a few officers tried to ask follow-up questions, he offered an exaggerated shrug. "You can't ask me to explain the Feds."

Inspector Ralph Davies had been put in charge of finding Leslie Thorne's killer, and Del didn't envy him. He was a blowhard and a jerk, but from what she'd seen he was a decently thorough investigator. She watched him blow off steam at a few junior officers. Then he started calling out everyone who'd been part of the original investigative team, which was nearly the whole station. When no one would respond to his taunts, Davies zeroed in on Del, saying that she'd done a half-assed job and he was sick of having to come in and clean up her messes.

Why he took his stress out on her and not Phan or anyone else, Del wasn't sure. But it didn't matter. She didn't take it personally. She'd been there herself, blind and behind the eight ball. They'd all been there, stuck with a nightmare of a case. And she knew Davies. He was one of those who wished these were still the good old days, when the whole department was populated with white men who looked and sounded like himself. The federal mandate requiring SFPD to diversify the ranks had long expired, and Davies had been one of those who cheered when it did.

She tuned Davies out when he muttered under his breath that she was incompetent. She and Phan were going over their overlapping to-do lists when Davies called her a bitch. Phan looked to Del for some cue, and she shook her head.

"Is there something I can do for you, Davies? If you need anything for the case, let me know. Until then, we're working."

Davies stalked away.

"Nicely handled," Phan murmured. "He's losing it."

"He'll be back," Del predicted. "And he'll up the ante. But I can handle Davies."

Phan nodded slowly, and they went back to reviewing their notes and task lists.

When Davies stalked up to Del an hour later, the partners were reviewing every piece of information they had on Mikey's murder.

Davies stood over Del, castigating her for failing to solve Leslie Thorne's murder. He ranted loudly, winding up by insisting she'd only been promoted to Inspector because she was a dyke and filled a quota.

Del looked up at the red-faced bigot. He was like a child with oppositional defiant disorder: if he could provoke any reaction that made her seem overly emotional or out of control or weak, he would feel victorious. She'd worked with dozens of guys like Davies. They were full-grown but acted like toddlers and would rage and scream when they got frustrated or upset. Davies was a bully. The way he stood over her, raining spittle on her from his lofty vantage, the way his eyes bulged and his arms waved around and his voice boomed over her—he looked like a blond, mostly hairless adolescent chimpanzee. She half-expected the guy to throw scat at her.

From the side she saw Phan lean forward in his chair, clearly resisting the urge to stand up and confront Davies. Phan would read her cue and let her handle Davies unless she seemed to want his help. He had her back. She felt the weight of the other officers' gazes on her. They seemed to be frozen with shock. Davies was out of line, and they knew it, but they weren't sure what they were supposed to do. It was up to Del to figure it out. If she lost her cool, they would lose respect for her. If she let Davies bully her, they would lose respect for her. Two decades of experience dealing with fellow officers, some of whom were bullies, had taught Del that only two things worked: calm and humor. She had to model both for the younger officers around her. They would all watch. They would all remember not only how she handled Davies but also how Phan had her back when she did so. This was a performance.

"Well, Davies," she drawled, her voice steady and cool, her face a mask of calm, "solve the case and maybe you can start to talk shit. Until then—"

There were a few smirks from the peanut gallery, and Davies seemed to grow more enraged. He turned purple. He said she was only a dyke because she was too ugly to get a man.

Del laughed and rolled her eyes. "You're calling *me* ugly? Do you own a mirror, Davies?"

This apparently startled everyone. Even Davies was momentarily stopped in his tracks. A couple of onlookers snorted, and Davies sputtered. Del stared up at him, one eyebrow cocked, a smirk twisting her lips.

Davies pushed her shoulder, the one she'd spent months rehabbing, and she fought the urge to jump up and punch the jerk. Six or seven guys came closer, watching Del for some cue. She reminded herself that if she lost her cool, there would be a brawl, which outcome would serve no one. She rose slowly, turning to face him fully. She resisted the impulse to get in his face. She kept her voice quiet, her face neutral. Her heart was pounding, and she took a second to make sure her voice would stay cool and low.

"Watch yourself, Davies."

Phan stood behind her. He'd come around the desks double-time and coiled, but she still ran the show. Now there was a tight circle of brother officers around Del, and she realized they were with her. Everyone watched and waited. If she broke the calm with anger or fear there would be chaos. Del felt like she was a kid in school again and being targeted by the newest bully to swing into town, the one who hadn't gotten the memo about how the skinny blond girl could kick ass. Only this time around there was a team on her side.

"Bitch," Davies growled. "Fucking bitch can't do the fucking job."

"That's okay, Davies," Del said in a light tone, turning from him with practiced indifference and breaking up the circle with deliberate casualness. "We don't hold it against you."

It was a lame joke but it broke the tension. Phan's laugh was the loudest. Davies's face turned to stone, and he stormed away. Del accepted verbal backslapping from her relieved peers. She didn't thank any of them, nor did any of them pledge undying loyalty. Their actions had spoken louder than words could have done. She was one of them. She wasn't sure when that happened, or why she hadn't been aware of it, but she was one of them. She went back to work, knowing that as soon as she normalized things everyone else would get back to work too.

"Nicely done," Phan murmured after the station's usual noise and activity had resumed.

"For now."

Phan tapped the desk with his fingers. "I wasn't sure how you wanted—"

"I appreciate how you had my back," Del said. "You let me handle it but you had my back. Perfect."

Phan nodded, pursing his lips. "Cool."

Del laughed. "You're such a surfer boy."

* * *

That night, she went home to find several messages waiting for her. From Lola, she guessed. Exhausted from the day and painfully aware of the late hour, she ignored them and dropped into bed without bothering to eat or shower or even brush her teeth. She'd been able to maintain her cool with Davies largely because she understood him. She got that he wanted a fight. He didn't even care who the fight was with or why. She'd felt like that plenty of times. Hell, she felt like that now—she was just too tired to get worked up. Even Phan was starting to get snippy, which wasn't like him. She decided to get him a coffee in the morning. He'd done that for her plenty of times, and she hadn't reciprocated. The thought of coffee made her remember she was hungry, but she couldn't muster the energy to walk all the way downstairs and find something to eat. Besides, her stomach hurt. Hugging her burning belly, Del knew she should take her ulcer medication but couldn't seem to talk herself into getting out of bed to retrieve it.

She thought of when she and Lola were together. Del would often come home late and find dinner in the fridge for her, a plate covered in foil with a heart drawn on it. Lola had done all sorts of sweet little things like that. Del had long ago gotten used to being taken care of by her girlfriends. She'd been spoiled by lovely, talented, brilliant women who while pursuing their own successful careers cooked for and cleaned up after her and let her do whatever she wanted. Until Janet, of course. Janet had made endless demands and rarely been satisfied by her efforts. Del had thought she'd learned something from that relationship. She had thought she'd learned not to take a good partner for granted. But then loving, thoughtful Lola came along and she took Lola for granted.

Janet had called Lola a housewife and clearly meant it in a derogatory way. Maybe they had fallen more deeply into the hetero-normed marriage roles than they'd meant to. While they'd kept their finances separate, they'd mixed their laundry and dishes and shopping, and Lola had done all of it. Del wondered how she would feel, being relegated to the role of somebody's helpmate. She'd hate it. Had Lola hated it? Sometimes it seemed like it, but sometimes it seemed like it was the way they both wanted to do things. Lola liked cooking and fiddling around in the house, didn't she? Baking and all that. Remembering the peach pie Lola had made her, back when they were together, almost tasting it, smelling it.

Daddy's favorite. She could almost smell the heavy sweetness of peach pie. She could picture him sitting at the table in the diner he took her to sometimes when she was little. She always sat next to him, by the window, Daddy's back to the corner. The main road that led to the freeway was usually empty of traffic, but the diner's parking lot was always full. The tables were what Daddy called God-bless-it yellow, and the waitress always wore a red smock.

Del remembered once asking if the smock was God-bless-it red. He laughed, ruffling her curls. She smiled up at him, delighted at having made him laugh. They were eating peach pie, he with coffee and she with milk. She took her first bite and widened her eyes to show him how much she loved it and he laughed again. He gobbled up his piece and they raced to finish first. He won, of course, and then he licked his plate to make her giggle. Now, remembering, Del was surprised to find that she was crying. When was the last time she'd cried over her dad?

"Pretty pathetic," she croaked. "You're forty-four goddamn years old, and you're crying over your daddy?"

Despite her tiredness, she woke early in the morning and went for a long run. She needed the exercise, that was for sure, but she also needed to clear her head. Davies might have another testosterone flash, and she needed to figure out a strategy. She pushed herself one step at a time in hopes she would find her stride, but after a mere three miles, she was struggling to move her body past the twin walls of gut pain and ennui. She slowed to a walk and trudged home to get ready for work. It would likely be another long, frustrating day, but she needed to get to the station and start dealing with it. By seven she was at her desk and checking email. By eight Phan was checking his and they were planning the day.

Davies had given each team a handful of suspects to run down, and Del was also focused on Teager, her original suspect, despite his having an alibi for one of the incidents. She spent the day working with Phan to build profiles and dossiers on each of their assigned suspects and going a bit further with her not-so-golden boy, running down Teager's former teachers and co-workers on the phone. No friends that she could find, no former girlfriends. The guy was a ghost. No one she reached remembered him. No one had any real impressions of him.

"Is he a nice guy?" Yes. They all agreed on that one, however halfheartedly.

"Is he funny? Smart? Creepy?" To these more specific questions their answers were invariably vague and noncommittal.

He's invisible, she thought. Totally invisible. Like Sofia Gonzalez had said of the man who peeped at her and laughed, covering his mouth with his hand when she fell down. Donette Williams' Boo Radley, invisible and strange at the same time. It wasn't until the end of the day that Del finally finished tracking down Teager's mother's friends and co-workers. Momma Teager been dead for several months, but Del figured surely her friends and acquaintances had opinions about her son. Del left messages for everyone she could find who was connected to the mother and decided to pack it in for the day. As she stood, she remembered her earlier thought that maybe Teager's mother's dying had triggered his crime wave. Funny, she thought, both of the suspects Davies gave us have lost their mothers within the last five years. Both to cancer. White's and Teager's mothers died within months of each other, both from well-documented causes. What if the only thing holding back scores of bad guys was their mothers? Neither of the men Davies had assigned her and Phan was a viable suspect. They both had solid, verifiable and verified alibis. Neither followed the patterns of behavior they were looking for. Davies had kept her and Phan busy all day with worthless nonsense. Shaking aside the thought, Del reminded herself she'd been given this scutwork because Davies hated her.

She and Phan walked out together, going over what they'd done over the course of the day.

"Davies kept his distance," Phan noted.

"Kept us busy with nonviable suspects."

"Yeah." Phan shrugged. "But they both showed up in your perv database. At least we can cross them off the list."

"True." Del nodded absently. "See you tomorrow."

She drove home thinking about Mikey. She had at some point stopped tracking how many days it had been since his death, and she felt strangely guilty about that. There was every possibility she would never solve his murder. She gripped the steering wheel, wondering about the kid. Had he learned to drive? Maybe not. Had he ever been on an airplane? Had he ever gone to Disneyland? How small was his world before it was taken away from him? He was just as invisible as Ronald Teager, just as invisible as the kidnapper, whoever he was. She'd read once that the worst thing you can do to people is render them invisible. She wondered if this was true. Had she rendered Lola invisible? Had she rendered herself invisible?

She turned onto 18th Street and saw Lola sitting on her front steps. Smiling hesitantly, she parked and found Lola standing a few feet away.

"How's it going?" she asked, realizing she probably should have returned Lola's calls.

Lola stared at her with an unreadable expression. "I've been trying to figure out how to talk to you, and I'm just going to jump in, okay?"

Del nodded. "Do you want to come in?"

Lola shook her head. "When we met I was a mess. I was just starting my adult life, really belatedly. I was scared and insecure, I thought I could never make it on my own. Never open my heart again. And if I did, I might once again choose someone who thought less of me and would probably hurt me."

Del started to interject, but Lola shook her head.

"No, wait. I felt broken. I was broken." She stopped to swipe at her eyes. "We fell in love. And it was amazing. I thought we were happy, I thought nothing would change. But I did change. I got more confident, in part because of you. I started to see myself as a whole person, not just somebody's property or whatever, and part of that was thanks to you loving me." She wiped her eyes and smiled. "You made me want to be more. Smarter and stronger and more independent. To be your partner, not just your girlfriend."

"You are." Del bit her lip. "You were."

"Not really. I lived for you. I only cared about what you thought of me and what you wanted. I was like an appendage to you, and I didn't want to be. I could lean on you, I could trust you. And that was such a precious gift! I wanted to give that same gift to you, be the person you could lean on, the person you could trust."

"You are!" Del's words burst out, and Lola's smile was gentle. Del bristled at what felt like condescension and worked to push away her urge to defend herself. She gestured at Lola to respond.

"No. I'm not," Lola answered quietly. "I'm the person you protect. I'm the person you give love to. But you won't take it back. You don't trust me enough to tell me what you really feel, what you really want. You act like I'm some helpless child that you love, but I'm not a child. I'm a grown woman."

"I know that."

"Del." Lola shook her head and looked away. "I love you more than anything in the whole world. I would do anything for you. But you need to be willing to trust me with your heart. You need to give up some of the control you always have to have."

Del decided not to argue that point. Hadn't Janet said something about that? At the thought of Janet, Del drifted away and heard Lola as if through a brick wall.

"I need you to decide you want a partner. I need you to lean on me. Tell me when you're scared or unsure or insecure. I want you to drop your guard around me. I want you to let me hold you up the way you hold me up. Can you do that? Can you give up some of that power? Can you let me be your partner for real?"

"You are." Del swallowed, wondering if her words sounded as false to Lola as they did to her. "You are my partner. I do lean on you. I trust you more than anyone in the world. I don't understand what you think I'm holding back."

Lola shook her head. "Please, just think about this. Please? I'm not trying to make you jump through hoops. I'm certainly not trying to change you into something you're not. I don't know how else to say what I'm feeling. I'm obviously not doing a good job of explaining it." She looked away. "I'm tired. I think I'm going to try to sleep. We'll talk tomorrow, okay?"

"Okay." Del fought the urge to argue. "Sure."

Lola nodded and turned to go. Watching her walk away, following her, Del suddenly realized she was blowing it.

"You're getting rid of me for not knowing my lines," she complained.

Lola shook her head. "No. What are you talking about?"

"It's like, if I do what you want, fine. But when I can't read your mind—"

"I'm not asking you to read my mind, and I'm not—I don't even—I just want you to talk to me. Is that so crazy?"

"What do you see when you look at me?"

Lola licked her lips and blinked. "The woman who means more to me than anyone."

"No, really." Del grimaced. "Tell me what you see."

"Beauty, intelligence, kindness—"

"Not compliments," Del protested. "What do you see?"

"I don't know what you mean."

"Neither do I."

Del fled to her house, where she sat on her bed feeling cold and lonely.

She felt the way her hips created a dent in the comforter. "Like a trench. Like I'm entrenched. Like Janet said."

CHAPTER THIRTEEN

Anton Jones, her favorite computer specialist, was waiting for Del when she showed up at work the next morning. He had folded his lanky frame into her chair and beamed at her with sparkling eyes. She bumped his toe with her boot.

"I see you got the memo."

Jones looked puzzled until Del pointed out their outfits. Both wore green sweaters with brown chinos. "Hey, only the cool kids know what to wear."

Del laughed. "I am not now, nor have I ever been, a cool kid."

Jones grinned widely. "Would you believe I have? No? Well, you're right."

"To what do I owe the honor of this visit, Jones? You just loitering?"

"Heh." He smirked at her. "Learned it from you, slacker."

Del smiled. "You're in a cheerful mood."

"Speaking of, I heard you and Davies are sweet on each other." Jones made a face.

"Yeah, he's just trying to pull on my pigtails."

Jones waved away the subject of Davies. "How's Lola?"

"Fine. How's your mom, she feeling better?"

"Actually, she's good. Sugar's stable most of the time, and she's doing an exercise class at the senior center. Listen, since you were too lazy to show up until the day was half over, I had to do your job for you."

Del smiled. Jones must have something good to offer or he wouldn't be teasing her. She reached into her desk and pulled out a candy bar, knowing Jones was a sucker for sweets. She waggled it in front of him and put it behind her back. "Want it? Spill."

"Nuh-uh." He swung his head from side to side and held out his hand. "Candy first."

"Nice try, smartass. Spill."

At that moment, Phan walked in and reached behind Del to grab the candy from her and wave it at the computer expert. "Jones, you don't have shit. If you did, Bradley would be here."

"Oh, really? Our fearless leader already did your job, and all before eight in the morning."

Del raised an eyebrow. "Tell me more."

"Warrants for Teager's place, his car? Remember that? Or did you forget all about working for a living?"

"Teager? Nobody thought he was good for either—well?" Del was tired of playing and let her tone show it. "How did it go down? What did you find on his computer?"

"Okay, boys and girls, preacher's gonna preach. Sit up and pay attention, 'cause I just made your lives very easy. Or at least very interesting."

He stood, shifting his weight from foot to foot. Del had trouble containing her excitement. They wouldn't have gotten warrants without something good.

"A couple weeks ago, Mason here—" Jones gestured at Del, "sent out an informal request for everybody's perv-on-the-loose files."

Phan nodded impatiently. "And submitted a formal request for info as well. We know."

"Because of that," Jones continued, shooting Phan a look, "a couple things happened. A few of our guys followed up on their guys who'd never been charged, guys they liked for sex crimes but they didn't have any evidence on."

"Jones—"

"So, one of them's retired—Garibaldi?"

Del nodded, recognizing the name of a retired officer she'd spoken with a few times. She kept her smiling mouth pressed in a thin line so she wouldn't interrupt Jones's circuitous progress.

"Thirty years ago, he served in the Marine Corps with a guy named Johnson, who was a Fed until he retired. His brother's kid followed in his footsteps. Johnson's nephew just happened to be one of the Feds assigned to this case after the second kidnapping. Johnson and Garibaldi are catching up one day, and they chat about the case. Follow all that, my congregation of two?" Jones took a deep breath. "Okay, the Patriot Act? Heard of it?"

Both detectives nodded, exchanging glances. Del had a flash of her dining room, an Ernie White-themed testament to her willingness to exploit the Patriot Act and invade the privacy of a citizen who wasn't actually under investigation.

"So Garibaldi talks to his fellow jarhead about this sweet lady at Mission Station who's curious about all these bad guys who never got charged. They talk about how nice it would be to know what those bad guys are looking at online."

"Oh."

"Yes." Jones nodded. "Garibaldi's buddy calls his nephew and tells him about their conversation. Something happens, who knows what, and some Fed boss we've never seen sends Bradley a long, formal email offering a 'higher level of assistance and interagency cooperation' without actually specifying what that will entail. What that ends up being is a data dump comprised of nine banker boxes of paperwork delivered an hour after the email was sent. Bradley thinks they're fucking with him, naturally. He's going to put some flunky on it. He thinks it's probably nothing but of course can't ignore these boxes stacked up in his office. The request goes out in a group email we all get."

"I don't remember anything like that," Phan interjected, frowning.

"Maybe because," Jones said, "Bradley forwarded the attached message the Fed told him to send the officers. The subject line said 'Redundant Data Overview Review.' Nobody read it. Bradley assigned some rookies to sort through the information. They're rookies, so they created a ridiculously complicated spreadsheet no one could understand. Bradley asked me if I could look at it, and—"

"What did you find?" Del forced herself to breathe normally.

"The Feds created a list of seventeen likely subjects, and Ronald Teager was one of them. For each likely subject there was a data set, and there was a lot of data on Teager. Two years ago, when he bought a new laptop, our man Teager was spending two or three hours a day online, looking at porn. He liked all kinds for a while, and then he got into the specialty stuff. That's what porn addicts do, they need more and more intense stimulation. Bondage, girls asleep or drunk or high, gang bangs, animals, torture, shit like that. He spent hour after hour watching and downloading really weird shit. Pretty soon all of it was freaky."

"How does this help us?" Phan sounded more irritated than curious, and Del shot him a look. Jones had been working all night, obviously. He clearly had something good to offer.

"Sit tight. Soon the porn was all one theme. Girls asleep, girls asleep and tied up. Girls passed out or drugged or whatever. I mean, he watched hours and hours of this. He's looking at porn just at night for a while, but then it's all the time. Twelve, fourteen hours a day or more. I don't know when the fucker sleeps or works or anything. He's saving shit on several external hard drives, he watches things over and over. He starts looking up criminal cases involving women and girls being kidnapped, drugged and raped. He downloads all kinds of info on rapes. He downloads books describing forensic science and investigative procedures, true-crime books."

"He studied." Phan's voice was flat.

"Our boy's a regular fucking scholar. His history tells the whole tale. Teager's watching the same shit over and over, he's reading the same shit over and over. He has three laptops and two tablets. He even has a desktop. He's taking notes, making plans and to-do lists. He's got a menu. Recipes for drug cocktails. He writes a journal detailing his hopes and fears. He starts hanging out in chat rooms, calls himself Prince Charming. He's cagey at first, asking guys if they like sleeping beauties."

"There are two of them." Del felt her mouth drop open. "That's why he has an alibi for some of the incidents. He has a partner. We talked about that—"

She saw Phan's gaze dart to her face. She chucked her chin at Jones so he'd continue.

"Ding, ding, ding, a prize for the little lady. About eight months ago, Teager finds a buddy. Guy calls himself The Sandman. Both capitals, you know? And they get to chatting about how nice it is when a girl is just a little sleepy. How it makes things so much better if she'll just close her eyes and go limp and let him play."

"Nice." Del pressed her lips together.

Jones's expression reflected a mixture of disgust at his topic and glee at whatever prize his work had netted. "Right? And, man, they go off! Teager and The Sandman spend a few weeks in a private chat room talking about all the shit they wanna do. How society is so judgmental and prudish. Women use sex to manipulate men, women are bitches and users and whores, a man ain't a man unless he can take what he wants. A man deserves all the pu—sex he wants, and any woman who denies him deserves to be punished. Our boys work each other up into a big, pervy lather. They exchange personal emails, start sending each other pictures, videos, links to websites. They swap tips about avoiding detection. Prince Charming—Teager—tells Sandman bad weather makes it easier to sneak up on a house. Sandman explains how important it is to establish plausible deniability. They're excellent collaborators."

"Gross." Del grimaced. "Like minds."

"Jones," Phan asked, "the videos, the pictures—are they useful to us?"

"Step off and wait for it." Jones dropped the candy onto the desk. "At that point, all the media is from websites. But then something happens. Teager is offline for four days, and Sandman starts freaking out. He wants to know where Teager is. Then Prince Charming—that's Teager—comes back and says his mom died. They go on for a while about how she was a whore like all women."

Phan made a face. "Do the dates line up with when Teager's mother died?"

Jones grinned widely. "Yes they do. Teager offers Sandman a present. It's a .jpg—that's a picture for you children of the dinosaur age—and it's crap. Blurry, dark, grainy—a woman in a nightgown, lying in her bed, under the covers, sleeping. The pic was taken through the window, looks like. Sandman asks who it is, and Teager says it's his neighbor."

Del exchanged glances with Phan. "So Teager sent Sandman, whoever that is, a picture taken from outside the window of his neighbor's bedroom? And this is just after his mother died?"

Jones nodded vigorously. "Yeah. And over the next couple weeks he sends dozens of .jpgs to Sandman. All taken from outside windows. They're grainy, distorted. Some of them, you can see bird shit on the glass, streaks, stuff like that. Women and girls, dressing, undressing, just standing there. Sleeping. At first, all ages, all races, all types. But after a few weeks, it's all skinny brunettes. Twenty to forty. Lots of them asleep."

Del smiled. "So Teager is the peeper?"

"Most of our peeper's victims are in there." Jones grimaced. "There are a lot more we didn't know about."

Phan jumped in. "Let me guess. Sandman likes the pictures, keeps egging Teager on. He wants him to do something besides take pictures. He keeps trying to get Teager to rape one of them."

"Right." Jones continued, "Teager isn't too sure, he's worried about getting caught. He says he just wants to look at them. He doesn't want to go to jail. So Sandman starts teasing him. Asks if he's a man or bitch. And Teager gets mad."

Del points at Jones. "He asks what Sandman's ever done."

"Bingo! And there's radio silence." Jones shrugs. "But after a week or so, Teager and Sandman start kind of reaching out to each other." Jones stretched out his long, thin arm and waggled his fingers toward Phan. "Like to make sure they're both still alive and not jailed. They're worried. I mean, they're porn buddies."

"Porn buddies?" Del frowned.

Phan laughed and mirrored Jones's gesture. "Yeah, you know, if I die suddenly, my porn buddy is supposed to go to my house and clean out all my nasty stuff so my wife or my mom or whoever doesn't find it. I do the same for him."

Del looked from Phan to Jones. "Is that a real thing? Do you guys have porn buddies?"

Jones laughed. "I'm a guy, remember?"

Phan raised his hands in a wordless protestation of innocence.

"Anyway," Jones continued, "Sandman sends Teager a movie. He's got a woman in a van. She's out. I mean, totally out of it. And he undresses her, messes around with her."

"Is it our first kidnapping victim?"

Jones nodded impatiently. "Teager gets it, he's shitting his pants. He thinks it was awesome. Sandman wants Teager to step up his game, but he's still scared."

"Let me guess," Del said, "Sandman keeps pushing him."

"Yup." Jones continued, perching on the edge of the desk, "Sends him a second video—yes, it's the second victim."

Del and Phan exchanged a glance.

"They take a vow," Jones said. "They're brothers. They'll alibi each other. They'll stick together no matter what. Sandman promises Teager he can help him get a girl and they can share her. Teager's eager but scared. Keeps backing out of the deal. They talk about how to keep from leaving any physical evidence. They make a plan. They—"

"So Teager was there with Leslie Thorne?" Phan rapped his fingers on the desk. "He helped?"

"He watched. Sandman messed around with her, and Teager freaked. He left and went to the station to file his phony report, and he didn't even realize she was dead until the next day."

Del touched Jones on the arm. "Question is, can we use this, keep Teager locked up?"

"They should both be locked up for a while." Phan grimaced. "If we can find out who Sandman is." He gestured a question at Jones.

"Yeah. Well, Teager's really been freaking out since he found out the girl died."

"Leslie Thorne," Del inserted, exchanging glances with Phan.

"Yeah, he's erasing stuff, warning Sandman. But as you know I'm a genius—archived everything related to Teager."

"Thank God," Del and Phan said in unison.

"See," Jones said, stretching arms up and out. "Preacher preached, and the heathens got religion."

"Hallelujah." Del put her hand over her heart. "Jones, I think I love you. Any chance you'll be able to figure out who Sandman is?"

"Who, me?"

"Who else?" Phan offered a sycophantic grin.

"I'm working on it. Fucker's going down." Jones tapped his forehead. "Feds are en route with our uniforms for support, got federal warrants for Teager's arrest, his place, his computers."

"You forgot your candy," Del called as Jones turned away.

"I'm on a diet," the computer specialist responded, waving over his shoulder as he walked off to his undersized cubicle. "Family history of diabetes means I don't eat candy anymore. Next time, bring protein bars. And hey, Mason? Thanks for asking about my mom, huh?"

Del nodded and turned to Phan. "This won't hold water unless we get something we can use that's not from the Feds and inadmissible."

"Yeah, so where are we?"

"Teager could turn on Sandman," Del suggested with more hope than conviction.

"You got a chicken or goat to sacrifice?"

By nine the station was full, as though someone had sent a message to everyone that things might actually move. How the word got out, Del never knew, but somehow everyone drifted in and started exchanging ideas for ensnaring Sandman.

Bradley arrived a little after ten, puffed up like a Friday night quarterback, and announced Teager's arrest. He had no further information to share, though, since the Feds were keeping their prize all to themselves.

Davies weighed down Del and Phan with the mountains of paperwork related to Teager's arrest and the search for his buddy, and Del was actually happy to do it. She and Phan didn't leave until nearly nine that night, but they were still on a high from the partial win. The ride home was so quick and easy, and the hour so late, Del didn't realize until she'd parked and gone into the front door that she had entered Lola's house instead of her own.

"Oops," she said aloud. Lola was at the top of the stairs. "Forgot which house I live in. Sorry."

"Don't worry about it." Lola headed down toward her. "Want some dinner?"

"Sure," she said, as casually as she could. "I'm starving. And I have good news."

"For good news, you might get dessert too." Lola seemed to realize then what her words implied, and she flushed and rolled her eyes.

"Only if it's homemade," Del said, following Lola to the kitchen. "If it's store-bought, I'll change the news to mediocre."

Lola giggled at her, and Del felt light and free at that sound. She waited until she'd washed up and eaten a giant bowl of Lola's beef stew before bringing up the case.

"Thanks for dinner," she said. "I forgot to eat today."

Lola smiled, but she seemed tense. She made a pot of tea while Del explained what Anton Jones had found.

"So you knew it was that man Teager even before there was any real reason to? How did you know?"

"Well," Del admitted, "I didn't know. I guessed, because of the way they described the peeper. Then I figured I'd guessed wrong, since he had alibis for some of the incidents. He also didn't seem sophisticated or experienced enough to successfully pull off the kidnappings."

"This Sandman guy committed some of the crimes, which is why Teager had an alibi for some of them?"

"Exactly."

"So how will you get Sandman? How'll you figure out who he is?"

"Jones is hoping to track him back from Teager's computer." Del made a face. "We're hoping Teager will turn on him. I think he'll turn if his interrogation is handled right. Which it won't be. Either the Feds will do it, and I'm not confident about them, or Davies will, and he doesn't have the self-control, or, frankly, the finesse."

"Why can't you—?"

"That's not how it works." Del rubbed her eyes. "There's a hierarchy, and I am nowhere near the top of it."

"But do you have any idea of who he is?"

Del hesitated. Part of her wanted to show off, let Lola think she was the world's most brilliant investigator. But she wasn't. And she didn't have the answer. She'd just about decided to put the case aside and try to talk to Lola about their issues when she heard herself talking.

"Five years ago there was this kid. Mikey. Ten or eleven years old. Single mom, poor, lived in a shitty, overpriced rental. Landlord raped the mom, according to Mikey. Kid freaked. Shot the landlord." Del shook her head. "Mom wouldn't cooperate, wouldn't get a medical exam, wouldn't corroborate the kid's story. I don't know why. I don't know if she'd had bad experiences with police before, or if there was some legal problem, or if the landlord bribed her, or threatened her, or what. Anyway, the rich white landlord got away with rape, and the little brown kid went to juvie for shooting him. The mom died. Cancer. Mikey went from juvie to a group home. Ran away about a year back. Then the kid got murdered a few weeks ago. Me and Phan got called on a body, juvie John Doe. It was our turn. I almost didn't recognize him. We still haven't been able to solve Mikey's murder, and I'm not sure we ever will. That's the case I'd like to solve."

"Oh, Del." Lola reached out and squeezed Del's hand. "How awful."

"Anyway, the landlord was a guy named Ernie White. There's no real reason to think he killed Mikey, not really, but

I keep thinking about the guy. Mikey was the only one who ever stood up to White. Not one woman or kid White had access to ever reported him or talked to police. Phan and I have interviewed over forty women who were tenants or employees of White's family, and not one will say a word against him. They just get the big, faraway eyes, you know what I mean. But Mikey stood up to him and now he's dead. I don't know. Jones and the Patriot Act basically solved the Teager case, and somebody else will break the rest of it and figure out who Sandman is. Or they won't. And we'll get called to work on it or not. Probably not."

"You sound kind of finished with the whole thing."

"Yeah, it's not my ballgame anymore, Davies has it. Ah, it's kind of a letdown and kind of a relief. Now I can focus on Mikey. I owe the kid. I have to know what happened. But there's nothing. We can't find out where he was that last year, who he hung out with, who might have killed him. There's nothing on him from the time he skipped school one day and never showed up at the group home again. Nothing."

"You have a hunch about what happened."

"No." Del smiled. "Yeah. Maybe. I don't know."

"And your hunches are right, time after time."

"I dunno about that. I have a hundred hunches, maybe two are right. Worse than a clock." Del smiled at Lola's confidence in her. "But I want to pursue White some more. Just 'cause I owe Mikey and I can't do anything else for him. Back when, White seemed to want to hurt Mikey. Like it was personal. He couldn't get to the kid while he was locked up, but once he was out—maybe I just didn't like the guy."

"Go get 'em." Lola's tone was matter-of-fact. "He sounds like a terrible person."

"He is," Del said. "I broke my own rules with White, got a buddy to give me this mountain of data on White, where he goes, his spending habits, all the digital footprints he's left over the last few years. My dining room is a war room on White. That can't be healthy. And it's useless anyway. I can't get anything on the guy even with all that data, which I shouldn't have." Forestalling the question she saw coming, Del shrugged. "You know I hate the way nine-eleven changed us."

Lola shook her head. "We've never talked about it."

"There's a lot of stuff we haven't done." She sat back, pushing away her empty bowl. "The Feds have gotten more and more intrusive, spying on private citizens, collecting data on all of us, using the Patriot Act and intrusive Homeland Security practices to push aside our civil rights."

"It's hard," Lola said, "they have to prevent terrorists. But—"

"Exactly," Del cut in. "Anyway, I got this huge file on White, just page after page of information on where he's been, what he's bought, who he's been in touch with, all this stuff. But there's mountains of it. I've been going through it, trying to make a timeline, trying to find patterns. If I can't find Mikey's killer, maybe at least I can get the asshole who put him in the place that made him vulnerable. And I'm getting nowhere."

"Sounds pretty frustrating."

"Yeah." Del looked away, gathering her thoughts. "On a totally different track, I was thinking about what you said. You know, about us?"

"Ah." Lola seemed to be processing the shift in topic at her own pace. "And?"

"You scare the hell out of me."

"I do?" Lola gave a nervous laugh. "What do you mean?"

"I don't know." Though she'd started it, Del wanted out of the conversation. "You just do."

"Good."

Lola smiled at Del's snort. "If you're scared and I'm scared, we're in the same boat. We can start from, we're both scared and trying to figure it out. Okay?"

"Yeah." Del nodded. "Okay."

CHAPTER FOURTEEN

They stood holding each other for a long time. Del felt Lola's warmth and breathing and wondered how she'd managed to forget how much Lola meant to her. She wandered home with her thoughts full of Mikey Ocampo and Ernie White. She started to disassemble her war room, sickened by the realization that she'd let the predator take up space in her home and in her head. But before she'd taken down more than a few sheets of paper, she was struck by a thought. On impulse she called Mac.

"You know it's the middle of the night here, right?"

"Sorry." She wondered if Mac understood that the apology was meant to cover more than the late-night intrusion.

"This about the lecherous landlord?" Mac sounded tired, and she mumbled an affirmative, struck by a sudden awareness that she had no idea how old Mac was. "Okay, let's update. Check your email in about ten, fifteen minutes. And Mason? Get some damn sleep and let everyone else get some too. Asshole will still be around tomorrow."

After a quick shower Del read the update from Mac. She texted Phan to ask if he could call her, despite the late hour, which he did.

"This better be good."

Del gripped her cell phone. "Sorry—listen, I was thinking about porn buddies."

"I'm not gonna be your porn buddy, Mason." Phan's voice sounded tired. "Especially if you can't let me get twenty minutes of sleep."

Del shook her head. "I've been assuming all these years that White did rape Mikey's mother. But we don't know. I don't know."

Phan huffed. "Unless you have something worth saying—"

"I know him, how he gets these women in the rental properties, how he insinuates himself in their lives. You know how these guys are too, they start violating the women's privacy bit by bit. They say they stopped by to check on the plumbing and stuff like that. Like it's perfectly legit, but it's not. Like the Feds do with us, violate our privacy bit by bit. They make it seem reasonable but it's not. It's the same thing pedophiles do. They groom their victims. They cross the line a little bit, then a little more. They acclimate the kid to grosser and grosser violations—it's the same pattern. It's always the same pattern."

"Jesus, Mason, where is this headed?"

"I started thinking, what about Sandman?"

"What do you mean, what about Sandman?"

"You and Jones, you were talking about it. Guys who like porn have a porn buddy in case they die or something. Now that Teager's popped, who's Sandman's new porn buddy?"

"It was a joke. I don't actually—"

"But some guys do, right? Sandman cultivated this friendship. He pushed Teager to go further than he would've on his own. Sandman groomed him. Like a pedophile grooms a victim."

"Ah." Phan sounded less sleepy. "Like Janet groomed Sterling."

Del bit her lip. "Anyway, one of the things these guys sometimes do is, they groom more than one. They're working one kid, they're working this other one just in case, maybe a bunch of kids at once. So what if our guy is the same? What if he was grooming Teager and some other guy too?"

"So, what are you saying?" Phan spoke in a quiet, reasonable tone. "Jones has already been looking at the chat rooms, trying to connect Teager and Sandman with other guys. He hasn't found anything significant."

"We have to pursue this aggressively, Phan, we—"

"And what?" Phan said. "Hack into his computer? Illegally monitor his Internet usage? What exactly are you talking about? You already did that, remember? You haven't come up with shit even after you got ahold of your Fed buddy—and don't think I haven't noticed how shy you've been about that—and broke your own protocol and still didn't come up with anything."

"I know, but listen." Del made a face at the phone. "If we try to rope Sandman in with a new pal, he'll just shut down. He's gotta be wary after Teager was arrested. And maybe he hasn't been grooming another Teager. Maybe. But if you were Sandman, what would you be doing right now?"

Phan remained silent.

"What would you be doing right now, what would you be thinking?"

"I'd be worried Teager would turn on me. If I couldn't get him released, if I couldn't have him killed, I'd be erasing my tracks. Cutting any possible ties between him and me."

"You'd make sure there was nothing tying you to it," Del said. "That's what Ernie White was doing after he got out of the hospital when Mikey shot him five years ago." Del stared at her dining room wall, tacked up with paper. "That was a natural thing to do, right? If you'd been breaking the law and maybe taking pics of your rape victims, or bragging to your buddies, or whatever—if somebody actually said you raped his mom, you'd want to cover your tracks, right? Even if you knew nobody would believe the kid, if you've intimidated the mom so much she'll never come forward."

"How do you know—?"

Del chuckled. "His financials. Back then we only looked for money moving from White to Mikey's mom. But that was all we knew to look for. A little while ago I called a friend in Homeland Security and just heard back. White paid somebody to wipe his tech clean. Bought a new phone, new computers where you can partition your hard drives, all kinds of fancy encryption software. He wanted to cover his tracks."

"So you want to prove White is Sandman by showing Sandman's doing the same thing. There's some kind of signature to the housecleaning process?" Phan spoke with a touch of belligerence. "Where's this going, Mason? You want to see who's been buying pricey electronics? I don't see what your plan is here."

"All I'm saying is, sometimes we catch them, not because of what they did to kill the victim, but because of what they did to cover it up."

"Okay," Phan said with finality. "I'm out. No more late night, random brainstorming sessions. When you have some kinda cogent plan, great. Until then, I'm going to head back to my girlfriend. Yes, she's actually thinking about taking me back, or was until you called me."

"Sorry!" Del grimaced. "Say sorry to Alana for me."

Del eyeballed her table, covered in dozens of stacked printouts of the data on Ernie White. There was so much paper covered in so much information that she couldn't seem to get anything useful out of it. She'd become so immersed in the past and the possibilities that nothing was clear to her. She was entombed in mental fog. But how could she get out of that? What were the blind alleys and what were the paths to redemption?

She thought of Nana and her weird religious fervor at the end of her life, how bizarrely evangelical and judgmental she'd become, convinced that everyone around her was a terrible sinner who was just covering up their tracks. Had that been part of what made Daddy fall apart? It couldn't have been easy, watching his mom lose her marbles like that. Had she been mentally ill or just pickled from alcohol and ignorance? Would Del end up going crazy too? Families could make a person crazy. Hadn't the job taught her that?

On impulse Del ran a quick check through all the paper to see what she could put together on Ernie White's mother. Eleanor Jane White had been born in Oklahoma and lived in Kansas, Missouri and Texas, picking up and surviving a well-to-do husband in each state. With her increasingly sizable inheritances, she dragged her young son Ernie with her to California, buying up one rental property after another and amassing an even larger fortune as the years went on. She'd died several months back, leaving her fortune to her only child. She'd been the defendant in dozens of slumlord lawsuits and the subject of two antitrust investigations, and she'd won or settled each of them. She'd let Ernie play property manager and given him a very generous allowance, but she'd stayed in charge until her short illness and death.

Del paced the house, trying to process what she'd learned about Eleanor White. Did any of it matter? All it really meant was that White had gone from playing errand boy to being the big man. Had his mother killed her husbands? Did White believe his mom had murdered her husbands? He'd taken control of an estate worth tens of millions and had done little with it other than live off the interest and dividends and fly to countries where he could buy sex with even greater impunity than in the United States.

Over the last weeks, she'd examined dozens of photos produced with her low-end printer: White in front of his mother's Los Altos mansion, White in front of his own Sunset-District mansion, White in front of his black Lexus, the fourth in five years, and now his old one because he'd traded that one in on yet another black Lexus a couple of weeks back. After her run Del emailed White's Redwood City Lexus dealer to ask if the dealership still had the model White had traded in. She wanted a carpet sample from the trunk. It was a longer-than-long shot but worth the time and effort to run it down, if only so she could put it out of her mind.

It was after three in the morning when she finally dropped into bed, shaking with exhaustion and trying to remember how many days it had been since Mikey's murder.

Five hours later she walked into the station to find Phan waiting for her.

"Okay. Talk to me, partner. Something obviously happened. Is it cake? Did Bradley get us cake?"

Phan rolled his eyes. "You know the Feds took Teager from us."

"And credit for his arrest, naturally. And?"

"He says he won't talk to anybody but you."

* * *

There was a fuss about it. The Feds didn't like it, and Davies did some grumbling, but Bradley played the proud papa and escorted Del into the block-long federal building on Golden Gate Avenue like he was walking her down the aisle.

"Any questions, Mason? Anything you need before you go in?"

Del shook her head. She wished Phan were with her, but she got it—Bradley might end up getting a promotion out of this, unless she messed up. He could move up to commander and maybe end up a deputy chief within a few years. This was good for Bradley, and she didn't begrudge him that. She would still be a lowly flatfoot, one of the nameless, faceless rabble the savvy step on as they ascend the ladder. But that was okay, she realized. She was doing what she wanted to do. Some of what she was feeling must have shown on her face, but Bradley misread it.

"It's perfectly natural to feel nervous. You'll do fine," he put in. "You've interviewed hundreds of guys smarter than Teager."

Del nodded and smiled her thanks. They were wanded into the lobby and scanned into some inner sanctum, where several very self-important men in suits tried to make them feel like yokels.

Del let Bradley play ambassador while she considered what to say and what to look for in Teager. Who was he, really? What would work best with him? She'd come a long way since her early years as an investigator. Even when she'd been working sex crimes, she'd been clumsy, relying on instinct rather than deliberate strategy. Homicide had helped her get better at that. She considered several approaches, keeping her face neutral and her posture relaxed. Federal agents pretended not to observe her while they made small talk with Captain Bradley.

Her first day at the Mission station came back to her with painful clarity. She'd been sloppy, letting her emotions guide her in her interview with Mikey. She'd been even worse when interviewing Ernie White in the hospital, letting him see her disgust and disdain. She'd handle both differently now. But that didn't do Mikey any good. She'd let him slip through the cracks with her sloppiness and carelessness. She'd ruined things with Lola by being sloppy and careless too.

She'd learned to be a better investigator. She could learn to be a better partner too.

She followed Bradley and the Feds out of the beige-and-fluorescent elevator into a beige-and-fluorescent hallway and a beige-and-fluorescent conference room.

There was a long meeting during which the Feds declaimed both their superiority and interest in helping the hapless yokels from SFPD. At least Del surmised it was something along those lines. She wasn't really listening. She made the right faces, nodded at the right times, and mentally ran through several different possible tactical plans for dealing with Teager. She realized everyone was looking at her expectantly and smiled with what she hoped was the appropriate balance of receptiveness and determination.

"Captain Bradley and the rest of the department and I appreciate this collaborative effort." Del looked around, noting the clear power struggle between the Fed who was overtly the boss and the other Fed who seemed to actually be running the show. Their teams were evenly divided along the two sides of the long conference table. "Is there anything else you'd like to share with us? Any insights you think might be particularly—?"

She didn't have to finish. The two competing Feds both jumped in, offering bland nothings about Teager and Sandman and sex crimes and their delight at a female officer's involvement in the interdepartmental investigation. It took seventeen minutes for them to run out of worthless things to say. Finally, after the requisite time-wasting, she and Bradley went on another interminable elevator ride to another bland hallway and another bland conference room, where they cooled their heels for another half hour. Bradley had by this time run out of small talk, and Del had settled into the half-life of waiting that had accompanied her every interaction with the federal government.

Finally she was led into an interview room where Teager sat shackled to a wide brown table. Close up, he looked less like Boo Radley than a preadolescent boy. He straightened up when she entered and actually smiled like they were meeting for lunch at Fisherman's Wharf. His teeth were too small, his chin weak, his eyes ringed with nervous fatigue.

"I hear you want to talk to me," she said, returning his welcoming grin. "I'd introduce myself, but I understand you already know me, Mr. Teager."

Teager sat back, a frown creasing his small, childlike features. He looked like a pouting kindergartener.

"Ronnie, call me Ronnie," he said.

"High school must have sucked for you," she said on impulse, "with that baby face."

"You don't know the half of it." Teager seemed pleased by her insight. "Mother didn't understand."

"I'm sorry for your loss," Del offered. "Or—?"

"Yes, thanks." Teager licked his lips. "She could be difficult at times, but she was my mother."

"Did she require much care before she passed?"

"No, no, Mother was ferocious right up until the end. I thought she was in perfect health."

"So her death was sudden. She passed, and you found yourself lonely and at loose ends," she prompted. "Vulnerable."

"Yes." Teager's head bobbed up and down. "I know I've made some mistakes."

"Yes." Del kept her expression neutral.

"I never really would have done all those things, I never would have—"

Del let silence follow Teager's faltering.

"I never intended—it's important you know I never wanted to hurt anyone."

"No?" Del shook her head. "Leslie Thorne—"

"No! That wasn't my idea! I didn't want to hurt anyone, I swear, I just—he made me!" Teager was red-faced, sweating. His eyes searched hers.

"Oh, come on, Ronald!" Del noticed she'd adopted a scolding tone and softened it only slightly. "'He made me do it'?"

"He did!"

Del shook her head.

"It's just," Teager whined, "I never had a father, I never had a male role model, and he was there for me in my time of need. I was vulnerable, like you said. You have to understand, you have to see how it was!"

Del crossed her arms. "How can I? Ronald, you haven't told me anything, you've just been making excuses."

"Call me Ronnie, please?" Teager gave her the big puppy eyes, and Del sniffed.

"Ronnie," she started, noting the beginning of a smile on his face, "is the name of a friend, someone who trusts you and helps you. You're not doing either."

"I don't know his name! I swear!" Teager actually stuck out his lower lip, and Del had to fight the urge to laugh.

"But you could tell me things." She leaned forward, let her expression soften. "You're the only one who can help me."

"I want to help you. Only I'm scared."

Aware of their audience, Del leaned even closer to Teager. "I need your help. I need you to be brave." She watched Teager's eager smile widen, his flush deepen.

Teager took a deep breath and nodded once. "He's weird-looking, Sandman. Like an albino or something. Like that movie with Chevy Chase and Goldie Hawn, remember? Mother loved that movie."

"With the cigarettes and the knitting needles," Del said, playing along. "He looked like an albino?" She let disbelief cover her budding excitement. Ernie White's eyebrows and eyelashes were light blond, nearly white. Was that what Teager meant? Or was he fishing, trying to see how close they were to Ernie White?

"Not exactly. He—I took a picture of him, but they have my phone. They took it!" He seemed to expect sympathy, but Del only nodded her comprehension. Unless Teager's picture showed White actually committing a crime, it could be explained away by a good defense attorney. If there was one thing she knew for sure about Ernie White it was that he could afford a good defense attorney.

"I'll check it out, but I need more." Del sighed. "I'm worried, Ronnie. What might this man do? He seems—"

"Dangerous? He is, he's very dangerous."

"Well," Del murmured, "before you met him, you never hurt anyone, right?"

"And I still haven't hurt anyone, I swear, Inspector Mason. I wouldn't. I couldn't. I'm not a criminal! I'm not some monster! I'm a decent guy, I'm a regular guy. I just had a hard time sometimes."

"Women can be very judgmental." Del worried she'd overplayed it, but Teager nodded eagerly.

"I just want to—Sandman made it all much worse. He scares me. He really scares me."

"I know." Del sat back, crossed her arms, gnawed as though absently on her thumbnail. "But unless we can identify him and convict him, this'll all get blamed on you and he'll just run free and keep pulling innocent guys into his web. And all the women! He'll hurt so many women."

"I know, I know, but what can I do? I don't know who he is." Teager's eyes brimmed, and Del watched him. She felt dirty, manipulating the little idiot, especially since she wasn't at all sure it would help anything. Suddenly she gasped theatrically.

"Something just occurred to me, Ronnie." She leaned forward again, reaching out her hand as if to take his. "A lawyer is going to show up, he's going to tell you to stop talking to me. Sandman will hire a lawyer to get you stop talking to me and then at the end of it you'll get blamed for everything. That's what I predict."

Teager gaped at her and looked at the door as though he expected a two-headed lizard in a three-piece suit to storm in and forcibly hold its feet over his mouth. Del looked too, hoping Bradley or one of the stupid Feds would take the hint. It took nearly ninety seconds by Del's count, but finally someone knocked on the door, some thirty-year-old in a blue suit who looked like all the other thirty-year-olds in blue suits. He couldn't have looked more like a Fed, with his standard-issue haircut and closed expression, but it seemed to work. Teager gasped. His gaze swung back to Del's face.

"No!" He leaned back against his chair, fighting his restraints. "I don't want a lawyer, I don't want one! I want to talk to her! I want her!"

The Fed backed away, his hands up, letting the door shut in front of him.

Del and Teager shared a conspiratorial grin. She debated giving him a thumbs-up and decided against it. He was a successful techie, so while he seemed naïve and easily manipulated he wasn't an idiot. His salary was easily twice hers. For all she knew, he could be playing her as much as she was playing him.

"Listen," she said, throwing caution to the wind, "maybe there are things you noticed, things you didn't even realize you noticed, and we could use those to—"

"His car," Teager said. "He had a fancy black car. We—he took the girl in the van, but he was in a black car."

"Do you remember what kind? What brand?"

Teager closed his eyes. She watched his lids move as he searched his memory.

"Fancy," he murmured. "Expensive, that's all I know. I'm not a car guy. It's not a good expenditure of money beyond a certain point."

"Okay." Del pushed her hair back off her forehead. She'd gotten it shorn just before Mikey's murder, and the curls were already outgrown enough to bug her. "Listen, you're tired, and so am I. Can we take a little break? You can get some food, I can go try to find something we can use to help you. Okay?"

Teager's disappointment was palpable, and Del let herself show some of her frustration and dismay too. She could imagine Teager's dragging this thing out until there was nothing meaningful left to find. He could offer her a million tidbits, half of them true, and White's lawyer would use those to poke holes in any case they managed to make.

Phan called her as she walked from the room. "Hey, you got a message, some car salesman? How's it going?"

"It's going," she said, clicked off, and checked her phone, seeing both a voice mail and an email from White's most recent Lexus salesman. The guy had made a ton of money off White, and he had to be wondering if she was White's friend or foe. She'd asked the dealership not to mention her query to White, but she couldn't be sure the sales manager or his star seller had complied.

"Mr. Devlin, this is a delicate situation." She kept her voice bright and let a note of chagrin creep in. "We're concerned about Mr. White."

"Ernie White is a very good customer, Inspector Mason." The dealer seemed rattled. "I wouldn't want to—"

"The thing is, we're not sure if he's been the victim of a crime or not, and because he is such an important man—you knew his mother, Eleanor, I presume? After her death, Mr. White came into a rather large inheritance, and sometimes folks in that position are good targets for a mercenary—well, we'd like to check it out and don't want to alarm him unless there's something to tell him about."

"I'm not sure I understand, ma'am. I—"

"All we need to know is if his old car is still there so we can take a look at it. I'm afraid I can't really tell you more than that. It's nothing to do with your dealership, but we'd like to prevent any embarrassment or upset for Mr. White. You understand."

Despite the fact that she hadn't said anything of substance, or perhaps because of it, the guy seemed eager to cooperate. The car was still there, as it happened. Of course he wanted to help. Of course he understood. Discretion was the soul of—blah, blah, blah. Del tuned out after that. She had to get back to Teager.

Bradley approached her, his face a show of curiosity. She asked him to get the Feds to start the process of getting a search warrant. She texted him the relevant information. Once they had the warrant, they could obtain samples from White's traded-in Lexus, which still sat on the lot. It had doubtless been cleaned, but Del couldn't ignore the possibility of a lead. Bradley hustled off, looking glad to have something to do.

An hour later she was again sitting across from Teager and could smell the navy bean soup and apple pie he'd eaten, courtesy of the federal government. She'd forgotten to eat, and her stomach rumbled loudly.

"They could get you something," Teager offered, gesturing at the camera.

"I don't know, how was the food?"

Teager wiggled his fingers in a gesture of ambivalence, and Del smiled and shook her head.

"Thanks anyway. Listen, I had a thought. I'd like to tell you a little bit about what I did instead of eating lunch."

Teager tried to smile but ended up grimacing instead. Del noted this but didn't acknowledge the expression.

"There was a fiber at this crime scene a few weeks ago. A murder. I have a suspect, and of course I can't say who it is. Anyway, I think you may have helped me solve it. What I'm hoping is that we can get him on that murder—this suspect—and then use that to gain leverage. Then we can help you. Explain how he pushed you to do things you didn't want to do. Maybe you were scared of him? Maybe he threatened you?"

Teager's eyes were wide, the pupils huge. His face got splotchy. Del kept her breathing steady, her expression neutral. She'd expected Teager to feel relief, not panic.

"So, we got hold of his car, the one he had when he murdered the victim, and we're taking samples now." She smiled brightly at Teager. "I imagine you'll feel much better when we can corroborate the theory with forensic evidence. It's amazing, the

FBI has this database of all the carpet fibers from all the cars from all the years. We can use it to identify—"

"I'm sick," Teager croaked, his hand over his mouth. "I'm gonna barf." He tried to stand but was shackled and stood hunched over and trapped, his whole body shaking.

Del was ushered from the room by a quartet of Feds who whisked her out of the building before she managed to blink more than a dozen times.

Bradley quizzed her on the way back to the station, but she could honestly say she didn't know what to think. When she recapped the brief meeting for Phan, he raised his eyebrows.

"What do you think it means?"

"I don't know." Del picked at a turkey sandwich Phan had set on her desk. "Could he have been involved in Mikey's murder? It just doesn't seem likely, does it? He knew Sandman—dammit, White—when Mikey was killed, but he was still tentative then. I think. I thought. God, I don't know anymore."

She thought about inviting Phan to her house and showing him the dining room she'd turned into a shrine to the investigation into Ernie White, but she didn't want to see his eyes turn cool, his demeanor reflect concern over her obvious obsession. She knew she'd come at the thing all wrong, personalizing it instead of maintaining her detachment. She'd been sloppy, just like she was always sloppy.

She knew the cost. Hadn't she paid that cost over and over, and inflicted that cost on everyone who'd ever loved or depended on her? She told Phan she was tired and left him staring after her as she fled the station.

At home she stood in the dining room, turning a slow circle to take in the evidence of her own mishandling of the case. She got a half-dozen banker boxes from the garage, which she still had yet to organize properly, and boxed up everything she'd printed out from Mac's gift to her. It had been a gift, all of it, and one she'd neither deserved nor properly thanked Mac for giving. She grabbed her cell phone.

"What now, Mason?"

"I'm sorry." Del knew her voice quavered but continued. "And thank you for helping me even after I—"

"You don't owe me anything, thanks or apologies." Mac's voice was quiet, far away. "We don't do things like that."

"I didn't—if anything, I—"

"Yes you did."

Del bit her lip. "Maybe we should do things like that."

"Jesus, kiddo," Mac retorted. "Hang up before this turns into a Hallmark moment."

Del felt a little better after that, though they really hadn't said anything. Maybe sometime they'd actually talk. Maybe not. Mac was a pretty closed book and always had been.

She'd hoped the distraction would give her some clarity on Teager's odd response to her mention of the carpet fibers. The truth was, even if the Feds did the lab work, even if the carpets were still the same, even if somehow they actually did get some kind of exclusion that said the carpet fiber was very, very likely to have come from the same exact model black Lexus owned by White at the time of Mikey's murder, that still didn't mean much without corroborating evidence. There were a lot of people in the city who owned the same model. A good defense attorney would eat that kind of circumstantial evidence for lunch. As if at the thought of lunch, Del's stomach rumbled. Three bites of the sandwich Phan had given her hadn't quite done the job.

She called him, thinking she owed him both thanks and an apology. It was an echo of her thought about Mac, and as she waited for Phan to answer she thought about how many women, Janet and Lola included, she owed both thanks and apologies to. Patterns, she thought idly, people always behave according to patterns that they mostly don't see clearly themselves. Even if they can see other people's patterns.

"He cut a deal." Phan said by way of a greeting.

"Just like that?" Del shook her head. "Seriously?"

"You know why?"

"Leslie Thorne," Del guessed.

"Mikey Ocampo."

Del sank into a chair.

In the silence, Phan filled her in. "Teager had a burner phone, Sandman had told him to get it so they could have nice little heart-to-hearts."

"And?"

"When Teager saw the Feds coming a-knocking, he used his burner to warn Sandman about his arrest, and Sandman threatened him. Told Teager he'd pin two deaths on him."

"Teager didn't know who the second death was." Del leaned forward as if Phan were across the dining room table from her. "It was Mikey. Sandman had killed Mikey and Teager didn't know about it."

"Teager's a little smarter than Sandman thought. After you left, Teager really did get sick. He was panicked you'd find out who Sandman was."

Del pushed her overgrown hair out of her eyes. "Okay."

"Yeah, the Feds got him to set the guy up in a follow-up call. Got Sandman to confess to Mikey's murder and implicate himself in the sex crimes."

"It's the same guy. It's Ernie White." Del sat back. "It was him all along."

"You got it. Since your buddy pulled White's info twice in the last little while, Homeland Security started taking a more focused look at him."

"More focused?" Del snorted. "They already had the data from his travel, his financials, his everything. They knew how he takes his coffee, Phan."

"Apparently they know a lot more about him now, but they're not sharing."

"So Teager goes to federal prison and White has to decide whether he's going to try his chances in court or plead out, which is what he'd be smart to do. Have they already picked him up?"

"Not as far as I know. But you know how the Feds are. They'll let us read about it after the fact. If they kept us in the loop they might have to share credit for the arrests."

Del processed all of this carefully, picking at a frayed cuticle and not saying anything.

"Hello?" Phan's voice sounded far away.

"I'm glad Teager's caught. I'm glad White is gonna get caught and pay for Mikey's murder. Which of them actually killed Leslie Thorne?"

"Teager still says it was White."

"Okay. Thanks for telling me."

"It sucks, doesn't it?"

"Yeah." Del pushed her hair back. "Glad they can't hurt anybody else, at least for now. But it's a major letdown. We weren't even there. And I'm guessing we don't get to chase him down."

"Yeah. But listen, it all happened because you set it all in motion."

"I guess." Del sighed. "Okay, thanks."

"Hey, we'll worry about the follow-up stuff tomorrow."

"It's like that poem—something about not a bang but a whimper. You know it?"

"Eliot." Phan's voice was as flat as Del's mood. "All too well."

CHAPTER FIFTEEN

Del tried to feel good about the fact that Teager was off the streets, at least for a while. She examined the gathering fog and realized the night would have been a perfect one for Teager if he were free, so there was all the more reason to be glad. Ernie White would be captured by the Feds, hopefully before he could kidnap and assault another woman. With any luck he'd get locked up too. There wasn't a whole lot she could do at this point to make things go better, and there were plenty of capable professionals who were working on building a legal case against both predators. Del was out of it. Things had gone about as well as they could have. Soon the women of the Mission would be a little safer, Mikey's murder was solved, and everyone would feel like they had done something worthwhile.

After a microwaved burrito, a couple of television shows and a slug of vodka, Del was still wound up and decided to go for a run. The sky was clear when she headed out, but, walking the last block home forty minutes later, Del found herself in a thick fog, both literally and figuratively. She felt her phone vibrate in her sock and pulled it out.

"What's up, Phan?"

"Okay don't give me shit for this, I'm just feeling—"

"Like it's unfinished." Del paused in front of Phil and Marco's house, chilled by the evening's mist but not ready to face her empty home.

"They'll catch White. You know that." Phan's heavy sigh pushed into Del's thoughts. "You and me, we're done with this one, we're not on point anymore."

"Yeah."

"Like we're pushed aside. Hey, you got to meet with Teager, I didn't even get that."

Del grimaced, wishing she'd thought about how Phan was feeling. "Yeah, sorry about that, I guess you're not pretty enough."

Phan's laughter filled her ear, and Del smiled.

"Listen, I gotta go, Kaylee's gonna call to ask me if she can do something I think I'm gonna say no to."

"Meanie."

Still feeling wound up, Del was trying to decide whether to go inside or take another loop around the neighborhood when she saw movement by Lola's house. The porch light was still out and the lights were off and the fog was blinding. Her peripheral vision had picked up motion but not a precise location, and she froze, trying to figure out if there was something to pay attention to or not. As she turned her head she felt mist dampen her drooping curls and eyelashes. Was the movement in the house or outside? Had she really seen anything, or had it been the roiling fog?

Del let out a slow, shaky breath. The movement could have been the fog, a cat, some innocent pedestrian, but Del's fired-up senses didn't buy any of those benign possibilities. She felt adrenaline surge through her body, igniting her awareness and tightening her skin. She forced herself to slow down and think. She'd replaced the bulb in Lola's porch light within six months. It shouldn't have burned out. Had someone tampered with the light?

Del felt her stomach muscles clench. Ernie White hadn't been apprehended, as far as she knew. Assuming that it was

Teager who'd gotten fixated on short brunettes, she'd failed to think through the details of White's possible psychosexual fixations. There was no reason for him to come after her, no reason for him to go after Lola. If he had any sense of self-preservation, he would stay as far from police officers as possible.

But what if there was something more important to White than self-preservation? What if his ego wouldn't allow him to consider the possibility that he could be apprehended or convicted? Del eased her way across the street, wondering if she was visible to any possible assailant, White or not. Suddenly impatient with herself, Del sped up her progress toward Lola's house. She reached the bottom of the stairs and saw movement out of the corner of her eye. Was the assailant now behind her? Was there even an assailant?

Del's hand was already hovering over her waistband, searching for her duty weapon when a creature, either a smallish possum or a huge rat, scuttled along the fence, heading toward the yard behind Lola's. Awash in relief and embarrassment over her panic, Del smiled, letting her shoulders sag. Her phone vibrated as if in response, and she jumped, startled. It was Sofia Gonzalez.

"Ms. Gonzalez. You okay?"

"No." The whisper was barely audible.

"You home?"

"Yes."

"I'll be right there."

Del texted Phan to call it in and meet her at Sofia Gonzalez's house, guessing he, like she, would remember the address the way they automatically recorded any data, never knowing when they might need to recall it in a hurry. Then she raced toward her truck. It was quieter than the bike.

The little bungalow, so cheerful in the sunshine, was gloomy in the fog. The gate north of the house was unlocked and open a few inches. All the lights were off, and Del turned off her headlights a hundred yards away. She left the truck as close as she dared and wished Phan lived closer. She should wait for him, wait for the Response Team. But the panic in Sofia Gonzalez's voice, the way she'd limited herself to whispered monosyllables, told Del time was of the essence. Someone, Del assumed Teager, had been there at least once. Del had figured the first incident, the one Sofia Gonzalez had been made to feel silly for calling in, was Teager too. What if it wasn't?

Skirting the perimeter of the house, peering in windows as she went along, Del made her way to the backyard. There were nine points of entry, from what she recalled, two doors and seven windows. The doors were good ones, heavy-duty with reinforced frames. The windows were the easiest points of ingress. If she were the intruder, she'd hit the window in the small bathroom across the hall from the bedroom. It was big enough for a medium-sized man to enter. There was a garden bench not far from it, wooden, light enough to move quietly and sturdy enough to use as a boost. She reached that farthest side and saw the bench under the bathroom window. She hesitated. Had that been too obvious? What if it was a trap?

That whispered voice had been Sofia Gonzalez's, Del reassured herself. Could it have been recorded? She shook her head. No, it had been Gonzalez. She'd been scared. Could she have been coerced by a captor into responding to Del without giving her a clue?

She pulled her phone back out of her sock and shielded its lighted face. She texted Phan, apprising him of her status. She heard a bang and a woman's quiet, inarticulate voice making some sad, scared little sound. Del vaulted toward the bathroom window, driven by instinct even as she thought of the Eliot poem. Was her world about to end? Or was it already over? Like Mikey's life, like Western civilization, like her relationship with Lola, like the case—had they all just sort of petered off into nothing while she was stumbling around uselessly?

Del pushed the random musing aside as she pulled herself in through the window, rolling into a crouch and peering out into the hall, gun in both hands. She couldn't see Sofia Gonzalez, couldn't see or hear anything. She was cold, damp from the mist that had gathered while she ran and then while she skulked around outside on her own street and then in Gonzalez's yard. She shivered. There was a morsel of sound, an excited, nearly inaudible exhalation. Not her own. She matched her breathing to the rhythm of the other person's breathing. It wasn't Gonzalez's. She had a wide rib cage and the low, slow breathing that came with it. This person was narrower in the chest, proportionate to his height. Tenth grade music class, Del thought with desperate distraction, had taught her to listen to sounds with their sources in mind. Or had it been her parents' drunken, depressed, raging inconsistency? She'd learned to know who was walking around, who was stumbling, who was falling against the fragile walls of their trailer. She'd learned on the job too, of course, how to hear what was barely a vibration and place its source, its velocity and direction. And of course Mac had taught her things she didn't even remember learning. She'd pushed Mac out of her mind, pushed so many things out of her mind.

She was synced with the intruder. He was to her left down the hall, in either the front room or the kitchen. She drew in air with careful deliberation, listening, listening, waiting, listening. She thought of her daddy and how he took her hunting in the woods, how he demonstrated without words how to listen, how to watch, what to do while stalking prey. Had the bad guy's father shown him how to stalk prey too?

He swallowed, a click she heard as clearly as if he'd made the autonomic sound just for her. Kitchen. The white, white, bare kitchen where Sofia Gonzalez didn't cook but ate toasted waffles over the kitchen sink. She listened and waited again but couldn't isolate him more than that. Del couldn't hear Gonzalez at all. She could try to go after him but it would be stupid to do so. Phan was on his way and so was the Response Team. There might be a patrol officer outside right now.

It had been eleven minutes since Del had texted Phan, thirteen since the first call from Gonzalez to Del. White had had plenty of time to prepare for whatever kind of showdown he was planning. Del stayed crouched in the bathroom, her shoulder stiff, her knees screaming, her body aching from the stillness, her head ringing with the effort of silent, attentive listening. She was stuck. She couldn't go back outside without risking leaving Sofia Gonzalez vulnerable and couldn't go forward without risking endangering Gonzalez, Phan, the other officers, and herself. Patience was all she had to offer, now that she'd impulsively, recklessly, stupidly entered the home.

The seconds slid by slowly, inexorably. Phan would come. The others would come. Ernie White preferred to attack women who were unable to defend themselves or get help.

Phan was coolheaded, but he operated on emotion more than he realized. He could be trusted to keep his head until he couldn't, like anybody. The Response Team was comprised of specially trained officers who had that rare and hard-to-keep balance of endless patience and ability to burst into action at a microsecond's notice.

"God." Ernie White's voice sounded exasperated and amused in equal measure. He was still, from what Del could hear, in the kitchen. Was he standing next to the refrigerator? It sounded like it. "I know you're there. I had her call you. You are really annoying. I can see why your partner—both your partners—lost patience with you."

Del remained silent. The team was surely here by now.

"He was a beautiful boy, you know."

Del closed her eyes for a second then snapped them back open.

He's baiting me.

"A prostitute. What else?" White laughed. "Not that I'm a fag or anything. I like pussy, as you astutely pointed out when we met."

Del kept her breath steady. She flexed her feet and adjusted her hands around her weapon.

"But I couldn't help myself. I kept tabs on him. Like you kept tabs on me."

White seemed to expect a response, but Del stayed silent and still, waiting him out.

"He wanted to find me. That's the thing. I'd considered letting him just fritter away his useless life, he would've been dead in a year the way he was going. No way he'd survive. But he was looking for me. He looked up my real estate holdings. Can you imagine that? He stalked me."

White sounded offended. Del smiled grimly. They always did, didn't they? The most predatory assholes always saw themselves as hapless victims and their victims as the ones who'd crossed some line only the assholes could imagine existed.

White shifted his weight. He wasn't used to exertion. A little golf, a little rape, but not a lot of exercise beyond that. Staying still and alert for a long time was exhausting in a way few people understood unless they were cops or soldiers or prisoners. White was used to being able to stalk his prey, strike and leave, returning at will without consequences.

"So you fucked the kid." Del heard how indifferent her voice sounded. She resisted the urge to shift her own weight. Her ankles were killing her more than her knees, which was saying something. She forced herself to tense and relax her major muscles, concentrating on that effort and on the labor of keeping her breath regulated.

"He didn't recognize me." White sounded offended by this. "He was looking me up, but he didn't even recognize me." He'd lost the thread of his intention to rile her up and was riling himself up instead. Surely he would regain his footing soon.

Del checked in with her internal clock. It had been fourteen minutes since her text to Phan. Was he outside now?

"Fifty bucks for a blowjob," White said, trying to keep his voice cool and detached. "A hunny to fuck him. Guess which I picked?"

Half and half.

"But I got impatient. No premature jack for me, though, don't get the wrong idea." White snorted. "The whole time he was on his knees in front of me, working away like a good little bitch, I thought about his mom. She could Hoover dick like a pro too." White laughed, a nasty sound Del thought might stain her if she let it. "I was planning to fuck him in the ass and tell him just before I came, but I thought about seeing his face while I told him and got a little too impatient."

Del squinted, fighting the urge to close her eyes to the image White was painting for her.

"He just sat back on his heels, his stupid face right in front of my dick, and I laughed. That made me jack all over his stupid face." White laughed again, the sound tinged with hysteria. "He couldn't believe it."

Del blinked, surprised at the dampness around her eyes. Her breath was tight, her body shaking. She could imagine all too clearly the shock and horror and shame on the boy's face. Had he felt guilty for not being able to protect his mom from this man, from cancer, from death? Had he felt humiliated and dehumanized and despairing? Del's chest ached. She felt Mikey's pain and grief as distinct things inside her, wounds she carried along with her own. Would she ever be able to breathe again and not feel Mikey's wounds lodged in her lungs?

"The beaner can't suck dick for shit. Kinda disappointing. I figured you were banging her, but you're just sitting there playing possum like it's nothing. So maybe you like to hit it and quit it, huh?" The tension in White's voice was building.

"Big ole dyke."

Del smiled.

"Goddamn city's getting taken over by the goddamn—"

Del tuned him out when her phone vibrated. Phan was outside. The twin aches behind her lungs were Mikey's wounds, keeping her still and quiet and nonresponsive to White. Angel's wings, she mused wildly, her guardian angel's wings were trying to protect her from her impulse to charge down the hall and tackle White and beat him to death with her bare hands. She could do it. He was soft. Del was struck by the chill inside her. The damp must have worked its way through her clothes and skin into her organs. Then she realized there was movement near the front of the house and maybe the far side.

She held still.

"They're going to shoot me," White announced, sounding smug and pleased. "And you'll never know about—"

"No they're not," Del interrupted. "They know your game plan. This isn't some soap opera where you get to go out in a blaze of bullets and don't have to deal with the consequences—"

"Don't try to play with me, bitch."

There was a hand on her shoulder, and Del let a burly officer in tactical gear help her up. Her legs were frozen, which the young officer seemed to anticipate, a thing Del noted only later. The kid shielded her with his armored body. She listened as somebody read White his rights and someone else disarmed him, searched him, cuffed him, led him away.

"Homeowner," she whispered to the Response Team guy as they exited the house. "Sofia Gonzalez."

"She's fine." Phan was there at her side by then. He chucked his chin at guy from the Response Team and smiled at Del. "The EMT will take her to make sure, but I saw her, and she's fine."

Del nodded, too shaken to say anything.

"You okay?"

Del tried to shrug but had a feeling it ended up looking more like a paroxysm, given Phan's grimace.

"Okay. Well, let's go face the music. Bradley's gonna shit a brick."

Del smiled and let Phan lead her to the car.

* * *

"It was really the man who hurt that boy's mom?" Lola gestured at Del to sit at her kitchen table.

"Crazy, isn't it?" Del shook her head. "Mikey Ocampo. He was a nice kid, I think. I mean, he seemed decent. Before everything. As far as I'm concerned Ernie White murdered that kid twice. White was just another selfish, destructive, heartless bastard wreaking havoc on the world without a second thought."

"Like Janet pushed Sterling."

"Yeah." Del nodded slowly. "True. Anyway, it's over. The ADA is turning cartwheels. Those two sicko perverts are gonna grow old in prison and maybe get some of the same treatment they dished out."

"I'm glad. You helped save a lot of women from those sickos, and I'm really proud of you."

"Thanks." Del flushed. "I'm glad it's over. I just wish I'd been able to stop Ernie White and save Mikey. I wish I'd been able to save Leslie Thorne. She should never have died. Mikey should never have died."

"You did the best you could." Lola shook her head slowly. "I know that can't be much consolation. But you can't change the hard truths, can you?"

"No, I guess not." But Lola was right. It wasn't much consolation and it certainly hadn't done the victims any good.

"I'm sorry. But I'm still glad it's over."

She watched Lola. Something was brewing behind those bewitching hazel eyes, and Del wasn't sure what that something was. "So am I," she offered.

"I bet." Lola slid steaming plates of pasta on the table and sat across from Del. "Can I talk to you about something? Is now a good time?"

"Sure." Del eyed her warily.

"I was thinking about you. How you were out there, looking for these monsters, hunting them. How dangerous that is. How you put yourself out there every day and how much that scares me."

"Yeah." Del pursed her lips. "I'm sorry. I know. But I'll always be a cop."

"I know." Lola gave a crooked smile. "I do know that. I accept that. And I'm proud of you. But I get to worry, too, don't I?"

"Only if I get to worry about you."

"Deal." Lola held out her hand, and Del shook it very gently then held on to it.

"I don't want to stay in this place where we're not really together and not really apart. I don't want to wonder where we stand with each other."

"Neither do I."

"So let's decide and stick with it, okay?" Lola stared at Del. "And be honest about how we feel and what we need and all of it."

"There's no question in my mind." Del swallowed hard. "I want to get back together. I want to spend the rest of my life with you. I really will work on being a better partner and treating you as my equal. I'll try harder to trust you and listen to you. Please take me back."

Lola's eyes overflowed with tears. Her hand shook. Del held on to it for a moment, then let go. She couldn't sit there and watch Lola decide it was too hard.

Why won't you answer me? Are you trying to tell me to leave you alone? Don't say that. Say yes, say you'll take me back. Please.

Del escaped the table to stand facing the backyard. She closed her eyes. It felt like they were at a crossroads, and she was afraid to say anything that would push them in the wrong direction.

How did we get here? What do I do?

She sensed movement and made as if to spin but felt a light hand on her hip, clearly signaling she should not turn around. Lola had gotten up and was standing behind her. She felt Lola's arms wrap around her waist. Del rested her back against Lola, feeling her words as much as hearing them.

"I love you. I was so afraid of losing you. And I never want to lose you again. I want to be with you. I want to spend the rest of my life with you. I want to marry you. I just want to be sure this time is forever. Okay? Can you understand that? I need for us to start over and take our time and make sure it's right. I need to know we are real. I need to learn to trust you again. I need you to learn to trust me. I need you to lean on me. You know?"

Del nodded. She felt the tension in her body release slowly, bit by bit. For the first time in months, her stomach didn't hurt. Her head didn't ache. She sagged against Lola and felt her solidity.

"I can't live without you," Del whispered. "I don't know how to do that." Her chest was constricted; she forced herself to take a deep breath and relax. She felt Lola's arms tighten around her and once more felt the tension seep out of her body.

"Yes, you can. Yes, you do. But we're gonna try real hard to make sure you don't have to. I'm here for you, Del, no matter what. Okay?"

Del nodded, unable to speak. When she trusted herself not to cry, she turned around and embraced Lola.

When did she become the strong one? When did I start leaning on her? She smelled Lola's hair, the clean, light, hint-of-lavender scent that she had come to know so well, and closed her eyes.

Home, she thought, I'm finally home.

Bella Books, Inc.

Women. Books. Even Better Together.

P.O. Box 10543
Tallahassee, FL 32302

Phone: 800-729-4992
www.bellabooks.com